BRED FOR BATTLE

Osis pulled his left arm free, allowing the armored sleeve to drop to the ground. He slipped his right arm from its shell, letting the small laser that capped it fall away. He flexed his arms and chest and allowed the SRM launcher assembly to crash to the ground.

"Do you know how I won my bloodname, Victor? I met and broke MechWarriors like you in single combat. To become an Osis, I had to destroy one who, like you, sat safely locked away in the cockpit of a BattleMech. From a cliff I leaped down and landed on his *Adder*. He could hear me there, so he crawled from the cockpit and tried to kill me. He failed, and his genetic heritage was discarded."

Victor's eyes narrowed. "You killed a man who clearly had been defeated? Why?"

"He wanted to die. He knew he was not the sort of material the Osis House would want to pass on to future generations." Osis stood and made no attempt to hide the hideous wound on his left leg. Victor punched up magnification on his holographic display and clearly saw sutures. *And there's blood oozing from the wound.*

Osis opened his arms. "I am the last of the Smoke Jaguars, Victor Davion. I invite you now to face me, man to man, and earn the honor you think you deserve. Come to me, Victor, and I will teach you things in seconds that men study lifetimes to learn."

BATTLETECH®

Twilight of the Clans VII:

PRINCE OF HAVOC

Michael A. Stackpole

A ROC BOOK

ROC
Published by the Penguin Group
Penguin Putnam Inc., 375 Hudson Street,
New York, New York 10014, U.S.A.
Penguin Books Ltd, 27 Wrights Lane,
London W8 5TZ, England
Penguin Books Australia Ltd, Ringwood,
Victoria, Australia
Penguin Books Canada Ltd, 10 Alcorn Avenue,
Toronto, Ontario, Canada M4V 3B2
Penguin Books (N.Z.) Ltd, 182–190 Wairau Road,
Auckland 10, New Zealand

Penguin Books Ltd, Registered Offices:
Harmondsworth, Middlesex, England

First published by Roc, an imprint of Dutton NAL,
a member of Penguin Putnam Inc.

First Printing, December, 1998
10 9 8 7 6 5 4 3 2 1

Series Editor: Donna Ippolito
Mechanical Drawings: Duane Loose and the FASA art department

ROC   REGISTERED TRADEMARK—MARCA REGISTRADA

To Faith,
My new niece. Welcome to the family. Don't worry.
Others of us Stackpoles have real jobs.

The author would like to thank the following people for their contributions to this book: Donna Ippolito, Bryan Nystul, and Randall Bills, for editorial direction and insight. Blaine Pardoe, Loren Coleman, Chris Hartford, and Thomas Gressman, whose work I've hopelessly mangled in here, and who, along with Dan Grendell, offered comments that fixed errors in the first draft. John-Allen Price, for the continuing loan of Galen Cox/Jerry Cranston. Steven Applegarth, for his generous contribution to charity in return for his appearance here and in future. And, as always, Liz Danforth, for putting up with me during the temporary insanity that masquerades as writing to a deadline.

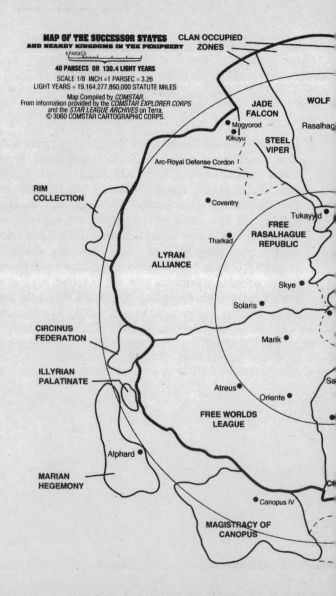

MAP OF THE SUCCESSOR STATES
AND NEARBY KINGDOMS IN THE PERIPHERY

CLAN OCCUPIED ZONES

8 PARSECS

40 PARSECS OR 130.4 LIGHT YEARS

SCALE 1/8 INCH =1 PARSEC = 3.26
LIGHT YEARS = 19,164,277,860,000 STATUTE MILES

Map Compiled by *COMSTAR*.
From information provided by the *COMSTAR EXPLORER CORPS*
and the *STAR LEAGUE ARCHIVES* on Terra.
© 3060 COMSTAR CARTOGRAPHIC CORPS.

JADE FALCON

WOLF

• Mogyorod
Kikuyu •

STEEL VIPER

Rasalhag

Arc-Royal Defense Cordon

RIM COLLECTION

• Coventry

Tukayyid

FREE RASALHAGUE REPUBLIC

Tharkad •

LYRAN ALLIANCE

Skye •

Solaris •

CIRCINUS FEDERATION

Marik •

ILLYRIAN PALATINATE

Atreus •

Sa

Oriente •

FREE WORLDS LEAGUE

Alphard •

MARIAN HEGEMONY

CO

• Canopus IV

MAGISTRACY OF CANOPUS

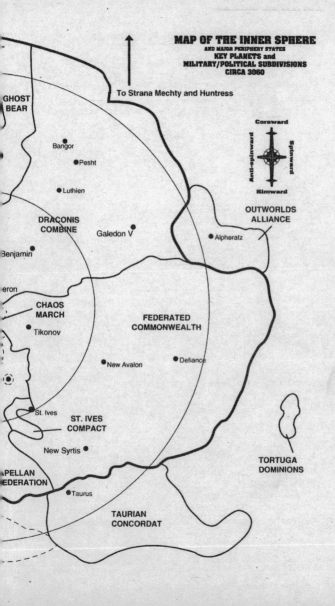

MAP OF THE INNER SPHERE
AND MAJOR PERIPHERY STATES
KEY PLANETS and
MILITARY/POLITICAL SUBDIVISIONS
CIRCA 3060

To Strana Mechty and Huntress

Coreward
Anti-spinward
Spinward
Rimward

GHOST BEAR

OUTWORLDS ALLIANCE

Bangor

Pesht

Luthien

DRACONIS COMBINE

Galedon V

Alpheratz

Benjamin

eron

CHAOS MARCH

FEDERATED COMMONWEALTH

Tikonov

New Avalon

Defiance

St. Ives

ST. IVES COMPACT

New Syrtis

TORTUGA DOMINIONS

PELLAN EDERATION

Taurus

TAURIAN CONCORDAT

**Star League Expeditionary Force Command Center
Lootera, Huntress
Kerensky Cluster, Clan Space
9 April 3060**

Prince Victor Ian Steiner-Davion slowly mounted the steps of the low dais at the southern end of the Field of Heroes on the edge of Lootera. He did so partially out of respect for the men and women following him, so he would not outstrip them as they ascended. They were the true victors of Huntress, the leaders of Task Force Serpent. They had come to Huntress and bested the Smoke Jaguars. They had inflicted so much damage that Lincoln Osis, Smoke Jaguar Khan and ilKhan of all the Clans, had fled the planet before Victor and his forces had even arrived in the system.

Victor's arrival had cemented the victory. His troops had come down and mopped up what little Clan resistance remained on Huntress. The Serpents had been sent out to completely destroy the Smoke Jaguar warrior caste. They were to erase every shred of evidence of its existence and, save for a few monuments and whoever escaped the system with Lincoln Osis, they had accomplished their mission flawlessly.

But not without cost, terrible cost, and the weight of that loss also slowed Victor. Ariana Winston, commander of the Eridani Light Horse mercenary brigade, had been slain along with the better part of her warriors. Countless others had perished, many of whom Victor had never even seen, much less had a chance to get to know. And then there was Morgan Hasek-Davion, his cousin and dear friend; a man who had shouldered an incredible amount of responsibility after the death of Victor's father. Morgan had led the Serpents, but had been cut down by treachery before they ever got to Huntress.

Victor reached the top step, then turned with his back to the crowd standing before the dais. As each of the Task Force commanders joined him, he thanked him or her. He also offered his heartfelt sympathies for their losses and praised them for their people's efforts. He fed them details of what their people had done, to let them know he *had* studied all the data beamed to his incoming DropShip. *I do know what you have been through, and I honor it more than you will ever know.*

When the last of them, Andrew Redburn, released his hand and limped over to the chair that had been set out for him, Victor turned and walked to the microphone mounted in the center of the dais. The day was overcast and humid, and a slight breeze ruffled the banners and regimental flags hanging from the shattered statues surrounding the broken stone that had once been a paved parade ground. He took his time, lowering the microphone to a proper height, then looked out over the troops assembled before him.

When first sent out, Task Force Serpent could have filled the field with rank upon rank of bright-eyed, eager warriors. Now, after some of fiercest fighting seen since BattleMechs first walked the fields of battle six centuries before, the Serpents occupied less than a third of it. The forward ranks were made up of people swathed in bandages, lying in beds that had been carried from the hospital, seated in wheelchairs, or gallantly standing with crutches to steady them.

Beyond them stood those who had no physical wounds, but who had been just as sorely used. Some of them seemed to sway with the breeze, as if their exhaustion would finally pull them down. Their uniforms were recognizable as such only because warriors of a particular unit stood together. This allowed Victor to piece together what a whole dress uniform might have looked like in better times. Not a few soldiers had appropriated pieces of Smoke Jaguar attire, supplementing their uniforms with the spoils of war.

Victor started to speak, then hesitated as his throat closed. He glanced down for a moment, forcing himself to breathe through his nose. Finally he clasped his hands at the small of his back and again looked out at the warriors arrayed there.

"Words fail when I try to think of a way to quantify what you have done here and praise you. You have accomplished what has never been accomplished before, and because you have done it, no one will ever have to do it again. Your children, and your children's children will never have to fear the Smoke Jaguars as we have, or hate them as we have, or kill them as we have. Their scourge is finished because of your effort. Your courage, your sacrifice, your determination will never be forgotten, and will always be praised."

Victor opened his arms. "Your mission was a most terrible one, and I know you have seen things and done things that are the fabric of nightmares. This war you have waged, the war the rest of us waged in the Inner Sphere, will stay with us forever. These things we cannot share with others who have not been here, who have not faced death in battle, who have not seen friends slain. They do not have the frame of reference to be able to understand. It is not their failing that they do not, but a monument to your spirit that you have experienced these things and have not been consumed by them. We have asked you to bear a burden for the Star League, for the Inner Sphere, that no human can compel another to bear.

You accepted it as your duty, and shall be lauded for eternity because of it.

"Even those of us who fought to retake part of the Inner Sphere cannot wholly know what you have experienced here." The Prince pointed to various places where Battle-Mechs could be seen patrolling the city's precincts. "I *can* tell you that every single one of the people I brought with me is prouder of you than you can possibly imagine, and we all feel honored to assume your burden so you may enjoy the respite you have so dearly earned. Your mission, Serpents, has been accomplished."

Mild applause started in the ranks, then swelled to echo from the buildings and the mountain to the north as the leaders behind Victor joined in. Victor stepped back from the microphone and turned halfway toward the back, so he could see the leaders and the troops both. He added his applause to theirs. As the crowd quieted, Victor flicked away a sudden tear, then approached the microphone one more time.

"To accomplish your mission, you paid a fearful price. As with all of you, I knew and loved some of those who died here, or on the way here. You who have survived do so not to bear a burden of guilt over your survival, but to live the lives and make real the dreams of your fallen comrades. You've succeeded in making one dream come true already by defeating the Smoke Jaguars; and another by rekindling the spirit that made the Star League strong enough to ward all humanity from disaster.

"If Morgan Hasek-Davion were here, standing where I am now, I know his heart would be bursting with pride in all of you. It would pain him deeply, and I think would pain your fallen friends deeply, if you allowed their deaths to become a weight that hobbles you. To do that denies the sacrifice they made, which was a sacrifice that is allowing you to live free—something they dearly desire for you. Accept their pride in your survival, couple it with your pride in victory, then take your rightful place in the Inner Sphere as the heroes you all are."

Victor allowed just the hint of a smile to find its way to his lips. "When you were sent here, you were asked to erase from existence every trace of the Smoke Jaguar warrior caste and culture. This you have done with one last exception."

He gestured to the north and everyone turned to look at Mount Szabo. There, incised into the mountain's southeast face, well above the Clan's genetic repository, was a gigantic smoke jaguar. Had the carving not been so fine, and the beast so magnificent, Victor would have found it vulgar. *Good thing Katherine can't see this, or she'd get ideas. I can just see her sculpting a moon into her own likeness.*

Victor produced a remote control from his jacket pocket, then turned and waved General Andrew Redburn forward. Limping slightly with a stiff right leg, the commander of the First Kathil Uhlans strode forward. His brown eyes glittered proudly, but Victor could see the tracks of tears on his face as he drew near. Redburn nodded wordlessly as he accepted the remote from Victor and flicked it on. His thumb hovered above the lit red button in the middle of the black box.

Victor smiled. "That edifice is the last trace of Smoke Jaguar warrior tradition left on this rock—not counting the 'Mechs you've left in scraps around here." He paused as laughter rippled through the crowd. "This is the last thing you need to do, to destroy it. Countdown from three."

"Three, two, one . . ."

Redburn's thumb mashed the button down with a vehemence that threatened to break the remote.

After a second's delay, a series of explosions started on the mountainside. Victor saw the bright flashes and gray plumes jetting into the air seconds before he heard the reports. The explosions marched in ranks up over the carving, shredding it from paws to spine. The last, biggest charge had been set in the head and when it went off, it arced pieces of the jaguar's skull over the mountainside. An avalanche of rock rained down the slopes, but rumbled past the genetic repository without crushing it. A gray cloud rose like a ghost above where the stone jaguar had once been.

A spontaneous cheer arose from the Serpents and Victor found himself thrusting his fists into the air, laughing and hooting along with them. Though he had not fought here on Huntress, he had helped drive the Smoke Jaguars from the Inner Sphere. That monument's destruction, symbolic as it was, marked the successful end of a brutal campaign.

And it heralds the start of another.

He took his place at the microphone one last time. He waited for the Serpents to quiet down once again, then resumed speaking. "There are two duties with which I must yet charge you, and I trust you will fulfill them as faithfully. The first is to remember that our battle was against the Smoke Jaguar warriors, not all of the people. You have destroyed the warriors, liberating those they have repressed for so long. Don't carry your war further, but turn instead to let them join with you, join with the Star League. The return of the Star League has ever been the goal of the Clans, and now they have realized it. Accept this and them.

"The second thing I ask of you, and a more difficult one for you, I am certain, is for you to wait. You have ended the threat of *a* Clan, but those of us who have followed you here now need to go to Strana Mechty and end the threat of all the Clans. With your example to follow, and your victory to build upon, we will not be denied. When we have finished this business that you so ably started, we will return here. Together we will return to the Inner Sphere, triumphant."

Victor snapped to attention and tossed them all a salute, then turned and saluted their leaders. As one, the Serpent commanders returned his salute, then Victor went to each and shook their hands. After he was done, the others filed off the stage and walked out among their troops, to be with them.

Alone on the dais, Victor looked out at the throng. *We asked of them so much, and they delivered so selflessly. Now*

*my people and I must go to Strana Mechty and be prepared to
make the same sacrifice they did.* A shiver coursed down his
spine. *Because we* must *succeed, we will, but I wonder if the
price we pay will be this high, or higher still?*

=== 2 ===

Star League Expeditionary Force Command Center
Lootera, Huntress
Kerensky Cluster, Clan Space
9 April 3060

"**A**ll right, what have we got?" Victor Davion leaned against the back of the chair set at the head of the table in the briefing room. The chair, which had been constructed to hold an Elemental, would have dwarfed him, so he refrained from sitting in it. Synthetic smoke jaguar fur covered all the chairs, and Victor had no doubt they would somehow find their way back to the Inner Sphere as spoils. *With so few men and machines to take back, the DropShips will be full of this stuff.*

He looked first to the blond, bearded man at his right hand. "Jerry?"

Jerrard Cranston smiled carefully and looked at his noteputer. "Concerning Morgan's murder, we've got . . ."

"No." Victor shook his head. "Morgan's death can wait. Give me the military data first."

Cranston hesitated for a moment, then hit a key on the

noteputer. "Okay, of the roughly ten regiments assigned to Task Force Serpent, we've got just under two left, and that's if we want to be generous. Morale among those people is up but not terribly solid. They've been through a lot and they're very glad it's over. I can't see any way we can pack them up and take them with us to Strana Mechty."

Kai Allard-Liao, a dark-haired, gray-eyed man of obviously Asiatic descent, frowned from Victor's left. "It *is* decided, then, that we're going to Strana Mechty?"

Victor shifted his shoulders uneasily. "That's a point to discuss in a moment or two. Whether or not we decide to go, we know the Serpents won't be with us."

At the far end of the table, Andrew Redburn leaned forward, a hank of ruddy hair tinged with white curling down over his seamed forehead. "I know our people are ragged, but they've still got fight left in them."

The Prince nodded solemnly. "No one is questioning their ability to fight, their courage or loyalty. As I said outside, your people have done their jobs. I'll need you with me, General, and some of your Uhlans, but that's because of something I learned on Coventry. I don't expect that trick will work again, mainly because the situations will be entirely different, but your presence will make things go a bit more easily."

Victor looked back at Cranston again. "What's the salvage situation?"

"There's stuff littered all over this planet, and stockpiled in warehouses. If standard salvage rules were applied here, the various units would come out very strong, provided they could find pilots to drive this stuff."

Seated just past Cranston, Anastasius Focht, Precentor Martial of ComStar, cleared his throat. "I have some of my people preparing a comprehensive inventory of supplies here and comparing it with the needs of our units for final refitting of Clan technology. I would expect we will require less than five percent of what is stored here to become fully operational. I'd like to refit the Fourth Drakøns with Clan machines, bringing them up to spec with the rest of the units that came here with us. Beyond that, I don't believe we will have a high demand for the materials here."

"Anyone else have needs like that?" Victor looked past Kai to the black-haired, dark-eyed man seated on his left. "Hohiro, how are your people set?"

"We are, as you say, good to go." Hohiro shattered the image of Japanese inscrutability he occasionally cultivated by smiling broadly. "Our people here struck a severe blow to the enemy, and the rest of us look forward to exploiting it."

"As do we all." Victor frowned as he thought for a moment. "Okay, what I'd like to do with the salvage is this: every unit gets its pick of what they took down. They can bring themselves up to full strength plus ten percent. Any salvage over that goes into a pool to be sold off and rolled into a trust for the survivors of those slain, and for those who've been wounded here. Also, let the units supplement their salvage from the warehouses. I want them rebuilding themselves while we're gone. It will give them something to do *and,* if things go bad for us, we may well need them."

Cranston nodded. "I'll have the orders cut and issued."

"Good." Victor straightened up and folded his arms across his chest. "Let's move on to discussing the journey to Strana Mechty."

Kai laughed lightly. "You make it sound like a stroll. We'll be invading the Clan homeworld."

Hohiro lifted a hand. "Are we certain we know exactly where Strana Mechty is?"

Cranston typed an inquiry into his noteputer. "We have a variety of independent sources pinpointing a particular star system nearby. It's one jump away and the observatory on the *Barbarossa* reports there are planets in the system. At least one seems habitable, and some indications sound like Strana Mechty's a touch on the dry side. We don't have a trace on the ilKhan's ship after it escaped Huntress, but it seems safe to assume he went to Strana Mechty.

"If he didn't, he's removed himself from political power, which means we don't have to deal with him."

Redburn's eyes hardened. "He's still a Smoke Jaguar warrior. He's got to die. Him and those with him."

The vehemence in Redburn's voice tightened Victor's guts. *We sent the Serpents here to destroy the warriors and they have, save for Lincoln Osis and his personal guards.* Victor knew he and his people would have to finish that job, but the idea of executing a man who abandoned his homeworld made him uneasy. *Fleeing, he proved himself no longer a warrior.*

The Precentor Martial nodded. "General Redburn has a very good point. From my experience with the Clans, I do think going to Strana Mechty and challenging them to a Trial of Refusal concerning the invasion is the only way to proceed."

Kai pressed his hands flat to the table. "We could go there and force the issue, or we could wait here for them to send a delegation to us. It could be they'll sue for peace. Making them come to a subjugated world to do so would humble them a peg or two."

Victor nodded. "I agree, Kai, but we all know the Clans are not a single unified front. A Smoke Jaguar surrender here wouldn't be seen as binding on the other Clans. We could delay deciding whether to go to Strana Mechty while we wait to see what they're going to do, but a quick move that links the defeat here with a challenge there is important."

"Victor, I think you must not look beyond Kai's point for a moment," Hohiro said. "While I am not afraid to go to Strana Mechty, we know that defending a world from an invader is much easier than invading."

Victor nodded. "I intend to invoke *safcon* when we arrive there."

Kai blinked. "Would you allow *them* to freely land troops on New Avalon just because they asked nicely?"

"No, but then I don't think my warriors are the pinnacle of a human eugenics program that makes them *homo sapiens parabellum,* either. Given their sense of honor, I bet they'll let us come down." Victor shrugged. "All I can do is ask, if they say no, we fight our way in and things get very messy."

Andrew Redburn sat back in his chair. "I'm for going to Strana Mechty before they can come here. Any time we give them allows them to prepare defenses or summon troops. No reason to do that."

Cranston looked up from his noteputer. "We also have the very real question as to whether or not any delegation will show up. If the Clans view this as a Smoke Jaguar problem, and the ilKhan has already fled, they may not think this involves them at all. It's up to us to make sure they know all of them are wrapped up in this assault."

"True, by singling out one Clan, we allow the others to distance themselves from the possibility of defeat." Kai nodded toward the Precentor Martial. "Notwithstanding the evidence of their mortality on Tukayyid."

Focht adjusted his eye patch with his right hand. "Tukayyid was eight years ago—a warrior generation and a half as far as the Clans are concerned. It's history to their minds, not current events. The push to Strana Mechty should be as soon as possible."

The Prince smiled. "I agree. We need to go, and go now. Here, on Huntress, we waged a kind of war virtually unknown to the Clans. Their style of warfare has forever limited the damage done because their ancestors knew all too well the horrors of war carried out unrestrained. By ritualizing warfare as they did, they were divorced from the true consequences of war. We've showed them we can win *our* kind of war here. Now we need to go to Strana Mechty, play by their rules, and show them we can defeat them, *all* of them, their way."

Redburn smiled. "I'll have a company ready to go by first light."

"Good." Victor's brows furrowed. "General Redburn, what do we know about Lincoln Osis and his departure here?"

Redburn scratched at his white beard for a moment, then hunched forward, leaning his elbows on the table. "There were scattered witness reports about his evacuation. Elementals carried him from the Jag command center a minute or so before it exploded. There was supposedly a nekekami team in here doing the demolition and its leader apparently challenged Osis to single combat with swords."

Kai blinked. "Nekekami?"

Redburn nodded. "I didn't know anything of their presence until I reviewed General Winston's files after her death. Apparently she didn't know of them either until she did the same with Morgan's files. They were a gift to Morgan from Theodore Kurita, or so it would seem."

Victor nodded. "Not a surprise. Spirit cats can be useful. I take it they were unsuccessful in killing Osis."

"After the challenge was issued, the rest of the team left before the fight was decided, so we don't really know. The leader hasn't showed up, nor have we identified a body. Osis was supposed to be grossly wounded, and a ship did lift shortly after the fight. Could be he's dead, but those Elementals, they take a lot of killing."

Victor glanced at Kai. "So I've heard."

"For an Elemental to have become ilKhan, he must be very resilient." Kai smiled sheepishly. "The Elementals I've known were all tough, but to be elected Khan and then ilKhan, this one must have been truly impressive. Until I saw the body and pumped a few kilojoules of energy into it, I'd not believe he was dead."

"So, we'll have to assume he's alive and either on Strana Mechty or running." Victor crossed his arms over his chest. "Precentor Martial, any idea how he would be greeted there, wounded, with his Clan's homeworld captured?"

Focht thought for a second. "Well, the fact that he was here at all is significant. The ilKhan is usually elevated above Clan fights, but Osis appears to have kept his hand in as far as Smoke Jaguar problems are concerned. The fact that there were no other Clans represented here could very easily mean that this whole fight *was* seen as a Smoke Jaguar problem. Very obviously, the Smoke Jaguars are finished as a power, so politically he's going to be weak. Even so, unless he's challenged to a Trial of Refusal, he will remain ilKhan until he's either dead or he steps down."

Kai looked over at Focht. "Is there a chance the Jags could have kept this secret from the rest of the Clans?"

"It's possible, I suppose, but with some of the Nova Cats coming over to the Star League, hiding what has happened in the Inner Sphere would be difficult." Focht shook his head. "We've spotted some Clan ships still making information runs on our systems, and they've certainly gotten plenty of broadcast data about our victories. I can't believe they wouldn't know, and that the Jaguars' foes haven't already pilloried Osis with his Clan's failures."

Victor frowned. "With his being weak, both physically and politically, it's not likely we'd win any real peace by defeating him and any scraps of the Smoke Jaguars still on Strana Mechty. We *will* have to offer a challenge to the Clans in general and see who responds."

Cranston sighed. "Oh, that will be fun. Then we'll have to sort out all the claims to fight this Clan and that from our side."

"Meaning, Jerry?"

"Meaning, Highness, that you'll have to pick and choose who gets to fight whom. The Rasalhague contingent will want the honor of defeating the Wolves, I'm certain. Hohiro will want the Smoke Jaguars, and so on."

Victor rubbed a hand over his jaw. "That's a point I'd not considered. We'll have to match our forces to theirs, allowing ourselves the best chances for success."

"Jerry is right," Hohiro said. "I'd want to take on the Smoke Jaguars, but if Osis is leading them, he should face you, leader to leader."

Victor blinked at Hohiro. "I don't know what surprises me more, my friend, your willingness to give me the Smoke Jaguars or the suggestion that I'd be nuts enough to face down an Elemental all by myself."

"I don't think you that stupid, Victor, but we know how important appearances are to the Clans."

"And, being from the Draconis Combine, you'd know nothing of form being as important as substance."

Hohiro laughed. "Consider my sensitivity to such things the basis for my suggestion."

Victor raised an eyebrow at him. "Besides, you've fought the Smoke Jaguars before and seen an Elemental up close, correct?"

"Victor, for the last seven months, as we traveled here, you have trained hard in single-combat techniques." Hohiro opened his hands easily. "I do not think you mad enough to engage Osis one on one, but if you did, he would be surprised at how difficult you would be to kill."

Cranston looked up. "I'll make sure you're issued a pistol to wear in your 'Mech."

Kai rapped his knuckles on the table. "Make sure it's a *big* pistol, and toss in a couple of spare clips."

Victor held his hands up. "We're getting ahead of ourselves here. We're resolved to go to Strana Mechty as soon as possible, right?"

Getting nods of assent from the others, Victor continued. "All right, then, we need to get our units loaded and headed back to the JumpShips. I'm going to leave Paul Masters in command here. General Redburn, you'll be coming with me on the *Barbarossa*. That should cover everything."

Kai frowned. "What about Morgan's murder?"

Victor froze, a chill puckering his flesh all over. *I know the rumors—the Combine did it, Katherine did it. I believe the latter, but proving it is vital. Can't do that here.* "If we succeed on Strana Mechty—*when* we succeed at Strana Mechty—we'll have a good, long trip home. *That* is when we can work on Morgan's murder and, when we get home, we can see justice be done."

3

Hall of the Khans, Warrior Quarter
Strana Mechty
Kerensky Cluster, Clan Space
10 April 3060

Khan Vladimir Ward of the Wolves waited until ilKhan Lincoln Osis had limped to his place at the head of the Grand Council chamber before he made his move. Head held erect, yet concealed by the enameled helmet displaying a snarling wolf's visage, he moved from his seat at the back of the hall over to the aisle bisecting the amphitheater. He descended from the highest rank of desks to the lowest, sliding into one of the two vacant spots beneath the Smoke Jaguar banner. As he removed his helmet and set it on the desk that had once been the ilKhan's own, Vlad's saKhan, Marialle Radick, slipped into the other empty spot.

Lincoln Osis' dark eyes burned with fury. His dusky flesh had an ashen hue to it, so his eyes seemed to project the only true life in the man. Vlad had heard stories of how seriously Osis had been wounded on Huntress, with the limp and the puckered scar on his forehead being the most obvious signs of his injuries. *And when he smiles, I can see where he lost teeth—though I doubt he will be doing any smiling today.*

Kael Pershaw, a misshapen lump of a man commingled with machinery, took his place in front of and below the ilKhan. "I am the Loremaster. I hereby convene this conclave under the provisions of the Martial Code laid down by Nicholas Kerensky. Because we exist in a state of war, all matters shall be conducted according to these rules and regulations."

"Seyla," the assembled Khans said as one.

The flesh around Osis' eyes tightened. "Khan Ward, what is the meaning of your occupying the Smoke Jaguar position here in the Grand Council?"

Vlad smiled slowly. "As I understand it, ilKhan, there are no Smoke Jaguar Khans available to the Council, and no Smoke Jaguars available to elect more. You and a handful of your warriors escaped Huntress—apparently even before Inner Sphere reinforcements arrived there, if reports are correct. Of those warriors who fled with you, only eight have bloodnames. Your Clan is effectively dead."

Vlad let an icy tone sharpen his words, but not a single one of his fellow Khans raised a protest. All of them, in fact, sat waiting, clad in their ceremonial uniforms, for Osis' reaction. *They want to know what is going on, especially those who have never faced Inner Sphere troops. A strike against a Clan homeworld is the last thing anyone expected.*

The ilKhan's hands tightened into fists, but he did not lash out. He hesitated, and in that moment Vlad read more weakness than he had ever seen displayed by a Smoke Jaguar before. *His spirit is bruised, if not broken. To be unhomed is to die without the release of oblivion.*

Osis slowly exhaled. "Huntress has fallen, yes." His statement hung in the air as heavy as the stink of the dead on a battlefield. "And, yes, I *withdrew* from Huntress because I fell unconscious from my wound and those caring for me believed I could only get the medical attention I needed here, on

Strana Mechty. At the time we left the system, the situation was far from lost and our assumption was that the invaders would be crushed within the week. I had full confidence in the commanders on the ground, and Khan Howell was left in charge of operations. Had I known of the Inner Sphere reinforcements coming in, I would have remained behind and led our forces to victory."

Asa Taney, a red-haired pilot of Clan Ice Hellion, removed his helmet. He rested a hand on the snout of the weasel-like creature that made up the helmet's faceplate, clearly attempting to strike a heroic pose. "IlKhan, when you say 'our forces,' do you refer to the Smoke Jaguars, or the Clans as a whole?"

Osis' shoulders slumped a bit beneath the question. "Yes, my fellow Khans, I recall well the discussions we had here regarding the aggression by the Inner Sphere. The assault against the Smoke Jaguars became framed as an internal Smoke Jaguar matter through political maneuvering right here in this chamber. At that time, it was a clever exercise by the Wolf Khan to destroy the Smoke Jaguars, but even you must see how much of a danger that was. A homeworld has been taken, sacked, destroyed. The warriors of a Clan have been slain. None of us is immune, now, to the wrath of this Star League reborn. Whereas you did not band together before, you must, now, *we* must *now* become a united front that will not rest until this threat is destroyed."

Vlad slowly clapped. "Bravo, ilKhan. I had not thought you capable of such passion any longer, misguided though it is."

Osis' lips curled in a snarl. "You mock the threat."

"No," came the voice of Jade Falcon Khan Marthe Pryde from the back of the hall. "Khan Ward mocks your analysis of the threat." She stood and opened her arms, taking in the assembly. "We have all heard the rhetoric coming from the Inner Sphere. We know this new Star League chose to attack *one* Clan. They are not so foolish to think they could defeat us all, nor are we so foolish as to believe they intend to defeat us all."

"But you have no idea, Marthe, what they did on Huntress," Osis broke in. "Their aim was to destroy the Smoke Jaguars, and they waged war against more than our warriors. They waged war against our culture. We have long held in the balance the twin realities of war: its destructive capabilities and its ability to hone warriors. By bargaining we limit the impact war has on our society, but they have done none of this. They destroyed warriors, equipment, monuments. If it had any connection to the warrior caste, it was not spared destruction. *That* is what we face, and if you are not frightened by it, your Clan will suffer more gravely than could be imagined."

Echoes of the ilKhan's words died slowly in the Grand Council chamber, largely because the fear he incited prompted others to repeat his words in low whispers. Vlad himself felt his guts begin to kink, but more out of revulsion than any fear. *How could they let themselves go and unleash total war on a people? Not even animals descend so low. The Inner Sphere has ever sought to prove we are not their superiors, but here they abandon any pretense of civilization to do so. The folly here is not ours for having gone to war with them, but in not prosecuting that war as fully and as fast as we could, to destroy this new scourge on mankind.*

Khan Taney pursed his lips, then lowered his eyes. "What do you suggest, ilKhan?"

"I suggest we immediately form a fighting force that will drive the Star League from Huntress, then we renew our assault on the Inner Sphere."

As the other Khans cheered, Vlad vaulted his desk and moved into the open area between the amphitheater's desks and the ilKhan's high bench. He waved his hands to silence the others, causing the jubilation to die a slow and strangled death. Once quiet again reigned, he rested his hands on his hips and slowly shook his head.

"You cannot let the ilKhan's madness infect you, too." Vlad looked over at Osis and sneered. "A task force, even if summoned from the homeworld garrisons, would arrive far too late to do anything to oppose the Star League troops there. Think of it, my Khans, think as *you* would, not as a Smoke Jaguar would. If you had successfully staged this long strike and been lucky enough to reinforce it in time to complete what had to be done, would you remain so far from home? Their supply lines are stretched impossibly. Huntress is not a viably defended place for them, and we hold many more worlds in the Inner Sphere against which they could devote their might. They will not remain on Huntress."

Vlad brought his hands together, pressing them palm to palm at the level of his breastbone. "They will be coming here."

Ian Hawker, the tow-headed Khan of the Diamond Sharks, removed his dorsal-finned helmet. "Impossible! They would not dare!"

"No?" Vlad looked up at Marthe Pryde. "You have met this Victor Davion. Would he dare?"

Marthe's laugh came low and sinister. "Would Victor Davion dare come here? He is already on his way, of this I am certain. On Coventry he and the Precentor Martial of Com-Star knew enough of us and our culture to use that knowledge to obtain their objectives. What the ilKhan has reminded us of is something they clearly know about our ways, and something they are using against us."

Hawker frowned impatiently. "What are you prattling on about, Pryde?"

"Something I would think was obvious to even someone such as yourself, Khan Hawker. Our way insulates us from the horrors of war. If my unit is bid away, I have very little fear that I will be forced to act in a particular battle. And, even if I die, I know my genetic legacy will live on beyond me. We have created an artificial box outside which warfare cannot touch us. The Star League leaders know that, and the action on Huntress was clearly designed to let us know that we are no longer safe in that way."

Asa Taney looked stricken. "He cannot be coming here to do to Strana Mechty what he did to Huntress."

Vlad laughed. "Calm yourself, Ice Hellion. There are those who will protect you."

"I don't need your protection, Wolf."

"Then you will fight, if he comes?" Vlad slowly shook his head. "Your blood is up? Remember, then, before you pledge yourself to something that will get you killed, Victor Davion did not destroy Huntress, he sent subordinates to do so. He sent his inferiors to send us a message. When he comes here, he will have a different message to send. They have defeated one of us *their* way on Huntress. When they come here, as Khan Pryde has indicated, they will use our ways against us to defeat us. And this will be a mistake."

Vlad let a smile slowly spread across his face. "We came to their world of Tukayyid and many of us knew defeat there. They now come to our world, and here they will know defeat." His voice rose to fill the room as he finished, and he felt the pride and enthusiasm of many of the other Khans rise with it. *Those who have not fought the Inner Sphere hunger for engagement. Those who have fought in the Inner Sphere may have already seen this day in their worst nightmares.*

Khan Karianna Schmitt of the Blood Spirits jammed a fist down on her desk. Decidedly tall for a MechWarrior, her blond hair was long enough to hang down over the shoulders of her red jumpsuit and cloak. "We *will* defeat this so-called Star League. I wonder, though, if our current ilKhan has the stomach for the fight. Perhaps we should depose him and elect Khan Wolf in his place."

"No!"

Vlad and Osis exchanged surprised glances as their hot denials of that suggestion meshed perfectly. Vlad got pure venom in Osis' hot glare, and met it with ice of his own. Vlad broke eye contact first, then folded his arms over his chest. "I will not be a party to such a move. A Smoke Jaguar started the crusade against the Inner Sphere. It is up to a Smoke Jaguar to sustain it, or let it die. If there is to be a new crusade, then there will be the time to choose a new ilKhan."

Osis posted both hands to his desktop and leaned forward heavily. "It is as Khan Ward has said. Now is not the time to make another choice. We will be faced with a severe test. I have seen what they did to Huntress, and I will not see that be done here. We must preserve our honor, our culture, our nature. I can and will preserve us, our ways."

Or die in the attempt. Vlad kept his face impassive. "Will we oppose them as they are inbound, ilKhan, or will we grant them *safcon*?"

Osis straightened up and lifted his chin. "We were granted *safcon* at Tukayyid. Can we offer them less?"

Taney, his eyes eager and bright, threw his arms wide. "We must not allow them to land without opposition. Our pilots will sweep them from the skies."

A light lilt ran through Marthe Pryde's voice. "That would be a first, Khan Taney. Superior we might be on the ground, but our aeropilots have always been evenly matched against theirs."

"You have not had Ice Hellions flying for you, Khan Pryde, *quineg*?"

"Neg, Khan Taney, but your pilots have never impressed me." Marthe's comment brought a ripple of laughter from the other Khans. "No, our victories have come on the ground. To engage them in space and the atmosphere allows them to destroy our aerospace assets without getting us a shot at their ground forces."

Khan Schmitt let a smile break the icy composure of her face. "Let them come here. Those of us who have not faced them before will teach them the lesson the rest of you failed to impart."

"Bold words from those who have not yet won the right to face the Star League." Vlad gave her a withering stare.

The Blood Spirit Khan affected not to notice, and instead slashed back quickly. "Just listening to you condescend earns

me that right, Khan Wolf. If we must bid or fight to confirm
this right, we shall. If they come here to defeat us, they must
defeat all of us."

A low growl rumbled from Lincoln Osis' throat. "Defeat all
of us, save the traitor Clan. What say you, Nova Cats? Will
you fight for the Clans?"

The ancient Khans of the Nova Cats, Severen Leroux and
Lucien Carns, slowly doffed their helmets. Countless wrinkles seamed their leathery faces, sending a shiver through
Vlad as he looked at the two old men. In any other Clan they
would have long since retired and had the good grace to die,
but among the Nova Cats their longevity and wisdom at in-
terpreting signs and portents had kept them in place. *And
those portents led them to believe this new Star League was
the fulfillment of true Clan goals, so their troops went over
with scant little fighting to become part of the new force.*

Leroux spoke, his voice surprisingly strong despite his age.
"Be advised, ilKhan, that the casual use of the term 'traitor' is
a trap in which you yourself could be caught. Our calling has
ever been to preserve the ideals of the Star League that gave
us birth. In recent times this has been reinterpreted to mean
we should return to the Inner Sphere to oust the unworthy and
install ourselves in their place, to recreate the Star League.
This we have done, though we are not the Star League. Our
actions have always been and are now compatible with the
goals of the Clans."

"How can you say that when your people preyed upon
mine?"

"Did they?" Leroux's eyes hardened. "Those troops who
fought against you were conquered, made bondsmen, and
then allowed to become warriors again. We have all converted captured troops to our own use in that manner. As
Khan Pryde noted, the Star League knows well our ways and
uses them against us."

Leroux held up a gnarled hand to calm Osis and the other
Khans. "Your core question, however, is not one I can answer

here and now. You want to know if we will fight for Strana Mechty and to preserve our way of life. Of course we will."

Osis frowned. "You have just answered the question you said you could not."

"Ah, but I did not say if we would fight for or against the Clans to do so." Leroux looked around at the other Khans. "The Star League is come to oppose us. The question is not whether we can stand against them, but if we *should* stand against them."

Vlad shook his head adamantly. "You are wrong, Khan Nova Cat. For you there is a question, but there is none for me. Not only can we stand against them, we *must* stand against them. The only noble remnants of the Star League that exist are the Clans. We were born of the last true members of the Star League, the last faithful members of it. For us to allow this usurper and pretender to destroy us only completes the destruction of the Star League that began so long ago.

"So, when Victor Davion arrives, he will find opposition, and anyone who is true to our mission will stand there beside me to fight him."

4

***DropShip* Barbarossa**
Inbound, Strana Mechty
Kerensky Cluster, Clan Space
12 April 3060

The Elemental's throw tossed Victor halfway across the cargo hold. Victor twisted enough in the air to land on his left shoulder and roll, but he was going too fast to get to his feet. Kai Allard-Liao caught him before he could slam into a bulkhead, steadied him, then gave him a little shove out toward the center of the floor.

"C'mon, Victor, she's just a girl."

Victor spitted his friend with an irritated glance. "Woman, and quite a woman at that."

The Elemental waited in the center of the floor, her feet spread wide apart, her knees bent, her hands out and ready to grapple with him. Tiaret Nevversan wore a sleeveless, khaki-colored leotard only a shade or two lighter than her skin. Her brown hair had been shaved from her head except at the back, where it hung in an abbreviated queue woven with a red cord.

Her light blue eyes seemed at odds with features that bespoke Terran African ancestry, yet reflected the strength of life in that body.

As Victor circled in toward her, he knew he was utterly and completely insane. She towered over him by fifty-five centimeters and had at least forty-five kilos on him. Her reach outstripped his, and she'd been trained since birth in hand-to-hand combat. While Victor had spent months honing his fighting skills on the long journey to Huntress, there was no way he could match hers. *And she's even seven years younger than me.*

He darted toward her, ducked beneath the swipe of a huge paw, and spun on his left foot. He hooked his right foot behind her right knee, intending to topple her, but he might as well have hooked his foot behind the leg of a BattleMech because she wasn't going anywhere.

Steely hands gripped the back of his neck and spun him off to his left. He whirled and rolled, then slid across the floor to Hohiro Kurita's feet. Victor sat there for a moment, then shook his head. "If this is the sort of fun you guys have planned for me on my thirtieth birthday, here, I don't want to be around you for my fortieth."

Hohiro helped him back to his feet. "Kai and I decided to do this to you so you'd have a chance at seeing your fortieth birthday. Now concentrate and go again."

With friends like these.

Victor balled his fists and raised them, then watched Tiaret straighten up and raise her fists. She cocked her right hand back by her shoulder, then slowly waved Victor in with her left hand. "Come, Prince Victor. I will show you why many warriors are retired by your age."

Victor groaned. "On my way." Clad in sparring boots, shorts, and a baggy sleeveless sweatshirt, Victor felt close to naked as he drew near her. *Fighting the Clans from inside a BattleMech is definitely less painful than this is likely to be.*

He stopped just outside her range and, remembering Hohiro's comment, took a second to focus himself.

Roughly the same second Tiaret chose to strike.

Victor slipped his head to the left as her left-hand jab sailed in at his head. In a nanosecond he saw her right fist coming in on a looping arc designed to mash his forehead into the back of his brainpan. Without thinking he began to twist to his left, and lashed out with his right hand. It locked over her right wrist and managed to steer her fist a fraction wide. The fact that he was turning within the circle of her arms took his head fully out of harm's way.

Pivoting on his right foot to make the turn, he extended his left leg in a rear kick that caught Tiaret in the stomach. It felt like kicking ferro-fibrous armor, but he got a gasp out of her. She spun away, ripping her wrist from his grasp. Victor felt good for an instant about having scored on her, then realized he couldn't see her and hadn't heard her hit the ground.

Her left leg scythed across his ankles and cut his legs from under him. Victor pitched to the floor and caught himself on his hands, but before he could leap up, she grabbed him by the waist and flipped him onto his back. She dropped onto his stomach, straddling him, then smiled down at him as her hands pinned his wrists to the floor.

"Not bad, Prince Victor, but not very good." A droplet of sweat hung on the tip of her nose, then splashed down on his forehead.

Victor frowned. "I couldn't dislodge you with pentaglycerine charges, could I?"

She shook her head, spraying a little more sweat over him. "And my sire you could not dislodge with atomic charges." Tiaret leaned back, then rose to her feet and dragged Victor up with her. "Remember that, please."

Victor nodded, wondering at the softness of her tone at the last. Tiaret Nevversan had led a Point of Elementals to take refuge in the sewers of Lootera. With them had gone a whole sibko of children barely ten years old—nearly fifty of them.

The Elementals had feared the youngsters would be slain in the Star League's attempt to destroy everything that was Smoke Jaguar, and had refused to surrender unless given assurances this would not happen by the commander of the Star League force.

Against the wishes of the task force leadership, Victor had met with her and assured her the children were safe. As the kids emerged from the sewers, the Elementals noted that five of them were missing. Victor immediately organized a search party and hunted for them along with Tiaret. When they were finally found, it was in a space far too small for her to fit through, so Victor had gone in and helped usher them out. Once on the surface again, she had surrendered to him. Victor instantly made her a bondswoman and freed her, welcoming her into the Star League force.

It was then he learned that she was Lincoln Osis' biological daughter. She knew little of her genefather in a personal sense because of the way the sibkos worked. In accord with the wishes of the various bloodname houses, Clan scientists combined sperm and ova in their laboratories to create the ultimate warriors. Osis and Nevversan blood mixed well in Tiaret, allowing her to win a bloodname while still a Star Captain.

Had the Smoke Jaguars been allowed to continue, she would have become a Khan. "I will remember this lesson, Tiaret. I'll remember it well."

The Precentor Martial, who had been standing back from the exercise area, now strode forward. He wore the white robe of ComStar, having chosen for some reason to abandon the military-style jumpsuit he usually favored. He tossed both Tiaret and Victor thick towels. "So, then, Victor, you won't be tempted to join Lincoln Osis in a Circle of Equals?"

Victor ran the towel over his face, giving himself a moment to think before answering. "As Tiaret has so easily demonstrated, I'm not a suitable match for an unarmed Elemental, but we've got reports that Lincoln Osis was badly wounded.

He might challenge me as a matter of bravado, and my refusal to engage a man in so weakened a state could be used as a mark of my cowardice."

Kai levered himself away from the bulkhead. "But your willingness to face and take advantage of so obviously crippled a man could be taken as even worse."

"Good point, Kai."

The Precentor Martial raised a finger. "Success or failure in a personal fight with Lincoln Osis would be immaterial. His power base has been destroyed. While we will end up dealing with him because he *is* the ilKhan, our objective is to show the rest of the Clans that they cannot continue their fight against us." He glanced at Tiaret. "Forgive me, but your father's defeat and death are now a sidelight to our battle on Strana Mechty."

Tiaret shrugged. "Though ilKhan, Lincoln Osis acted as if he were still a Smoke Jaguar Khan. In doing so he did not serve the Clans or the Smoke Jaguars. We all fought according to our orders, and we are not pleased with our defeat, but without proper leadership, there was little chance of a victory."

The Prince stripped off his soaking sweatshirt and toweled down, then settled the towel over his right shoulder. The tails on both sides hid the scars from the sword-wounds he'd taken on Luthien. *That seems so long ago, so far away.* "Well, inbound as we are, the Clans know we're coming. We have, what, three days to deceleration turn-around? We won't pick up any aerospace fighter contact before then, right?"

Anastasius Focht shook his head. "Unlikely. Since we came in at the sun's zenith jump point, there's no place for fighters to be hiding between here and Strana Mechty itself. If we're going to meet resistance, it will be closer in."

Jerry Cranston popped in through the hold's hatchway. "Highness, we've just had radio contact with Strana Mechty— data only, no voice or holo. Message came in over Martha Pryde's signature. In the name of the Grand Council of Khans, out of respect for ComStar's largesse at Tukayyid, we have been granted *safcon.* They will allow us to land uncontested. They want to meet with you in six days to discuss the bidding for the battle of Strana Mechty."

Victor threw back his head and barked a quick laugh. Smiling, he looked at his companions. "Now, *that,* gentlemen and lady, is a birthday present."

Kerensky Sports Centre
Strana Mechty
Kerensky Cluster, Clan Space
18 April 3060

Victor's hovercar slowly settled to the ground and a shiver ran through him. Air hissed as the gull-wing door slid up, but before he could even unfasten his restraining harness, Tiaret eclipsed the opening and was out the door. That she'd appointed herself Victor's bodyguard had been a matter of concern to some of the other commanders, but the Precentor Martial convinced them that her presence would be of enormous value, especially in the negotiations they were entering into this morning.

Victor slowly exhaled, then followed Focht and Redburn out of the hovercar. Green grassy fields stretched out before him and not a cloud appeared in the sky. Far to the south he saw the black outline of mountains that trapped purple light between their peaks, but elsewhere the dawning sun had risen enough to brighten everything he saw.

Over a dozen pavilions, large and small, dotted the fields in front of him. They varied in color and design, but all appeared muted and utilitarian, despite the Clan pennants flying from their highest points. Some of the crests he recognized: Wolf, Jade Falcon, Ghost Bear. Try as he might, though, the only sign of the Smoke Jaguars he could see was on a smaller tent closest to him, and that flew beneath a six-star pennant he assumed to be the insignia of the ilKhan.

Victor tugged at the cuffs of his jacket. He'd chosen to appear in the kind of jumpsuit MechWarriors wore over their shorts and cooling jackets pre- and post-battle, and his was the light Steiner blue and gray of the Tenth Lyran Guard unit he commanded. Over that he pulled on a dark blue canvas jacket festooned with Star League Defense Force patches and rank insignia.

Andrew Redburn wore his black and gold Kathil Uhlans uniform, but with an SLDF patch sewed over the left breast. The Precentor Martial had donned his ComStar robe, showing not only the Order's golden star insignia on the breast, but an SLDF patch added to the left shoulder. Tiaret wore a dark blue SLDF jumpsuit, but had cinched it around her narrow waist with a belt bearing the Smoke Jaguar mottling.

The quartet set off for the ilKhan's tent, making their unhurried way along a gravel path that looked newly incised into the ground. At the tent's mouth, four Elementals in their armor stood guard. The two on the left were from the Ghost Bear and Wolf Clans, and easily recognizable by the white and gray motifs painted on their armor. To the right stood a Jade Falcon and an Elemental from a Clan Victor couldn't place. The paint scheme involved whites and blues suitable for wintry battle, but the insignia had a verminish look to it.

"Tiaret, what's the white one on the right? What Clan?"

Contempt dripped through her reply. "Ice Hellion. As long as the war is with words, they are very brave."

"Always good to know." Victor lifted his chin as he passed through the Elemental phalanx. He paused a couple of steps inside the tent's opening and immediately recognized Marthe Pryde, the tall, dark-haired Khan of the Jade Falcons. Next to her stood a shorter, flame-haired man Victor took to be the Ice Hellion. Standing on either side of the desk occupying the center of the tent was a scar-faced man in Wolf Clan leathers and a slightly older, blond man wearing white clothing and a cloak of white fur adorned with pale gray claws—*presumably a Ghost Bear.*

The ilKhan rose smoothly from behind the desk, looking as big in a jumpsuit as the two armored Elementals behind him. Muscles bunched beneath ebon flesh and Victor sensed no unsteadiness or weakness in him. *If he was cut badly, aside from the scar on his forehead, I can't tell it.* Any last fantasy about meeting Lincoln Osis in single combat that might have lingered after Tiaret tossed him about died abruptly.

Victor took one step forward and extended his hand. "I am Victor Ian Steiner-Davion, Commander in Chief of the Star League Expeditionary Force."

Osis' eyes widened. "*You* are Victor Davion? Impossible. You are so . . . small."

The Prince's blue-flecked gray eyes narrowed. "Your underestimation of Inner Sphere forces has brought you to this point, ilKhan. Why compound your folly now?"

Shock registered immediately on Osis' face. The Ice Hellion also reddened as anger started him trembling, but the other three Khans managed to keep their reactions largely hidden. Only on Marthe Pryde's face could Victor detect the twitch of a smile.

The ilKhan balled his fists. "The folly here is yours, Victor."

Victor smiled, realizing that the ilKhan had refused to use his surname because the right to bear a bloodname was the highest honor existing among the Clans. *He seeks to shame me by addressing me so familiarly, but a first name really can't hold all the contempt he wants to project.* "Shall I then retreat to Huntress? I would feel safe there, I think. No one left there to fear."

With that remark even the Wolf Khan allowed himself a smirk to match the one that flashed across Martha Pryde's face. This Ghost Bear Khan took half a step forward. "I am Bjorn Jorgensson, of the Ghost Bears. I suggest this exchange is not productive, and not what we are here for. Victor Davion, you and your forces have been granted *safcon* and summoned here to bargain a battle. We should proceed."

"I agree, Khan Jorgensson." Victor half turned and pointed

to the trio standing behind him. "I would like to present my aides. Captain Tiaret Nevversan is late of the Smoke Jaguars. General Andrew Redburn commands the first Kathil Uhlans and had overall command of operations on Huntress for our final victory there. And this is Anastasius Focht, Precentor Martial of ComStar, victor of Tukayyid, and forger of the truce won from your invasion's second ilKhan."

The Prince turned back to face the other Khans. "The truce was very useful, but would expire, which is why we have come all this way. We challenge you to a Trial of Refusal concerning his whole invasion. When we win, you will forswear any attacks on the Inner Sphere."

Osis folded his arms across his broad chest. "And when we defeat you?"

"You won't."

The Wolf Khan smiled slyly. "Hardly a bargain you are offering us, Victor Davion. If we win, we should be rewarded."

Victor nodded. "If you win, the Precentor Martial is prepared to release you from the truce agreement he struck with Ulric Kerensky. You will again be free to attack the Inner Sphere."

The Ice Hellion spat out a sharp laugh. "If we win, you give us Terra."

Victor smiled. Word of Blake, the reactionary splinter group of ComStar, had wrested Terra from ComStar's control two years earlier. Word of Blake mixed mysticism with paranoia in a way that produced fanatic followers capable of all manner of lethal and insane actions. *I'd gladly give them Terra, and any other Word of Blake world, but they really aren't mine to give.*

"No, you don't get Terra." Victor shook his head slowly. "We've come here to fight for peace. You're fighting for the opposite, you're fighting for war. You win. You'll get all the war you want, and you'll get it in the Inner Sphere, and here, too."

Jorgensson's blue eyes half-closed. "If you were to win,

what would be the status of the worlds we've taken in the Inner Sphere?"

"If we win, I no longer see a state of war as existing between us." Victor carefully considered his words. "I cannot tell you that powerful people may not try to influence the Star League to drive you from your occupied worlds, or that wealthy people will not hire mercenaries to liberate those worlds. Economic integration of the Clan worlds into the Inner Sphere would be much more productive than war, and if that avenue were open, I suspect it would be preferred."

Marthe Pryde arched an eyebrow at Victor. "You think your people are tired of war?"

"I sincerely hope so." Victor let his gaze pass over each one of their faces. "You've based your culture on war and the need to prepare for it. We fight when pressed to do so, but that is not our preference. When we are forced to fight, as you know, we adapt quickly. This is the first expedition to your homeworlds. It can be the last. It will be, if I have any say in the matter.

"So, there it is. We challenge you to a Trial of Refusal of this invasion. Let us know what you will defend with, and we'll match you strength for strength."

Victor again looked from one Khan to another. "Here, on Strana Mechty, this thing will be decided. The best warriors will win, and the fate of mankind will be determined."

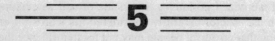

5

Hall of the Khans, Warrior Quarter
Strana Mechty
Kerensky Cluster, Clan Space
18 April 3060

Vlad turned around to watch the apoplectic Asa Taney explode from his seat in the Grand Council chamber. The small man's face had become a darker red than his hair, giving the impression that the hair was really a spray of blood fountaining up from his scalp. His balled fist slammed into his desk and made a surprisingly loud thump.

"We cannot allow ourselves to be trapped by this Trial of Refusal. The Inner Sphere forces—this ersatz Star League—have no right to use our traditions to bind us so."

Lucien Carns of the Nova Cats rose to that point. "Khan Taney, you forget that since the inception of the invasion we have issued challenges to the Inner Sphere troops and on Tukayyid we engaged in a similar trial. To refuse to honor a challenge now would be base chicanery and unworthy."

"Unworthy? It is *they* who are unworthy." Taney thrust a

finger toward the west, where the Inner Sphere forces had been allowed to land. "You were not there, Khan Carns, when this Victor came before us. He mocked the ilKhan. He mocked us. His language was full of contractions and he brought with him a bondswoman taken from Lincoln Osis' own genetic legacy. She is a harbinger of what we face if we accept this challenge."

Vlad allowed a low laugh to rumble from his throat. "She is a harbinger only if we are defeated, Khan Taney."

Taney shook his head. "*That* will not happen."

"If not, Khan Taney," asked Bjorn Jorgensson, "why the concern about accepting the consequences of defeat? Your protests seem out of place. Do you not want to fight?"

"Do not question my bravery, Khan Jorgensson. My Hellions and I will fight."

Vlad barely suppressed a smile. *And why do I think your air wing will be bid away first, Asa Taney?*

Kael Pershaw banged his gavel down. "The ilKhan's report on what the Inner Sphere offered at negotiation was not made a voting issue. To refuse such a challenge without becoming *dezgra,* the Grand Council would need only a simply majority vote to void the challenge."

Taney raised a hand. "I demand such a vote."

The Ghost Bear's Jorgensson nodded. "I would second that call."

Vlad ignored the buzz of voices around him. The Clans had long ago split into two camps along political lines. Wardens held that their true mission was to act as guardians for the Inner Sphere, waiting in their self-imposed exile until a crisis called them back to save the worlds that had spawned them. The Crusaders knew the truth and knew it was their destiny to conquer the Inner Sphere and provide leadership for all humanity. Until recently the Wolves had been a strong Warden Clan, but Phelan Kell had culled the Wardens and had taken them to the Inner Sphere, leaving behind the hard-core Crusaders.

Looking around the room, Vlad did a mental inventory of the Clans and their leanings. Of the sixteen Clans present—including the Smoke Jaguars, though Lincoln Osis was the only Jaguar in the room—seven were Wardens. That left nine Crusader Clans, though it would have been ten had the Star Adders not recently completed their absorption of Clan Burrock. *This provides the Crusaders with the needed votes to void the challenge.*

Vlad felt a shiver run down his spine. The conditions laid down with the challenge were not unexpected, and for his Clan the consequences would be far from disastrous. The Wolves had driven deep into the Inner Sphere. Their holdings exceeded all the other Clans. *If there is peace and we cannot attack the Inner Sphere, other Clans may be tempted to prey upon the Wolves. We are not so strong yet that we can scoff at the likely attacks to come our way.* By voting to void the challenge, another set of conditions would be negotiated, or the Inner Sphere would continue its war and the Wolves had the Ghost Bear and Jade Falcon occupation zones to serve as buffers against attack.

On the other hand, peace would work well for him and his people. His covert alliance with Katrina Steiner-Davion and her Lyran Alliance meant the Jade Falcon occupation zone was caught between his hammer and Katrina's anvil. The Wolves could fall on the Falcons, destroying a hated enemy, and help the Lyrans liberate worlds of their own. A formalization of his alliance with Katrina would unite the Wolves with the Inner Sphere, giving him a much more powerful base to work from. *And it would oust Phelan Kell and his rogue Wolves from their safe haven.*

Before Vlad had reached a decision on how he would vote, Kael Pershaw spoke. "The senior Khan will issue the vote for each Clan. Since the ilKhan is still the senior Khan of record for the Smoke Jaguars, he will vote for them. I will have your votes now, by Clan."

Things began much as Vlad anticipated. The Blood Spirits

and Fire Mandrills, Crusaders both, voted to void. They were balanced out by the Cloud Cobras and Diamond Sharks, who chose to sustain the challenge. That brought things to the Ghost Bears, another Crusader Clan.

Kael Pershaw looked up at Bjorn Jorgensson. "What is the will of the Ghost Bears?"

The flesh around Jorgensson's eyes tightened. "To void this challenge would be to repudiate the whole of our tradition. Ghost Bear votes to sustain."

Vlad blinked. The Ghost Bears had the most to lose if the challenge were upheld. Though they were the strongest of the invading clans, without the Smoke Jaguars in place, they now bordered the Draconis Combine. The fanatical Kuritas would undoubtedly continue to press for the reconquest of their worlds, leaving the Ghost Bears vulnerable. *They must have some trick in mind.*

The voting continued to split along Crusader and Warden lines, leaving Vlad the last to vote. Since the Wardens possessed eight votes because of the Ghost Bear defection, the challenge could not be voided. As Pershaw called for his vote, Vlad smiled. "The Wolf Clan chooses to abstain."

Marialle Radick shot him a quick glance, but Vlad waved away her mute inquiry. *Why waste a vote in a decided matter, when by doing the unexpected I can sow chaos and uncertainty?*

Lincoln Osis looked up from the ilKhan's bench. "The challenge stands. Next we shall decide who shall fight for us."

Taney stood. "We should all fight."

Marthe Pryde scoffed from the top rank. "Those who have earned the right to fight should fight."

The ilKhan nodded. "Khan Pryde is correct. The original four invading Clans shall fight, of course . . ."

"You will forgive me, ilKhan." Bjorn Jorgensson rose slowly behind his desk. "The Ghost Bears have no desire to participate in this battle."

"What?" Osis' face screwed down into a sour frown. "How can you refuse this honor?"

Jorgensson leaned forward. "How can you call this an honor? We have defined ourselves as warriors down through the centuries. We have refined our skills and our weapons, and have even resorted to altering the basic structure of human culture to create a martial ideal in our people. When we first invaded the Inner Sphere, our victories, our *easy* victories, confirmed what we had long held true: we were the physical, intellectual, and moral superiors of those who had been left behind.

"You, ilKhan, stand here, wounded, stripped of your Clan, exiled from your homeworld with no hope of return, seeing your bloodkin serving your enemy. We all saw an Inner Sphere warrior, Phelan, rise from bondsman to Khan of the Wolves. Both of you put the lie to what we have thought of ourselves. By defeating you, by having one of their own rise to high rank among us, have we not been shown that our superiority was an illusion?"

Vlad looked up at Jorgensson. "You have not forgotten our victories, Khan Jorgensson."

"No, Khan Ward, I have not. They burn brightly in my mind, as do the images from our defeats. On Tukayyid, ComStar showed us our vulnerability to prolonged warfare. Since then, our major efforts have been thwarted. The Huntress campaign showed that even here, in our own stronghold, we are vulnerable. Our supposed invincibility is a sham, as is our superiority.

"The reality of things is quite clear to us. As Crusaders, we embraced the invasion because it was clearly our destiny, and our early, easy victories made that plain. Our defeats have undercut our conviction in *destiny*. After long consideration, the Ghost Bears have come to question our commitment to the Crusader philosophy, and now consider ourselves Wardens, so we can avoid the sort of self-deception that has brought the Clans to this state. We now stand with our Warden brethren, apart from the Crusaders, so they may defend an invasion that has defined them, and likely will destroy them. Take heart, though, ilKhan. I am certain there will be no end of Clans willing to take our place.

Vlad shivered. *This is a serious realignment by the Ghost Bears. They will require close watching, especially with their holding being next to mine in the occupation zone.*

Osis stared with disbelief plain on his face at Jorgensson, then slowly shook his head. "Are there others of you who do not wish to fight against the Inner Sphere?"

Not unexpectedly, the other Warden Khans answered the ilKhan's question in the affirmative. Severen Leroux stood in the back rank of the room. "The Nova Cats applaud the Ghost Bears and the other Wardens who are wise enough to look for something other than blood to fulfill their lives. Shed a single drop more of Inner Sphere blood and you will doom yourselves for all time. This is your chance to be welcomed back into the fold of humanity. We took ourselves apart so we would not be consumed by the Inner Sphere's squabbling, and we have united them against us. Let us not fall prey to their unity."

Taney laughed aloud. "We will not fall prey to it. We will shatter it."

Leroux hissed. "Seek that course, Asa Taney, and you walk a path more evil than you can imagine. A wound has healed. Reopen it, and the diseases that fester there will consume you. You cannot be allowed to do this."

The Ice Hellion sneered contemptuously at the Nova Cat Khan. "Your brain has atrophied with age, Khan Leroux. We will go and fight the Inner Sphere. We will break them, then we will turn our eyes to you and your Clan. Your days are at an end."

"This I know, Asa Taney, but I also know how they will end." Severen Leroux sighed heavily, letting his shoulders slump. "Your choice forces mine."

"I am certain." Taney turned back toward the ilKhan. "The

Wardens and their ilk clearly have no stomach for a fight. So be it. There are eight Crusader Clans. We will defend the Clans and our honor."

Osis nodded. "Seven Clans fought on Tukayyid, eight will fight here. Smoke Jaguar, Ice Hellion, Jade Falcon, Blood Spirit, Fire Mandrill, Star Adder, Hell's Horses, and the Wolves. On our shoulders will rest the fate of the Inner Sphere."

Vlad nodded. "We are defending, ilKhan. What shall we defend with?"

The ilKhan shifted his shoulders uneasily. "They said they would match us, strength for strength, which is good. Of my Clan's warriors, all I have left are the Elementals who carried me from Huntress and my bodyguard Binary here on Strana Mechty."

"That is well and good for you, ilKhan." Asa Taney's smile grew quite broad. "The rest of us can summon more troops from our homeworlds."

"Why would you need more than a bodyguard unit?" Marthe Pryde looked down on the red-headed Ice Hellion. "I see no reason to require more than a Binary to defeat any unit of Inner Sphere forces. BattleMechs have ruled warfare since their introduction six centuries ago, and have decided outcomes as momentous as this one before. We need nothing else to defeat the Inner Sphere."

Vlad echoed Marthe's words in a low voice. "Khan Pryde has it right. An incompetent leader will lose as easily with a Cluster as he will a Binary. A superior leader will win no matter the forces he's given. Each of us should prepare a Binary and choose wherever it is we wish to defend."

Taney stared hard at Vlad. "Is this it, then? You would have us cripple ourselves when we face the greatest threat to the Clans we have yet known?"

Vlad laughed. "It strikes me, Asa Taney, that this is the *only* threat the Ice Hellions have faced since before the Invasion. If I fear for the Clans, it is because of your participation, not the size of your contribution to our effort."

"You will pay for your temerity, Khan Ward."

"Will I?" Vlad narrowed his eyes. "I have fought against the Inner Sphere and defeated them, Ice Hellion. Once you have done the same, then you can come to me and talk of payment. Until that time, your bluster does not frighten me. If you survive your next battle, come see me."

Osis slammed a fist against his desk. "Enough of this squabbling—you are worse than a sibko. Determine your forces and submit them to Kael Pershaw. He will communicate them to our enemies. Prepare yourselves and your people for this battle. We cannot afford to lose."

6

Star League Expeditionary Force Headquarters
Nicholas' Ford, Strana Mechty
Kerensky Cluster, Clan Space
19 April 3060

Victor closed his eyes against the burning and craned his head back. His shoulders felt like stone and the top of his skull seemed to have a massive weight on it, pressing down on his brain. He opened his eyes again and let the world swim back into focus. In the center of the tent, in the middle of the U-shaped conglomeration of long tables where his advisors sat, a holographic representation of Strana Mechty's southern continent burned. On it a series of eight stars blinked, each one indicating a battlefield chosen by the defending Clans.

"Thank you all for coming back here. I know we're all short on sleep, but I'm interested in your analysis of the data we've been sent. We have to figure out how much we're going to send against them and who is going to take on what force."

The Precentor Martial leaned forward at his place on the

far end of the U's right arm. "It appears, with only a couple of exceptions, that we are facing a Binary of 'Mechs from each participating Clan. The Ice Hellions have added a Point of aerospace fighters, but I suspect that is because one of their Khans, Asa Taney, is a pilot. Hell's Horses have included a Star of armor in their force, in place of a Star of 'Mechs. I suspect it is less because they are contemptuous of us than that they have a tradition of employing armor."

"And a company of twelve of our 'Mechs pretty much matches the ten 'Mechs they have in a Binary, right?"

Focht nodded at Victor. "Correct. Given the information we have here, we can match their firepower fairly closely— even taking into account the new 'Mechs we've never seen in combat before. The datafiles are revealing, but I see no true surprises."

Kai frowned. "It looks as if the Smoke Jaguars shorted themselves a BattleMech and substituted a Point of Elementals."

Victor scratched at the back of his neck. "Osis is an Elemental. It makes sense."

"Highness, if you will permit me, please, I wish to make a request." The woman seated at Focht's left hand glanced at Victor with fiery green eyes. "I would ask that you allow the Free Rasalhague Republic's Third Drakøns to fight the Wolves. No other Clan did so much to destroy our nation."

"I appreciate your desire to face the Wolves, Overstë Dahlstrom, but we cannot pick and choose partners as if this were a dance."

Joan Dahlstrom's head came up. "But you will fight the Smoke Jaguars, will you not? It will be you, our commander, against the ilKhan?"

Hohiro Kurita frowned at her. "Is there someone who has a better claim on the Smoke Jaguars than Victor?"

Dahlstrom nodded adamantly. "I would think you do, Kurita-*san*. You were made prisoner by them, Luthien was attacked by them, and they carved their empire out of your nation."

Hohiro smiled easily as his voice came low and confident. "*Hai,* all these things are true; but here, I am not Hohiro Kurita of the Draconis Combine. Here, I am Hohiro Kurita of the Star League Expeditionary Force. If I let my personal desires interfere with my duty, I let the same forces that brought us here tear us apart. We are a united force, each of us playing our parts. I ask for no favors and expect none."

Joan Dahlstrom chewed her lower lip for a moment, then nodded. "I stand corrected. Please, Highness, ignore my previous request. Use my people where you will."

Victor gave her a reassuring smile. "Thank you, Overstë, for being so cooperative. I hope we can get through the decisions here smoothly so we have time to plan for our attacks. I have some thoughts, and if you will permit me, I'd like to have your feedback on them. Jerry, bring up the Wolves, please."

Jerrard Cranston hit a button on his noteputer, and the display shifted to show an area with a few rolling hills, but otherwise clear terrain. "This is the Kawlm District the Wolves want to defend."

Victor pointed a hand at the display. "As you can see, it is very open and favors their extended-range weapons. What I would like to do is throw a fast force against them, one they've not seen before, and one that can chew them up. Kai, I was thinking you might build a company out of your St. Ives Lancers to take them."

Kai's gray eyes sparkled. "You want me to go after the Wolves?"

"Truth be told, I want you to go after Vlad Ward. Because the Lancers haven't fought the Wolves before, I bet he'll underestimate you. Frankly, this fight is also going to be more freewheeling than most."

Kai shrugged. "Can't be anything I haven't seen on Solaris."

"That's my thinking." Victor hesitated. The Wolves were likely to be one of the toughest units in the field. *Here I am sending a good friend out to die.* "Are you willing to take the assignment?"

"Victor, if you think this is where my people and I will serve best, we'll be there." A bit of a smirk tightened the corner Kai's mouth. "You remember, back on Arc-Royal, Phelan and I shot each other out in a simulator battle? Phelan had some run-ins with this Vlad. I don't mind finding out how good he really is."

"Let's hope he's not as good as Phelan was." Victor looked next at Hohiro. "Jerry, bring up the Neegdye area."

The image changed from rolling plains to a broken landscape with brush-choked ravines and forests of twisted trees. "Hohiro, this is the area the Blood Spirits have chosen to defend. It's really a maze of ravines and hills, with lots of forest. It completely negates their range advantage, so I don't know why they picked it. Your First Genyosha Regiment is very good at adapting to new situations. I'd like to have you take the Blood Spirits."

Hohiro nodded confidently. "I am reminded of a story of feudal Japan in which a bandit was known for fighting with a *kusari-gama*—a sickle with a weighted chain attached to the haft. He would ensnare his foes with the chain, then finish them with the blade. Many samurai tried to end his career, but he defeated them all until one wise man engaged him in a bamboo stand. If the Blood Spirits wish to be so foolish as to limit themselves, we will be happy to destroy them."

"Good. They are yours, then."

The next terrain image flashed to life. The holograph showed a mountainous region with a lake in its center. Victor couldn't tell if he was looking at the broken-down remains of an old volcano, or just a mountain that had been savaged by millennia of weather, but outcroppings of rock and boulders dotted the landscape.

"This is Zhaloba Mountain, which the Jade Falcons will defend. We know their troops are pretty sharp, thanks to the training they got on Coventry. The personnel records appended to the Falcon data indicated that all the warriors they will deploy against us did serve on Coventry, including Martha Pryde. I want a crack unit to go after them. I was thinking, Precentor Martial, of using elements of your 394th Division."

Focht nodded. "I will inform Precentor Harvison to prepare his people."

Before Victor could continue the briefing, shouting arose from outside the tent housing him and his staff. The flap slid open and Tiaret stooped to poke her head in. "Forgive me, Highness, but there is a situation you may want to address here. You, and the Precentor Martial."

Victor looked at Focht and sighed. "Okay, we'll be back in a moment or two. Anastasius, after you."

The two men filed from the tent and followed Tiaret through the SLDF encampment. She led them to the makeshift detention center and swung the door open. Victor stepped in first and saw three men seated on a bench, two rather calm and the third very agitated. Four security officers with stun batons stood around them.

Victor frowned. "We're not going to have trouble here, are we?"

The two calm men shook their heads. The third man, who wore a ComStar uniform, frowned, then shook his head. Victor vaguely remembered having seen the man in the Precentor Martial's company, but he couldn't recall his name.

"Very well. Good work, men. You may leave us alone with your charges here. Tiaret, you can stay." Victor let the guards slip past him, then turned to the two older gentlemen. "I'm Victor Davion. I would have to guess you are Nova Cats."

Both of them stood. "I am Severen Leroux and this is Lucian Carns. We are the Nova Cat Khans."

Victor blinked. "I, ah, I didn't think the Clans allowed so venerable individuals to hold power."

"All of the Clans are not the same, Victor." Leroux half-closed his eyes. "The Nova Cats, as you already know, are different. You have seen that in how we have dealt with the Star League reborn."

The Prince nodded slowly. The Nova Cats had held worlds that once belonged to the Draconis Combine and had recently entered into negotiations with the Combine concerning those worlds. Though Victor did not understand everything concerning the Nova Cats, he had been told they tended to believe in portents and omens, and acted accordingly. One of the Khans had seen a vision that suggested resistance against the Star League was wrong, so the Nova Cat units had come over to the Inner Sphere with scarcely more than a shot being fired.

"What can I do for you?"

Before Leroux could answer, the third man shot to his feet. "They want you to do for them the thing I was promised and have been denied."

Victor turned to look at him, ignoring the scars that twisted the side of the man's face. "Something you were promised? Refresh my memory."

"I am Trent. I was a Smoke Jaguar. I gave you the Exodus Road." The man's voice came low and full of frustration. "If not for me, you'd not be here, none of you. I gave you the route to Huntress in return for the Precentor Martial's promise of a command so I could show the Smoke Jaguars the error of their ways. He promised I would be able to fight the people who have betrayed the Kerensky vision."

Trent glanced at the Nova Cats. "I was walking through the camp and I came across these two. They said you were deciding who would fight against the Clans, and that I did not figure into your considerations."

Victor met the man's incendiary gaze without flinching. "How they determined that fact, I don't know, but it is a fact. They were right. You don't figure into my considerations."

Color drained from Trent's face. He turned to the Precentor Martial. "But you promised."

Focht nodded. "I did."

Victor spitted Trent with a merciless stare. "And his most persuasive arguments will not prevail because your considerations and his considerations are not *my* considerations. *My* considerations are directed at stopping a war that has affected the lives of trillions of people. Your petty vendetta means nothing to me. I've just told the representatives of nations that I'm not going to let them pick and choose which Clans they will fight just because they feel they owe them or were wronged by them.

"I apologize to the Precentor Martial for voiding this promise he made to you, but I do not apologize for denying you what you want. You sold your people out. You say it is because they have strayed from Kerensky's vision, but the reason does not matter to me. Did you not look around on Huntress? You were there. Did you not see what you'd done? Isn't that enough? Is killing someone yourself so important now?"

"Yes."

"Then you have my pity."

"You don't understand what it is to be Clan, to be a warrior."

"No, Mr. Trent," Victor said, pointing a quivering finger at him, "you don't understand that the Clan way is finished. You've been avenged—your Smoke Jaguars have been taught a lesson from which they will never recover. It's over for you, too."

The Prince watched anger and frustration color the man's face. He felt sorry for Trent in some ways. The man had an agenda that he clearly saw as important, but in comparison to the forces that were driving the expedition to Strana Mechty and the gravity of the outcome, his wishes were inconsequential. Moreover, he'd betrayed his own people and, no matter what his provocation or reasons, Victor knew he could never trust him. *Traitors have no friends because they have proven capable of turning on friends.*

Severen Leroux laid a hand on Victor's shoulder. "Prince

Victor, please. Khan Carns and I have come on a mission of importance. We have a Binary that will—that *must*—fight with you against the Clans. We must fight the Ice Hellions. If we are not there at the Lyod Glacier to oppose them, disaster will result and you will never know peace."

Victor rubbed a hand across his brow. "Did you just miss what I told him?"

"No, Prince Victor, I heard it all. It has no bearing on this situation." Severen Leroux frowned. "This is the way it will be, the way it must be. I have seen it. This is the choice you must make if you want peace to last. If we do not fight the Ice Hellions, they will defeat your forces and the war will continue unabated."

The Prince closed his eyes. Two years earlier he would have dismissed the story of a vision with a skeptical laugh. But in the last two years he had seen the Nova Cats embrace the Star League because of one of these visions. *And I visited my dead father and told him I would find my own way in the world.* He knew he had no business accepting their offer, believing in their vision, but the conviction in Severen's voice sank through him. The fact that the Nova Cat Khans had not seemed surprised at the revelation that Trent had betrayed the Clans did not escape him, adding weight to their argument.

He glanced at the Precentor Martial. "We've trusted them in the Inner Sphere and proudly added their troops to the Star League Defense Force. Do we trust them now?"

The Precentor Martial thought for a moment, then nodded. "If joining us is what they believe stands between war and peace, I am willing to have them fight on our side."

Victor nodded, then turned to the Nova Cat Khans. "I accept your service. You will oppose the Ice Hellions."

"What? Do you know *no* honor, Victor Davion?" Trent took a half-step forward, his clawed hands reaching for Victor's throat. Before Victor could react, or Tiaret could grab Trent, Severen Leroux lashed out with an open-handed slap that spun Trent to the ground. The elder Nova Cat Khan landed on the man's chest, driving the wind out of him, and grabbed Trent's right wrist. Around it he twisted a cord he'd drawn from his pocket.

"There, Trent, you are now my bondsman. You belong to the Nova Cats." Leroux straightened up and let the cord slip from the man's wrist. "I now accept you as a warrior in our Clan. If you wish, you may join us in fighting the Ice Hellions."

Trent coughed and rubbed at the red mark on his cheek. "Ice Hellions? I will fight them for you."

"Good. Go to my Alpha Galaxy headquarters. They are waiting for you." Leroux glanced at the Precentor Martial. "You have no objections?"

"He will fight well for you." Focht helped Trent to his feet. "Go, Trent. You have what you wanted now. Finish what you started."

Trent left the tent, and Victor turned to Leroux. "So a traitor does have a friend. You didn't have to do that."

"His role in this was foreseen as well." The older man smiled. "He will only know peace when he dies as a warrior."

Victor smiled. "I've heard that said of a lot of us."

"Yes, but some will have that release denied them." Leroux's mouth twisted into a quizzical smile. "Trent will have his release. It was really the only way for him. To know the future can have value when disaster can be averted, but knowing when someone will die, and making it possible, that is wearying."

Lucien Carns patted Leroux on the shoulder. "It is his burden to see too much, and mine to see too little. What I do see is this: the Nova Cats pledge themselves to the Star League. We will devote a Binary to this fight, then the rest will be for you to command, Victor. When you use them, use them wisely."

The Prince shivered. "I will ever and always do so."

Carns nodded. "We know. That is the other reason we

came. You will fare well, Victor Davion. Yours will not be a life without pain or adversity, but perseverance is your strength. Remember that always and the promise of your name will be fulfilled."

ComStar Command Center, Zhaloba Mountain
Strana Mechty
Kerensky Cluster, Clan Space
23 April 3060

With his head encased in the Interactive Construct Reality helmet in the command center at the foot of Zhaloba Mountain, Anastasius Focht felt entombed. The ICR suit he wore kept him snug and even a bit warm, as if he were in the cockpit of a BattleMech. As the feed came in from the computer to which his ICR gear was attached, the world brightened and above him a wheel of images slowly spun.

Reaching up with his right hand, which appeared ungloved in the simulation environment, he pulled the wheel down and let it spin around him until he found the image he wanted. He selected it and it expanded, filling the blue expanse that had surrounded him. In an instant the datafeed from Precentor Harvison's *Black Knight* appeared. The gyrostabilizers connected to the camera-mount kept the image surprisingly still as the 'Mech lumbered toward Zhaloba Mountain.

The visual of the battlefield that Focht had seen in the briefing room was an aerial shot taken from the east. Had he been looking at it now, he could have made out the dozen ComStar 'Mechs making their way across the last hillside to the foot of the mountain. Coming in from the west was really the only way to approach the objective, a point Focht was fairly certain had not been lost on Marthe Pryde. ComStar would be attacking up-slope in an effort to dislodge the Jade Falcons, and that was not going to be an easy battle.

Focht had a moment's regret at not being there with Harvison, strapped inside a 'Mech. All his life the image of being a MechWarrior had been the apex of human achievement. To be one of the best required skill, courage, and a willingness to accept the utmost in responsibility. A single BattleMech had the power to level buildings—in warfare it was implacable and all but invincible unless pitted against another ten-meter-tall 'Mech. All BattleMechs were grim, mechanical avatars of Death, grouped into legions of automatons piloted by the finest warriors a nation could produce.

For a moment he wondered if his refusal to join the unit had come from cowardice. That specter lurked at the back of every warrior's mind, most often buried deep beneath tradition and honor, but there were times it dug itself from that grave. In those times everyone ended up wondering if it was his turn, if that next shell had her name on it, if that laser bolt was meant for him. Fear like that seemed irrational, but Focht realized it was the only rational aspect to being a warrior. *We willingly put ourselves in a position where we can be killed to protect those who cannot protect themselves. It goes against every instinct for survival we have, yet we do it. Fear reminds us we're acting in an insane manner.*

He scanned the rim of the lake area, looking for any 'Mech deployed to oppose the incoming ComStar unit, but he saw none. Harvison's *Black Knight* came equipped with a Beagle Active probe that enhanced his ability to find hidden 'Mechs, but it detected nothing. This also did not surprise Focht, since he would have had his 'Mechs waiting back away from the rim to avoid damage. *There will be time enough to move them forward when we get in range.*

Focht didn't find fear inside himself. He'd made his decision to stay behind despite a desire to be there. Though he was eighty-seven years old, he was still more than capable of piloting a BattleMech. He managed to continue training and maintaining performance testing scores that kept him on ComStar's active pilot roster, but he knew his scores were closer to the minimums needed than to the highest marks he'd ever posted. His decline in skill was natural, a product of aging, and it left him far behind the best ComStar had to offer.

And the best was what Harvison and his people were. They had all volunteered to be part of the company being sent against the Jade Falcons. None of them harbored illusions about how difficult the fighting was likely to be. Casualties and even fatalities were to be expected, as the Clans were fighting for their lives. *And yet they volunteered.*

Focht admired the way Harvison had put together his company. The 'Mechs had a decent mix of long and closer-ranged weapons, so they'd be able to engage the Clanners as they came in. All of the 'Mechs were also humanoid in configuration, so as they fanned out and around the *Black Knight,* moving to take advantage of the cover offered by granite boulders and outcroppings, they almost looked like a company of armored infantry. Resplendent in their white paint with the gold ComStar device worked on the left breast and the dark blue crest of the Star League Expeditionary Force circling the arms and thighs, the 'Mechs moved forward and up the mountainside. Despite having lost a *Black Knight* to a hip-actuator failure as the march to the mountain began, the ComStar force was formidable indeed.

Focht caught a flicker of movement at the crest of the slope. Five Clan 'Mechs, all painted the Jade Falcon's bright green, came into view. He felt ice ripple through his guts as this first line of defense presented itself. All five of the 'Mechs—a *Black Hawk,* two *Turkina*s and two *Black Lanner*s—all had very low profiles with back-canted bird legs. The 'Mechs could pop up to fire down at their enemies, then squat to minimize the effect of incoming shots.

The *Black Hawk*'s pilot targeted Harvison's *Black Knight*. All six of the extended-range medium lasers built into the 'Mech's right wrist blazed away, but the shots went low, burning a line in the golden meadow ten meters from the ComStar 'Mech. One of the lasers in the other arm sent a shaft of ruby light stabbing at the *Black Knight*'s head. The diagnostic icons in the corner of the view painted the 'Mech's head red, but pilot status remained green.

Harvison fired back with the particle projection cannon built into the *Hawk*'s right arm and the large laser mounted in its right chest. The large laser's green beam missed high, but the PPC's cobalt beam drilled straight into the center of the Clan 'Mech's torso. Half-melted armor plates dropped away, leaving a blackened scar on the *Black Hawk*'s chest.

One of the *Turkina*s turned its weapons on a *Grim Reaper*. The medium laser built into the *Turkina*'s left flank vaporized armor on the center of the bulky *Grim Reaper*'s chest. The twin large lasers mounted in the 'Mech's right arm bracketed the *Grim Reaper,* boiling off some of the protection on both arms. One of the two large pulse lasers in the Clanner's left arm missed, but the other sent a hail of green energy darts to chew away at the armor over the *Grim Reaper*'s right hip.

The ComStar 'Mech shuddered under the assault, but the pilot kept the machine upright. The pilot even managed to return fire. The LRM launcher built into the right side of the 'Mech's chest launched a volley of long-range missiles that streaked up at the *Turkina*. The majority of them blasted armor from the 'Mech's right shoulder, but two chipped away at the armor on the other arm. The *Grim Reaper*'s large laser sizzled off armor on the Clan 'Mech's left breast, sending molten ferro-ceramics streaming down its torso.

Another of the ComStar BattleMechs, a broad-shouldered, bullet-headed *Excalibur,* chose that same *Turkina* as its target. The spread of LRMs it launched savaged the *Turkina*'s left chest, ripping away at the already damaged armor there. The Gauss rifle in the *Excalibur*'s right arm sped a silvery projectile at the Clan 'Mech. The ball smashed into the *Turkina*'s left thigh, shivering armor plates from it, but leaving it far from unprotected.

The company's second *Excalibur* opened up on a small, squat, bird-legged *Black Lanner.* The ComStar pilot's Gauss rifle slug struck the ridge in front of the Clan 'Mech, skipping the projectile high over the target. The spray of LRMs did hit, carving armor from the *Black Lanner*'s left chest and right leg, but really did no serious damage. Another ComStar 'Mech, a heavyset *Shootist,* pointed its right arm at the *Black Lanner* and fired with the large laser built therein. The green beam carved armor from the Clanner's right arm, leaving smoke rising from a blackened furrow.

The *Black Lanner* fired back at its primary tormentor, the *Excalibur*. The PPC in the *Black Lanner*'s right arm sent an azure bolt of synthetic lighting out, stabbing it deep into the left side of the *Excalibur*'s torso. Armor exploded outward, leaving the ComStar 'Mech's left flank naked, and the support structure below it blackened.

The second Jade Falcon *Black Lanner* drew fire from a trio of ComStar 'Mechs. The cylindrically built *Spartan* pointed the PPC built into the left side of its chest at the smaller 'Mech and fired. The blue bolt ruptured armor plates on the *Black Lanner*'s left breast. A second *Spartan* likewise used its PPC on the Clan 'Mech, roasting a similar amount of armor on the other side of the *Black Lanner*'s chest. The company's second *Shootist* fired its large laser at the Jade Falcon, but missed low, instantly igniting grasses into a smoldering blaze.

The *Black Lanner* answered the assaults by attacking the *Shootist* with its extended-range medium lasers. Of the five beams used, only three hit. Two blistered armor off the ComStar 'Mech's right flank, while the last carved a nasty scar across its left shin. The *Shootist*'s pilot kept the 'Mech on its feet, and Focht realized the two *Black Lanners* were of different battlefield configurations.

The final Clan 'Mech, a massive *Turkina*, vented its wrath on the second ComStar *Grim Reaper*. The twin large pulse lasers scattered a storm of laser needles over the *Grim Reaper*'s chest and right arm, reducing armor to a greasy black mist. Of the two extended-range large lasers in the *Turkina*'s right arm, only one hit. It shriveled yet more armor over the ComStar 'Mech's breast. The torso-mounted medium laser speared the 'Mech's right leg with a ruby beam, dissolving armor plates into fluid ceramic sludge.

The *Grim Reaper* fought back, hitting with both LRMs and its large laser. The missiles gnawed armor from both arms and blew a chunk of it off the *Turkina*'s chest. The large laser sent a beam into the 'Mech's right arm, slicing through armor to leave a crescent-shaped wound burned though the green paint.

Another ComStar *Black Knight* fired at the *Turkina*, but missed with its PPC and one of its large lasers. The second green large laser beam slagged armor on the *Turkina*'s chest, expanding on the damage done by the missiles. The *Turkina* remained visible and did not shrink back despite the damage, the pilot seeming contemptuous of the ComStar efforts to kill him.

As the 'Mechs set themselves for another exchange, Focht had a feeling of dread crawl up his spine. Though his people had given as good as they'd gotten in the first round of fighting, they'd only engaged half of the Jade Falcon force. ComStar's pilots had softened up the enemy, but two ComStar 'Mechs had taken serious damage, leaving the pilots very vulnerable.

The Precentor Martial frowned for a moment. The Jade Falcon commander wasn't using her *Black Lanners*' speed to its obvious advantage in flanking the ComStar force. Briefly, he wondered why, then cold dread filled his stomach. *She doesn't need to employ them in that way. She has us at a disadvantage and is willing to fight hobbled to prove her superiority.*

Focht reached out but stopped himself before he opened a radio frequency to Harvison. He wanted to advise the man to hang back. With the damage to the head of Harvison's *Black Knight* being so severe, another shot could wipe out the cockpit, killing him and leaving his force leaderless. *He has to know that, but his 'Mech still continues to press the attack.*

The Precentor Martial held back. *I gave the battle to Harvison, now it is his to fight. He knows what he's doing, and concentrating fire seems to be effective. Will it be effective enough, though?*

Harvison's *Black Knight* targeted the *Black Hawk* again. The PPC again struck the Clan 'Mech in the center of the chest, all but denuding it of armor. The green beam of the large laser gobbled up armor on the *Black Hawk*'s right arm, reducing the protection there by half.

The *Black Hawk* engaged the *Black Knight* again, cutting loose with its medium lasers. This time, however, it shot all six of the weapons built into the 'Mech's left arm, and only one from the right. The red beam in the right arm shot low again, confirming Focht's suspicions of a serious malfunction there, while five of the other beams nailed their target. Three combined to claw away all but the last of the armor on the *Black Knight*'s right arm, while the other two ablated armor over the center and left sides of the 'Mech's chest.

Focht's virtual world whirled. He fought vertigo, then reached up and pulled down another datafeed from the unit's other *Black Knight*. Off to its right he could see the smoking form of Harvison's 'Mech down on the ground. Little grass fires—ignited by super-hot armor shards—surrounded the 'Mech, making it look almost like an ancient knight laid out for a funeral. Harvison's 'Mech did move its arms and legs, so Focht knew the pilot was still alive, but riding a ten-meter-tall BattleMech to the ground seldom did any pilot much good.

The first Clan *Turkina* again shot at the *Grim Reaper* it had attacker earlier. Twin pulse lasers hit, peppering the 'Mech over its right and center chest with green energy darts. The pair of large laser bolts ripped along the *Grim Reaper*'s right leg, burning away the last of the armor there, then started in on the myomer muscle fibers that allowed the 'Mech to move. The medium laser in the *Turkina*'s left flank drilled into the *Grim Reaper*'s right flank, leaving only the thinnest layer of armor in place.

Even as the *Turkina* targeted it, the *Grim Reaper* fired back. The LRMs swarmed from its chest-mounted launcher and rode argent jets in toward the target. The group blasted armor from the 'Mech's middle and right flank, as well as compounding the earlier damage done to the 'Mech's thigh. The *Grim Reaper*'s large laser added to the destruction done to the *Turkina*'s right breast, leaving the 'Mech's torso armor tattered on both flanks. Yet, despite having done that damage, the *Grim Reaper*'s pilot could not keep his 'Mech on its feet. It crashed down beside the *Black Knight*.

The *Excalibur* went after the *Turkina* again and sent a Gauss rifle slug into its left arm, reducing armor plates to dust. The LRMs it launched peppered the *Turkina*'s right arm and flank, grinding away at the armor, but failing to open a breach. Regardless, the savaging the Clan 'Mech took unbalanced it enough that it went down, disappearing behind the hill crest.

The first Clan *Black Lanner* blazed away at the *Excalibur* that had attacked it before. Its first pulse laser sent a stream of scarlet energy darts through the gaping armor on the left side of the Mech's breast, melting support structures. The PPC completely vaporized the armor on the right side of the Com-Star 'Mech's torso, then the second pulse laser drilled through to seriously shred the 'Mech's frame. A huge gout of black smoke jetted from the holes, telling Focht that the *Excalibur*'s engine shielding had been damaged, spiking the heat output and all but rendering the 'Mech useless. And yet, despite the pounding the *Excalibur* had taken, the pilot kept it upright and returned the *Black Lanner*'s fire.

The *Excalibur*'s Gauss rifle hammered a projectile into the *Black Lanner*'s left flank, crushing the armor and seriously warping support structures. The LRM barrage scored armor on the 'Mech's left leg and over its heart and poured more damage into the naked left flank. The *Black Lanner* shuddered, but didn't go down under the *Excalibur*'s assault.

The *Shootist* that partnered with the *Excalibur* shot at the *Black Lanner* again. The large laser raked its green beam across the Clan 'Mech's right thigh, then the heavy autocannon in the *Excalibur*'s left breast vomited a torrent of depleted-uranium slugs that pulverized the remaining armor on that limb. Their fury unabated, they shredded the myomer muscle on the 'Mech's lower leg, yet somehow the pilot managed to keep his 'Mech upright.

The second Clan *Black Lanner* fired its medium lasers at the *Shootist* again. With the shrinking range, four of five hit in this second attack. Two melted more armor on the 'Mech's left leg, while one scored an ugly furrow over the 'Mech's right thigh. The last beam played over the center of the 'Mech's chest and cored through. A plume of black smoke began to trail from the hole it opened, betokening another damaged engine.

If the *Shootist*'s pilot knew how gravely his 'Mech had been hit, his own targeting appeared not to have been affected by it at all. His large laser poked its beam into the *Black Lanner*'s right hip, blackening armor there. The heavy autocannon also hit in the same location, tearing away the last of the armor and working on the rest of the limb.

The two *Spartan*s again attacked the *Black Lanner*. Each 'Mech hit with its PPC. One azure lightning bolt skittered over the armor on the 'Mech's chest, frying all the armor it touched. The second blue beam flayed most of the armor off the *Black Lanner*'s arm. Had either one been fortunate enough to hit the stricken 'Mech's right leg they would have burned it off, but attacking up a hill seldom allowed for precision shooting.

The final *Turkina* turned its weapons on the *Grim Reaper* it had attacked earlier. Its large pulse lasers burned away the last of the armor over the ComStar 'Mech's heart and began working on its right flank. The large lasers in its right arm played their beams over the *Grim Reaper*'s right leg, paring away all the armor there and beginning to roast the artificial muscles beneath. The medium laser missed clearly, and the *Grim Reaper*'s pilot kept his 'Mech from falling.

The *Black Knight* supplying Focht with his datafeed targeted the *Turkina*. Both of the large lasers hit the target, pumping kilojoules of energy into the armor on the *Turkina*'s left arm and right leg. The *Black Knight*'s PPC ripped a jagged gash along the *Turkina*'s pristine right thigh, sending liquefied sheets of armor raining down the leg.

The only 'Mech in the ComStar force that had not fired yet was a humanoid *Quickdraw*. Its weapons were well suited to fighting closer in, and it had finally closed to where it could fire effectively at the Clan forces. It fired four medium lasers at the *Turkina* but hit with only three. Two melted more armor from the 'Mech's left leg while the third slashed away armor sheets from the center of the 'Mech's chest.

Finally the *Grim Reaper* unloaded on the *Turkina*. The large laser fired wide, sending its verdant beam to play along the mountainside behind the lake. Most of the LRMs missed, but those that did hit only chipped away at armor on the 'Mech's left leg and flank. The heavily armored *Turkina* remained upright and defiant, its armor damaged, but its killing ability yet unimpaired.

Focht shook his head and felt his mouth go dry. *They've put two of my 'Mechs down and severely damaged several others.*

We've hurt two of theirs and put one down. Marthe has gotten the better of the battle so far, and when she commits her reserves . . . He shivered. *I can only hope the others are having better success with their battles.*

8

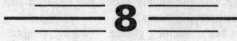

First St. Ives Lancers Headquarters, Kawlm District
Strana Mechty
Kerensky Cluster, Clan Space
23 April 3060

Kai Allard-Liao allowed himself a smile as he walked into the hangar area and saw the BattleMech he'd be piloting in the battle with the Wolves. The Inner Sphere had designated it a *Ryoken,* though he knew the Wolves called it a *Stormcrow.* Given that his force contained *Raven* BattleMechs that traveled as fast as the Clan 'Mech, he chose to think of it as a *Stormcrow* as well. It even had the appropriately styled bird legs, with a tapered cylindrical cockpit mounted above them, and arms that contained his weapons systems. The left arm had no hand and instead ended in the muzzle of a heavy autocannon, while the right arm had a swollen forearm that housed six extended-range medium lasers.

Colonel Adele Tsang, a woman in her forties who commanded the Lancers, came over to stand beside him and study the 'Mech. She had assumed command when her predecessor,

Caroline Seng, was bumped up to become Candace Liao's military advisor back on St. Ives. She folded her arms over her cooling vest and slowly shook her head. "I still do not think this is wise, Highness."

Kai shot her a sidelong glance. "Piloting a captured Clan 'Mech into battle isn't really going to be a problem, Colonel. I've been fully checked out on it."

"Yes, sir, I don't doubt that. What I'm talking about is the paint job you ordered. We're going to be in green fields and you've got this *Stormcrow* painted up like a ghost. It will stand out."

Kai glanced down for a moment, then smiled at her. "The reason for the white color, and the red and blue yin/yang crests is because those are from Cenotaph Stables on Solaris, my stable. Those are the colors I wore when I was proclaimed the Champion of Solaris."

"I know that, Highness."

"Kai, please, I've told you to call me that." He sighed. "My mother rules the St. Ives Compact, but here I am not a ruler, I am just a warrior."

"A warrior who's just had his 'Mech painted up to be a big target." Tsang frowned, her brown eyes narrowing. "Do you think this Vlad won't be hunting for you anyway?"

"Oh, I intend he should hunt for me. And I mean for him to be angry at my audacity in having this paint job on my 'Mech. If he knows about Solaris, this should infuriate him. It means he's going to go after me, and after me exclusively. I'll be well-matched to his *Timber Wolf,* so that means the rest of you can deal with his people."

The colonel's frown deepened. "Well-matched to his *Timber Wolf*? How do you calculate that? His OmniMech masses twenty tons more than yours, is more heavily armored, and is bristling with weapons. He's going to be only slightly slower than you are, and he's supposed to be a hot hand in a 'Mech."

Kai's smile shrank somewhat. "Your analysis is correct, but with the autocannon I can pack more of a punch when I get in close. I tighten a spiral on him and he ends up getting hurt bad. Regardless, the purpose of this exercise is to drive them from the Kawlm box. Whoever ends up in possession of it wins our little contest, and while I'm occupying the attention of their commander, I expect you to pound the rest of them."

"That's our plan." Tsang tossed Kai a salute. "Good hunting, Kai."

"And you, Colonel. Let's mount up." Kai returned the salute, then climbed up the gantry. He moved along the catwalk, his steps echoing mechanically. Reaching the *Stormcrow,* he dropped through the top hatch and secured it, then lowered himself into the command couch. He fastened the lap belt, then the restraining belts that criss-crossed his chest. They felt snug against his cooling vest. *Good, I'll stay where I'm meant to stay.*

From a pocket on the left side of the cooling vest, he took out a pair of plastic lines and clipped their metal ends into the sockets on the command couch. Because the fusion engine and the 'Mech's weapons produced tremendous amounts of heat, pilots wore as little clothing as possible in the cockpit and all donned a cooling vest. Aside from the cooling vest, his only other clothing were his armored boots, which covered him to mid-shin, and a thin pair of shorts. He knew that, by the end of the battle, he'd be sweat-soaked and exhausted, but the cooling vest would keep him from being poached alive in his sweat.

From a rack above and behind his head, he grabbed his neurohelmet and pulled it on. The heavy helmet settled onto the cooling vest's padded shoulders, and Kai felt a familiar ache begin there. He tightened the chin strap to hold the helmet snugly on his head. The neurodetectors built into the helmet allowed a pilot's own sense of balance to work with the 'Mech's gyroscope to allow for movement and recovery from the devastating damage inflicted in battle.

Kai flipped up the padding on the command couch's right

arm and pulled out four small, disk-shaped pads and four wire leads. He peeled open the adhesive on the back of the pads and stuck them onto his thighs and upper arms. He clipped one end of the wires to the metal button in the middle of each white circle, then snaked the wires up through loops on his cooling vest and plugged them into the neurohelmet at the throat. The sensors on his arms and legs would further aid in balancing the 'Mech.

Kai closed the compartment's lid, then reached over and punched the ignition button. An inhuman voice crackled through his helmet's speakers. "Authorization code request."

BattleMechs, being the fearsome war machines they were, had been fitted with security devices that did not allow unauthorized users to operate them. The first was a simple voiceprint check. "Kai Allard-Liao, Star League Expeditionary Force. Check Code 413256."

"Voiceprint match obtained. Personal authorization request."

Each pilot filed a personal authorization code, guaranteeing *his* 'Mech would remain his alone. Some pilots recorded simple nonsense, assuming that would be tough to crack, while others went with family mottoes or other phrases that seemed suitably martial. Kai always tended toward some thought that would set the proper mood for the battles he was facing.

He cleared his throat. "To *try* is to court failure. To *do* is the path to victory."

A rumble shook the *Stormcrow* as the fusion reactor kicked in. The various monitors scattered around the cockpit flashed to life and data began to scroll over them. The weapons monitor reported that all six of his lasers were on-line and charging. The ultra-heavy autocannon was shown to be operational, and all the ammo seemed ready to be fed without a hitch. The heat monitors showed everything to be cool and blue.

Finally, the holographic battle display materialized in front of him. It condensed a 360-degree view into about 160 degrees, with gold lines designating his weapons' forward firing arc. A golden cross hairs floated across the semi-transparent display in response to his working the joystick on the command couch's right arm. When it swept over another of the Lancer 'Mechs, the computer flashed a gold dot in the center of the cross hairs, indicating he was on target.

He punched up the unit's tactical frequency on his communications unit. "Colonel Tsang, this is Kai. I'm good to go. Shall we? The Wolves await."

Kai's *Stormcrow* and two birdlike *Raven*s formed the vanguard of the St. Ives force. In addition to being faster than the *Pillager*s, *Cataphract*s, and *Blackjack*s that made up the rest of the company, the *Raven*s were equipped with a lot of electronics that made detection of the enemy easy, and also jammed some of their sophisticated fire control systems. The Kawlm District's gently rolling hills and sparse tree stands didn't really allow for much in the way of hidden 'Mechs, but the Guardian Electronic Counter Measures suites on the *Raven*s did offer some protection against ambush.

Kai held the *Stormcrow* back from top speed since he had no desire to outstrip the 'Mechs coming up behind. Colonel Tsang, piloting one of the massive *Pillager*s, had the three of them spread out in the unit's second rank, so their Gauss rifles could provide a devastating salvo. The blocky *Cataphract*s and the long-legged *Blackjack*s in the third rank had more speed and a full array of longer-ranged weapons that would suit them well in engaging the Wolves.

One of the *Raven*s dashed over to a small stand of trees near the crest of a long swell of hill. Kai noticed that the Lancers' dark green and black camouflage really did help hide the *Raven,* but with the flick of a finger he could switch his holographic display over to infrared or magnetic resonance and the 'Mech would stand out from the landscape as if outlined in neon. *And I will do that in visible light.*

The radio crackled with the *Raven* pilot's report. "I have

visual. Ten of the Clanners. One *Timber Wolf*, two *Man O'*
*war*s, three *Fenrise*s, and four *Nova*s."

Aside from the *Timber Wolf* and the *Man O' War*s, the Clan
'Mechs were smaller and very fast. While under-powered
when compared to the Lancers, their speed would make them
difficult to hit. *Seems this Wolf is keeping to his namesake*
and has sent against us a force that will hurt in a pack. Kai
took in a deep breath and exhaled slowly. *But how well will a*
pack do without its alpha male?

The St. Ives force moved forward and at the sight of it, the
smaller, faster Clan 'Mechs began to spread out. The *Man O'*
*War*s came forward, but the *Timber Wolf* held back a bit. Kai
knew it wasn't out of any fear, but in invitation. The *Man O'*
*War*s began to exchange ranging shots with the *Pillager*s,
shooting well past his *Stormcrow. They're letting me pass, no*
doubt at Vlad's orders.

Kai kicked the *Stormcrow* up to speed and moved in
toward Vlad. He took the 'Mech on a looping course to the
right, cutting in front of one of the broadly built, macro-
cephalic *Man O' War*s. The Clanner didn't shoot at him, but
as Kai swung past, he twisted the *Stormcrow*'s torso to the left
and pointed the autocannon at it. A great golden gout of flame
vomited from the weapon's muzzle. The storm of depleted-
uranium slugs ripped into the armor on the 'Mech's right
flank and arm. The shots didn't completely strip the *Man O'*
War of armor in those spots, but any shot from the Lancers
could get through what was left without a problem.

He allowed himself a grim smile. *That ought to infuriate*
Vlad. Here he gives me safe passage and I blast one of his
compatriots. He's seeing this as some grand battle between
good and evil, but I know it's just a war for turf. He's look-
ing for honor and I just want to drive his people from some
computer-designated box.

Coming out from the *Man O' War*'s shadow, Kai braced
himself for Vlad's first shot at him. The boxy, shoulder-
mounted LRM launchers on the *Timber Wolf* blossomed with

fire as twin salvos flew out at him. The larger laser mounted in the right arm, and the medium laser underslung on it, both missed wide and almost caught the *Man O' War* Kai had previously hit. The medium laser on the 'Mech's left arm did hit, carving semi-molten armor ribbons from the *Stormcrow*'s right flank. The missiles blasted all over the 'Mech's extremities, chipping away at the armor, but coming close to breaching nothing.

Kai conquered the tremors the LRMs had started in the *Stormcrow* and dropped his cross hairs over the *Timber Wolf*'s forward thrust fuselage. He triggered five of his medium lasers, but only hit with three. Two pared armor off each of the 'Mech's birdlike legs, and the third drilled the armor over the 'Mech's right flank. *We've taken similar damage, a little factoid I'm sure gives him great confidence.*

He smiled. "Time to wipe the smirk off his face."

Keeping the *Stormcrow* running at top speed, he tightened his approach to bring the 'Mech in very close to Vlad's *Timber Wolf*. Vlad had already been turning his war machine to continue tracking Kai's spiral course, so this sharper approach forced an adjustment. *He knows that for me to close is crazy, and now things aren't going the way he planned them. That's the thing about the Clans and bidding—it eliminates as much chance from warfare as possible, so they don't handle this kind of chaos very well.*

At point-blank range, Kai dropped his cross hairs on the *Timber Wolf* and triggered an ultra burst from his autocannon. The flickering muzzle-flash tracked shadows over the *Timber Wolf*'s torso as autocannon fire pitted the armor on the 'Mech's left leg. The weapon came up, playing the second volley into the Clanner's right flank. That shot ate away the last of the armor and chewed into some of the internal structures, but hit nothing critical.

Two of the medium lasers on the *Stormcrow*'s right arm blazed. One ruby beam knifed into the right arm, boiling off armor plates. The second slashed at the right leg, liquefying more armor there.

Vlad's counter-attack came swiftly and savagely. The large and medium lasers played their red and green beams over the *Stormcrow*'s right flank. Warning klaxons screamed in Kai's cockpit as the lasers melted the last of his armor and started on the 'Mech's frame. Kai glanced at a monitor and watched his right flank redden, but he saw no vital systems getting hit, and knew he'd been very lucky.

The beams from the *Timber Wolf*'s left arm caressed his 'Mech's right arm, dissipating all the armor and roasting the limb. Despite the beams' fearsome power, they failed to damage the arm's weaponry. *Next shot and the limb goes, but he's still got to hit it and I don't want to give him that chance.*

Kai fought the controls and kept the OmniMech upright. *That pass was a bit too close for comfort, but Vlad didn't expect it.* Kai smiled as his 'Mech shot past the *Timber Wolf* and into the area behind the Clanner's original deployment. *There are plenty more things he won't expect, though, and if that ties him up, Colonel Tsang can win the day.*

First Genyosha Command Center, Neegdye District
Strana Mechty
Kerensky Cluster, Clan Space
23 April 3060

Hohiro Kurita, clad in a black silk kimono embroidered over the right sleeve with golden stars, walked across the 'Mech compound, keeping his tread even despite the depressions 'Mech feet had made in the ground. He wove his way around puddles and did not hurry himself, even though he could see the eleven warriors waiting in a circle for him. The sun poked through broken clouds and warmed him, but he knew that heat was only a prelude to the hell his 'Mech's cockpit would become in battle.

He came around to the eastern edge of the circle and knelt at the low lacquered table there. He could feel the sun on his back and was glad he'd delayed the ceremony until an hour after dawn. Had it gone off as his subaltern had wanted, the warriors with whom he was going into battle would have only seen him as a silhouette backed by a rising sun. The symbolism would not have been lost upon them, but Hohiro knew they needed no mythical omens to spur them on to their utmost performance.

His willingness to be seated at the east had been a concession he granted his aide, but only after he forced the man to arrange the tables in a circle, instead of in two ranks. *If only Shin were here to serve as my aide. He'd have no part in these games.* Hohiro refused to be exalted above the warriors he would lead, especially here, on Strana Mechty, going into battle against the Blood Spirits.

Hohiro rested his hands on his thighs and smiled as the other warriors bowed to him. They made their bows low and held them out of respect for him. He returned the gesture, not going quite as deep as they had, but holding it just as long. He meant to show them respect, and to inject some solemnity into their meeting.

He straightened up. "This is a good day to meet an enemy. The clouds are present not to shield us from the sun, but to shield the sun from us. It would be jealous of the brilliance we will display on the battlefield. When warriors gather to recount tales of battles won, they will revel greatly in their own victories, but someone will say, 'Yes, but if only we had been at Neegdye, fighting the Blood Spirits.' "

Hohiro reached down and grasped the sake flask on the table with his right hand. It had been fired black and decorated with golden stars, as had the small cup that he filled. He poured twice, filling it halfway, hesitated, then poured twice more. In doing so he avoided filling the cup in four motions. Since the Japanese word *shi* meant both four and death, by taking the care he did, he avoided invoking an ill omen.

He set the flash down again. "I know there are among you those who would have wished we were fighting the Smoke Jaguars, but I must ask why? Did we not defeat them at Wolcott? Did we not break them at Luthien? Have we not driven them from Combine space and ravaged their homeworld of

Huntress? To engage them now would be to hunt a foe who is too weak to pose a threat."

Hohiro raised his cup and sipped the sake. The potent liquid burned its way down his throat. He set the cup back down and waited for his pilots to drink, then he continued. "We have been given a new foe to fight. In this choice Victor Davion has honored us because these Blood Spirits are a fearsome lot. Of the Clans who did not invade, they are the most militant. From them will come the impetus to continue the invasion."

He let that thought sink in for a moment. "Our task, then, will be to shatter their force and break their resolve. In defeating them, we will bleed white the dreams others have of conquest. Victor Davion and the others fight to lay the past to rest, but we battle to secure the future.

"The First Genyosha is a storied unit. My grandfather ordered it created to allow a great warrior to redeem himself. Here and now, we will redeem the honor of the Combine and guarantee that those who suffered under the Clan invasion never again need fear for their futures. This is our mission, this is our destiny. The Blood Spirits await us in thickets and ravines, hidden among hills and valleys. We, the elite of the Combine, will root them out as we would feral beasts and slaughter them."

Hohiro laid a hand over the top of his cup and smiled. "Leave the rest undrunk. When we return here we will finish it, reveling in stories of our battles, knowing that other warriors will wish they, too, had been here to drink with us, fight with us, and know victory with us."

The *Daishi* Hohiro piloted had the gray paint scheme of the Genyosha, with the Combine's dragon crest on its right thigh, and the black tsunami with gold stars crest on its left flank. The OmniMech trotted forward on bird legs, exploding a deadfall log with a crackling crunch as a foot came down on it. Both arms ended in a quintet of weapon muzzles, and the boxy launcher for a rack of LRMs hunched its left shoulder. Though the weapons array was more suited to a longer-range battle, the large lasers, medium lasers, and autocannons would do some serious damage in the close fighting the Neegdye District offered.

Hohiro knew beyond a shadow of a doubt that the Blood Spirits expected his people to break down into smaller and smaller groups so they could be ambushed. *They believe of us what early reports said—we were not at all prepared for the Clan style of Combat. Even winning against the Smoke Jaguars will mean nothing since that Clan's defeat clearly showed them to be inferior.*

The heir to the Combine's Dragon Throne smiled. *They will discover we are more disciplined and more than ready for them.* The fact that he knew as little about the Blood Spirits as they did about him did disturb him a little, but his people had fought and bested Clans who had won the right to invade. Had the Blood Spirits been that good, he'd already have engaged them and beaten them in the Inner Sphere.

Out in front of his 'Mech was the only other non-humanoid 'Mech in his group of five, a *Dragon Fire*. The 'Mech had little more than vestigial arms, with a Gauss rifle and autocannon taking up most of the room in them. It packed a trio of lasers built into the torso and head, but most important of all it had a Guardian ECM suite. With it in place, the enemy's ability to concentrate their fire would be hampered.

Flanking the *Daishi* came two *No-Dachi*s. The humanoid 'Mechs were a special Combine design whose left arm ended in a PPC muzzle. The right arm bore a four-meter-long katana designed for use during close-in combat. While Hohiro had never been much of a proponent of physical combat between BattleMechs, the image the *No-Dachi*s projected was pure samurai and heartening in battle.

The last 'Mech in his entourage likewise projected an image suited to its name. The *Akuma*—demon in English—had a positively diabolical cast to its head and a left arm that ended in a PPC muzzle. Like the *No-Dachi*s, it also sported a medium-range missile system that fired unguided rockets at the enemy. While lacking the accuracy of LRMs, the MRMs were smaller in size, so more could be loaded and launched than with the smarter missiles. Because the battling with the Blood Spirits would occur at closer ranges, the MRMs became even more potent.

The 'Mechs moved through a deep ravine choked with brush and deadfall trees. Though the ravine had obviously been formed by seasonal runoff, only a small trickle of water now ran down the center. The trees growing up on the hillsides and above formed a green canopy, filtering the sunlight to make everything seem softer and more peaceful. Hohiro looked around, trying to burn the sights into his brain because at any second he knew a battle would transform the place from a haven for the living to a domain of death.

Ranging up over the hillside to the north came three Clan 'Mechs painted blood-red with black stripes. In his holographic display he saw another Blood Spirit 'Mech enter the ravine at the rear of his position, and a fifth topped the hill to the south. Towering above the Combine 'Mechs, the Clan machines looked magnificent and, as their weapons swung toward his force, Hohiro felt a jolt of fear.

The first of two *Kingfisher*s on the northern slope targeted Hohiro's *Daishi*. The heavy autocannon that made up the *Kingfisher*'s right forearm spat fire and shells that hit the *Daishi* in the center of its torso, shredding a third of the protection there. Spent shells rained out of the ejection port of the weapon, dropping steaming to the ground. Hohiro wrestled with his 'Mech's controls, struggling to ride out the hideous impact of the *Kingfisher*'s assault.

The large and medium lasers built into the *Kingfisher*'s left arm raked their beams across the *Daishi*. The green beam further stripped armor from the 'Mech's chest while the red beam obliterated the Combine crest on the *Daishi*'s right thigh. Another scarlet laser splashed out from the *Kingfisher*'s right flank and boiled armor scales off the OmniMech's right arm. The armor monitor showed the damage to his 'Mech's chest as moderate, but the loss of armor elsewhere to be insignificant.

The *Battle Cobra* blocking their exit from the ravine turned its weapons on the *Akuma*. It missed with the PPC built into its right arm, but the left-arm PPC on the flair-shouldered, no-necked BattleMech struck the *Akuma* solidly. The errant beam exploded a leafy tree, casting flaming splinters all about, while the other one skewered the *Akuma* over its heart. The Combine 'Mech wavered, telling Hohiro that the gyro had been hit, but the pilot kept his machine on its feet.

The *Crossbow* on the south slope targeted the *No-Dachi* nearest it. The Clan 'Mech was handless, its arms ending in cylindrical forearm pods sporting a ring of missile ports surrounding the muzzle of a medium pulse laser. The beam weapons flashed with a volley of energy darts that scoured armor off the target's chest and left leg. The LRM launchers released two swarms of missiles that hit the *No-Dachi* in the right flank and left leg, but neither of those attacks breached the armor. The short-range missile launchers also built into those pods shot their full complement of missiles, scattering explosions all across the *No-Dachi*'s chest.

The other *Kingfisher* on the north slope attacked the second *No-Dachi*. Twin bolts of artificial lightning ripped jagged lines through the armor on the Combine 'Mech's right leg and left arm. Ruby beams from the 'Mech's arms slashed at the *No-Dachi*'s face and left breast, stripping away much of the armor shielding the pilot. The last two medium lasers, built into the center of the *Kingfisher*'s torso, slashed out and melted armor from the *No-Dachi*'s chest and right flank.

The last Blood Spirit 'Mech, a huge, ugly hunk of machinery also with handless arms, blasted away at the *Dragon Fire*. Hohiro had never seen that machine before, but datafiles from the Clans allowed his computer to tag it as a *Blood Kite*. The green beams of large lasers glowed from the weapons in the *Blood Kite*'s head, chest, and left arm. One of them missed, transforming a fallen log into ash in a second, while the other two bubbled armor from the *Dragon Fire*'s left leg and right arm. The LRM launchers mounted on each of the *Blood Kite*'s shoulders sprouted fire. The missiles corkscrewed down the hillside, blasting armor from the *Dragon Fire*'s legs, right arm, and chest.

The *Akuma* brought its left arm up and pointed the PPC muzzle at the *Battle Cobra* that had attacked it. A cobalt spear plunged into the Clan 'Mech's right thigh, ablating over half the armor covering the limb. The autocannon mounted in the *Akuma*'s right breast vomited fire. The shells traced a line of craters up the *Battle Cobra*'s left arm, leaving bare fragments of armor behind. Then the MRM launch pod in the 'Mech's left shoulder erupted into a fountain of smoke and flame. Nearly half the unguided rockets missed their target, sowing fire and explosions back along the ravine. Those that did hit ground away at the armor on the *Battle Cobra*'s right arm and flank.

The *No-Dachi* that had been shot at by the *Crossbow* on the southern slope turned its attention toward its tormentor. The MRM pods in each shoulder sent a staccato stream of missiles up at the *Crossbow*. They blasted armor from the chest, right flank, and left arm, but failed to open any gaping rents. Three of them did detonate against the 'Mech's domed head and snapped off a decorative armor ear. The *No-Dachi*'s red laser missed low, but the SRM launchers scattered shots over the *Crossbow*'s right side, leg, and arm.

Hohiro twitched his right hand to float his cross hairs over the outline of the *Kingfisher* that had blasted his 'Mech. *Now you will get a real taste of how the Combine fights.* Once the gold dot pulsed at the heart of his holographic display, he tightened upon his triggers.

He fired one each of the large lasers built into the *Daishi*'s arms. They incinerated armor on the *Kingfisher*'s right arm and flank. Only one of the two autocannons he fired actually hit its target. Its fire cratered its way across the 'Mech's chest. The four medium pulse lasers all put their stuttering fire on target. They liquefied armor on the *Kingfisher*'s left flank, chest, right leg, and right arm. Though Hohiro's shots failed to lay any part of the Clan 'Mech bare, he'd begun nibbling away at its protection rather significantly.

The *No-Dachi* on the north side of the formation likewise targeted the *Kingfisher* that had attacked Hohiro. The MRMs peppered the Blood Spirit 'Mech, hitting it on both flanks, the left leg, and the center chest. One of the chest shots got through, releasing a plume of black smoke trailing up from the 'Mech's angular chest. The *No-Dachi*'s head-mounted medium laser vaporized more armor from the target's right flank. Its SRMs exploded more armor from the *Kingfisher*'s chest and left flank, spinning broken sheets off like playing cards.

The *Dragon Fire* cut loose with all of its weapons, employing them against the battered *Kingfisher*. The Gauss rifle's silver ball smashed the *Kingfisher* in the left shoulder and shivered off the last of the armor over that portion of the 'Mech's body. The autocannon mounted in its right arm savaged its counterpart on the Clan 'Mech, leaving the armor on that limb in tatters. The *Dragon Fire*'s large laser linked the two 'Mech's chests for a moment, and in its wake left molten armor running down the *Kingfisher*'s belly. The twin pulse lasers scattered their scarlet energy needles over the Clan 'Mech, burning more armor from the right flank and drilling deep into the naked left side.

Hohiro watched with amazement as the *Kingfisher* soaked up damage. In the blink of an eye it had gone from pristine to a raggedy hulk cloaked in gray armor vapor. Around it, trees and bushes ignited by missiles and lasers smoldered. The Clan 'Mech wavered for a moment, then pitched over backward.

Even though the *No-Dachi* on that flank likewise fell—

landing face-forward to the ground—Hohiro barked a laugh. *The Dragon is strongest when it does not allow itself to be distracted and its efforts divided.* He smiled. "And against the Clans, my friends, it is very easy to be united in effort and result."

10

Bloody Basin, Lechenka District
Strana Mechty
Kerensky Cluster, Clan Space
23 April 3060

From the initial scans of the Lechenka District, Victor thought the Smoke Jaguars might have been looking for the same divide-and-conquer sort of battle it appeared the Blood Spirits wanted to offer Hohiro's people. Bloody Basin earned its name from the color of the rocks, which indicated a high iron content. That made magnetic resonance scanning useless and because of the high heat in the arid area, infrared scanning likewise was taken out of the equation.

Though the area was dry now, the canyons and hillsides had clearly been molded by thousands of years of rain and rivers. Little in the way of plant life survived here and tended to be either lichen dwelling in shadows or clusters of succulents with broad pads that held as much water as possible. The background temperature already had the heat sinks on Victor's *Daishi* working a bit more than the march toward the battlefield should have required. *I don't think they chose this area to try and overheat our 'Mechs. At least, I hope not.*

Victor felt very good about the company he was leading into battle. The core of it came from the Tenth Lyran Guards—his Revenants. They'd all been trained in anti-Clan tactics for years, and had fought with distinction against the Smoke Jaguars before and during the counter-offensive. He'd hand-picked his people for the operation and was pleased that no one had refused his invitation.

One whole lance of his company came from the First Kathil Uhlans, but the only way to tell that was by identifying the golden lion crest on the 'Mechs' left breasts, since all the 'Mechs in the company had been repainted in the dark blue of the Star League Expeditionary Force. Andrew Redburn led the four of them and, along with two of Victor's own people, brought up the rear of the formation.

The only outsider in the group Victor had included for political reasons. Danai Centrella came from the Periphery state called the Magistracy of Canopus. She had petitioned to join one of the anti-Clan units and, after reviewing her records, Victor had accepted her. He'd assigned her to a *Falconer,* which was the closest 'Mech he had to the *Banshee* she normally piloted. She was a valuable addition to his force and, if she acquitted herself well on the battlefield, could be a hero for the Magistracy.

And a thorn in Sun-Tzu Liao's side. Though Victor's focus during the trip to the Clan homeworlds had been on rescuing the force on Huntress and putting an end to the Clan invasion, he did, from time to time, try to imagine what was going on back in the Inner Sphere. Sun-Tzu Liao had been made First Lord of the Star League and Victor was fairly well certain that would not prevent him from committing mischief. *Better that than mayhem.* Having Danai in a position to rally her people to resist Sun-Tzu's influence could easily be a help upon their return.

If we make it back. The narrow draw through which Victor's people had been moving widened into a broad, red-rock valley with soaring cliffs on either side that dwarfed the BattleMechs. In an instant Victor imagined the sort of torrent of water that had carved the sinuous shapes into the rocks coursing again through the valley. *We'd all be swept away in an instant—Nature again reminding man that our hopes and desires and hatreds are insignificant.*

The Smoke Jaguars had arranged their line across the valley approximately two-thirds of the way into it. Victor counted only nine BattleMechs, but kicked some magnification into his vislight scan. The holographic display before him sharpened and details grew, allowing him to see the Elementals waiting in and around the Clan 'Mechs. *Not a surprise. Osis is an Elemental, after all.*

Victor glanced at his secondary monitor, then keyed his radio. "I've got a *Cauldron-Born,* a *Masakari,* and three *Stormcrows* that look the most dangerous, at least as far as I can tell here. They've got to go first."

Redburn's voice came back through the speakers. "Roger. Consider the *Cauldron-Born* our primary. We'll adjust depending on the performance of others."

Danai's *Falconer* trotted forward and pointed her left-arm PPC at a lone figure silhouetted on top of a small rock outcropping. "Single Elemental, Victor. Think that's the ilKhan?"

"Could be, but let's not make him a primary target. It would be a waste of ordnance, and splashing him might just make them angry." Victor double-checked his 'Mech's weapons' status. "I am all green and good to go. Let's move."

As the Revenants moved eastward, two smaller, barrel-chested 'Mechs began a hook toward the south. The *Jackals* relied on speed to keep them safe, and a right-shoulder-mounted PPC to make them dangerous. Each carried an anti-missile system and a small SRM launcher, but the PPC was what they used to pack a punch. While they were not seriously powerful, if they managed to get into the rear of the Clan formation, they definitely could contribute to bringing some of the Smoke Jaguars down.

Three humanoid Clan *Hankyu*s moved south to lengthen the Clan line and make it tough for the *Jackal*s to roll up that flank. Steven Applegarth trotted his boxy, bird-legged *Penetrator* out in the *Jackal*s' wake. The twin large lasers his 'Mech sported could provide some long-range cover for the smaller 'Mechs and, if the *Hankyu*s didn't scatter by the time he caught up with the *Jackal*s, the *Penetrator*'s array of pulse lasers would prove devastating to them.

Their flanking motion left Victor's *Daishi*, Danai's *Falconer*, and the broad-shouldered *Devastator* as the core of the Inner Sphere front line. Redburn's four *Longbow*s and two *Rakshasa*s made up the second line. The movement in the Clan line brought the *Cauldron-Born* and *Masakari* to the fore, with the smaller *Stormcrow*s and a *Nova* moving around toward the north.

As they maneuvered, Victor could see the battle already beginning to evolve. The northern hook would pressure his left flank, forcing him to curve around south. Redburn's people would lag or be exposed to the *Stormcrow* and *Nova* attacks. If the heaviest of the Clan's 'Mechs managed to drive toward the southwest, they could sever the *Jackal* and *Penetrator* right wing, using the *Hankyu*s to keep the right wing busy. The northern forces would attempt to get into his formation's rear and break up Redburn's group.

That's got to be what they're planning, but, as von Moltke noted so long ago, no plan survives contact with the enemy. Victor smiled sheepishly. *Let's hope that doesn't apply to mine this time.*

The Smoke Jaguars made good use of their weapons' superior range by getting off a first round of shots before the Inner Sphere troops had reached their firing ranges. Two of the *Stormcrow*s fired large lasers at Redburn's group, cooking armor on a *Rakshasa* and one of the *Longbow*s. The *Cauldron-Born* only hit with one of its two large lasers and sliced some armor from Victor's *Daishi*.

Victor looked at the damage on his monitor and laughed. "You've taken worse, Prometheus, and it'll be our turn soon."

The forces closed, and the gold dot in the center of Victor's cross hairs flashed as he drifted it across targets. He let it linger for a second on the low-slung, almost insectoid outline of the *Cauldron-Born,* then shifted to the *Masakari* coming in to the right of it. The dot pulsed and he cut loose with the Gauss rifle that made up his 'Mech's left forearm and the trio of large lasers built into the right arm.

Engaging the target so far away meant only two of his four shots hit. The silver ball from the Gauss rifle blasted away over half the armor on the bird-legged *Masakari*'s left arm. The verdant laser darts from the pulse laser scorched armor over the right flank, burning away the gray and black jaguar markings there. Neither bits of the damage was serious, but another Gauss rifle slug to the left arm and it could come off, costing the Clan 'Mech the use of two PPCs.

The *Masakari* fired back at Victor with three PPCs. The two in the damaged left arm missed wide, but the single beam from the right arm tagged the *Daishi* in the left flank. Smoking armor plates sloughed off like dead skin and littered the ground in Victor's wake.

The *Cauldron-Born* also shot at the *Daishi*. Only the large laser built into its right arm hit its target. The beam vaporized armor on Prometheus' left arm, matching the damage previously done to the right arm. What Victor found significant about the *Cauldron-Born*'s attack, and the *Masakari*'s attack before it, was that the Smoke Jaguars had clearly abandoned any pretext of honor by maintaining their warrior tradition of single combat against a single foe.

Either they've decided to deny me that honor, or they figure I'm in here and want me to die here. He shrugged. *No matter. Just makes what we're going to do that much easier.*

He keyed his radio. "General Redburn, you are free to fire."

The *Longbow*s Andy Redburn commanded were vaguely humanoid in shape, at least from feet to shoulders and head, but at the arm the resemblance ended. Instead of having fully articulated arms as did so many other 'Mechs, the *Longbow*s sported only massive cylindrical pods intended to launch LRMs. And the *Rakshasa*s, with their forward-thrust torsos and bird legs, looked nothing like the *Longbow*s except that on their shoulders rested boxy LRM launchers, and they carried large lasers just like the one built into the *Longbow*'s chest.

The missile barrage arrived in waves that washed fire over the *Cauldron-Born*. The Clan 'Mech jerked up and down with each battering spread of missiles. The green beams of the large lasers slashed through the dust and smoke, evaporating armor and starting in on the myomers on the Clan 'Mech's left leg and arm. As the cloud surrounding it cleared the only pristine armor it still had covered its chest. Its arms had been stripped bare along with the left leg.

Danai Centrella fired at the *Masakari* with her ranged weapons. An argent blur sped from her Gauss rifle to crater armor on the center of the Clan 'Mech's chest. The PPC in her 'Mech's arm drilled a bolt of blue fire into the *Masakari*'s right flank, doubling up on the damage Victor had already done. More important, the *Masakari*'s pilot couldn't counter the devastating physical effects of Danai's shots. The Clan 'Mech crashed down on its left arm, scraping armor as it came to a sparking stop.

The *Devastator* on Victor's left did not contribute its fire to killing the *Masakari* or *Cauldron-Born*, but instead targeted one of the *Stormcrow*s coming around to the north. The Gauss rifle in each arm spat out silver projectiles that streaked across the scarlet landscape and smashed into the *Stormcrow*'s left arm. The first shattered the armor and the second carried the limb off. When the arm hit the ground, the heavy autocannon in it exploded, spraying shells everywhere. The *Devastator*'s twin torso-mounted PPCs then stabbed forks of cobalt lightning into the *Stormcrow*'s right flank and left leg, obliterating armor.

Victor keyed his radio. "Nice shooting, Jerry. *Devastator*'s a nice change from that old thing you used to drive, isn't it?"

"No complaints here, boss."

Looking like a robotic fledgling moving about the nest, the *Masakari* regained its feet and delivered three PPC shots to Danai's *Falconer*. Two stripped armor from each arm, but the third nailed the *Falconer* dead center in the chest. Victor saw her 'Mech shake and lurch to one side. He knew it was going down, but Danai fought it and got her own shots off before the *Falconer* plowed into the ground.

Danai's Gauss rifle shot skipped off the *Masakari*'s left flank, scattering pulverized shards of armor in its wake. The PPC strike drilled into the center of the Clan 'Mech, mirroring the shot that had hammered her *Falconer*. The Clan 'Mech likewise wavered and again crashed to the ground in a shower of armor fragments.

The *Cauldron-Born* fired at Victor's *Daishi*. The large lasers hit Prometheus in the chest and right flank, with a medium laser jabbing its red beam into the damaged right flank as well. The Clanner's assault reduced the armor on that side by nearly two-thirds, yet despite the loss of a ton of armor, Victor kept the OmniMech upright.

The second missile and laser volley from Redburn's people pounded the *Cauldron-Born*. Explosion after explosion bloomed like flowers all over the Clan 'Mech. Jets of black smoke erupted through the gray haze surrounding it. Green laser spears skewered the cloud and more explosions splashed light throughout the cloud. Bits and pieces of 'Mech, most unrecognizable, bounced across the ground, some trailing long, stringy myomer fibers. As the dust settled, Victor could make out what looked to be the cockpit and a thin lattice of metal connecting it to what probably was a leg, but of the rest of the *Cauldron-Born* all he could see was debris and a black stain on the ground.

A shiver ran through Victor. It was easy to project himself into the pilot's place. *I know our being here is insanity, but the Clanners seem to embrace and cherish it. They should see they've lost here, but, then, that wouldn't really matter, to them or us.* He set himself and turned his guns on one of the *Stormcrows* to the north. *We all agreed on Tharkad that the Smoke Jaguars must die. It's time for me to finish the job so many others have carried to this point.*

Victor's Gauss rifle nailed the *Stormcrow*'s right arm, shivering most of the armor from the limb. His large pulse lasers scattered shots over the smaller 'Mech's chest and right flank. One of the darts pierced the armor over its heart while those that hit the flank scraped away all the armor there and lit up internal structures. Black smoke started trailing from the chest and flank, and a greenish-yellow fluid started leaking from the right hip.

Jerry Cranston's *Devastator* unloaded on its target. The Gauss rifle projectiles slammed into the 'Mech's left leg and flank, shattering all the armor there. The shot to the flank even dented the 'Mech's frame. Of the PPCs, only one hit, but its cerulean lightning played over the *Stormcrow*'s head. Armor exploded and the cockpit canopy burst apart. Trailing black smoke from where the pilot had once sat, the *Stormcrow* pitched forward, scattering stones before it, as it skidded to a halt.

Victor stared mutely at the dark, smoking pit where the Clanner had once sat. A sour taste stole through his mouth, but he knew it wasn't fear. *Disgust. That warrior didn't need to die, none of them needed to die. That's why this is all insane, but no more. Here, today, the insanity that was the Clan invasion will stop.*

11

Khan Marthe Pryde, seated high in the cockpit of her *Summoner,* keyed her radio. "Second Star, we engage now. You have your targets logged. Good hunting." As her Starmates acknowledged the order, she started her humanoid 'Mech forward, even as the first Clan *Turkina* went down.

Her blue eyes narrowed at that sight. Her people had taken more damage than she'd expected, but the datafeed to her secondary monitor indicated that the ComStar force had been pounded. All her 'Mechs save one were operational and, more important, the damage done to the ComStar 'Mechs had left them strung out along the mountain slope. Her second Star would engage them and break them, sending them tumbling back down to the plains where they had grounded.

Marthe brought her *Summoner* to the edge of the slope, standing beside the *Nova* piloted by her saKhan, Samantha

Clees. She immediately settled the golden cross hairs on her holographic display over one of the broadly built *Excalibur*s on the field. A gold dot flared in the center of the cross, and Marthe tightened on her trigger, firing all three of the *Summoner*'s weapons systems. The autocannon devoured armor on the target's right leg, and the LRMs picked away at the protection on the 'Mech's middle and right arm. More missiles might have hit, but the *Excalibur*'s anti-missile system picked a number of them off. The PPC sent its cobalt scalpel stabbing deep into the *Excalibur*'s right flank, withering away all the armor there and starting on the 'Mech's frame.

Part of Marthe knew that as devastating as her attack was on that previously unblemished 'Mech, it could have been even more harmful against one of the damaged ones. The attack that merely softened up her target could have put one of the other 'Mechs out of the battle. The ComStar forces had shown no compunction against having multiple warriors target one foe to heighten the damage done.

She refused to participate in such barbarity. The Jade Falcons had always prided themselves on single combat, a contest of equals. The ComStar pilots, no matter how skilled, would never be the equals of her Jade Falcons. To gang up on them would be to suggest that somehow they inspired fear. *They bested us at Tukayyid, but we will beat them here, regaining our honor. We have no reason to fear them. Multiple assaults might be fine for the Wolves or others, but not us.*

The *Excalibur* fired back at Marthe's *Summoner*, impressing her with the pilot's cool reaction despite the damage his 'Mech had taken. His LRMs crumbled armor on her *Summoner*'s right leg and middle, sending tremors through the 'Mech. A silver blur launched by the *Excalibur*'s Gauss rifle slammed into the *Summoner*'s left arm, slewing the giant machine around to the side. Marthe fought the controls to keep the *Summoner* standing, stabilizing it after only taking a few steps backward.

The downed *Black Knight* climbed back to its feet and

exchanged shots with Clees' *Nova*. The ComStar pilot cut loose with two large laser shots and a blast from his PPC. The PPC boiled armor off the *Nova*'s left shoulder, while one of the large lasers vaporized armor on the right flank. The second large laser's beam drilled through the last of the armor on the 'Mech's chest and began to eat away at core structures.

Clees kept her 'Mech upright and fired back, again relying on the 'Mech's left arm to supply most of the shots. The single medium laser in the right arm missed again, and Marthe knew Clees would have the hide off the leader of her tech crew for the misses. All six of the other lasers hit. Two scoured more than half the armor off the 'Mech's left arm, and one each blazed into the *Black Knight*'s legs, broiling armor off in great slabs. The last two hits did the most damage, though, destroying the last of the armor on the 'Mech's left flank and beginning to work on its interior. Despite the fearsome damage Clees delivered, this time the ComStar 'Mech did not go down.

The first *Turkina* and the *Grim Reaper* it faced both rose up at the same time and resumed their battle. The *Grim Reaper*'s missile spread came in tight and wreathed the squat *Turkina* in fire. Armor exploded from both flanks and fell off the right arm in huge chunks. The large laser's beam sliced the last of the armor from that limb, then angled up through a heat-sink pod and half-melted the myomer muscle controlling that arm.

The *Turkina* targeted the *Grim Reaper* and cut loose with all its weapons. Both pulse lasers sent a storm of green laser bolts screaming through the *Grim Reaper*'s weakened chest armor. They evaporated the last of it, then incinerated internal support structures and engine shielding. One of the large lasers melted through the last of the armor on the *Grim Reaper*'s right arm and started on the myomers beneath, while the other combined with a medium pulse laser to completely gut the *Grim Reaper*, collapsing the 'Mech and driving its engine out through the back.

The other weapons shredded yet more armor, but that damage meant nothing as the ComStar Mech slammed into the ground. The 'Mech's faceplate exploded outward in a gout of flame, then the pilot shot into the sky aboard the ejection seat. The pilot quickly corrected the chair's rocket course, curving around and heading back toward the distant ComStar headquarters.

Marthe switched her holographic display over to infrared, then shielded her eyes as the other ComStar *Excalibur* drew a bead on the most damaged Clan *Black Lanner*. The engine hits must surely have the *Excalibur*'s heat spiking, but it raised its right arm and pointed its Gauss rifle at the *Black Lanner*. At the same time the *Black Lanner* fired back.

The *Excalibur*'s silver ball slammed into the *Black Lanner*'s naked right leg, splintering the ferro-titanium limb and severing it right above the knee joint. The lower half of the leg careened back toward the lake, while the damaged 'Mech dropped to its right flank.

The *Black Lanner*'s fire at the *Excalibur* proved just as devastating. The PPC incinerated almost all the armor over the 'Mech's midline, and one of the two pulse lasers burned armor from the left arm. The other pulse laser's red needles sailed through the gaping hole in the *Excalibur*'s right flank and melted what little frame remained there. The *Excalibur*'s right arm fell away, taking with it the Gauss rifle. Heat spiked yet again, and the *Excalibur* froze in position. Black smoke poured from it, and the pilot ejected nanoseconds before the unshielded engine exploded, consuming the upper half of the 'Mech in a roiling golden ball that had once been the fusion reaction that gave it life.

A *Night Gyr* in Marthe's Star targeted an untouched *Shootist,* bringing all of its weapons to bear. The two large lasers that made up the 'Mech's right forearm splashed their beams over the *Shootist*. One scored the armor on the heavy-set 'Mech's centerline, while the other disintegrated the armor on its head. A shower of sparks from the cockpit signaled the failure of some system or other, but the 'Mech did not go down. The two small autocannons that fired each nicked up the armor on the *Shootist*'s arms. The *Night Gyr*'s medium lasers hit with their ruby beams even as the *Shootist* fired its weapons. One of the mediums boiled more armor off the 'Mech's right arm, but the other one bathed the 'Mech's head with a bloody beam that obliterated the structure, both cockpit and pilot vanishing in one hellish second.

The decapitated 'Mech crashed to the ground, but not before the shots it had taken hit their target. The *Shootist* had not aimed at the *Night Gyr* that killed it, but had instead targeted the *Turkina* that had gotten this far without having its armor breached. The *Shootist*'s autocannon fire ripped its way up the 'Mech's left arm, scouring all but a thin crust of armor from the limb. The dying 'Mech's large laser ablated more armor off the *Turkina*'s midline, while the two pulse lasers burned armor from the left flank and finished the last of the armor on the 'Mech's left arm. The last of the scarlet darts chewed into the *Turkina*'s skeletal structure, but the pilot weathered the assault.

The *Turkina*'s other foes turned their fire on it as well. The *Grim Reaper* fired everything it had at the Jade Falcon 'Mech. LRMs blasted into either leg, further worrying the spotty armor on the left leg and the left flank. The large laser in its right arm flashed out to caress the naked left arm with an internal beam. Myomers smoked and the ferro-titanium bones began to glow a dull orange. The pulse laser's red bolts peppered the *Turkina*'s midline and one pierced the 'Mech's breast. Black smoke began to pour out of the hole and heat spiked, telling Marthe the *Turkina*'s engine had been hit.

The *Black Knight* that had attacked it before now centered its weapons on the large Clan 'Mech. It fired two large lasers, a large pulse laser and the medium pulse laser mounted in its right arm. The large lasers cored armor on the 'Mech's right arm and left flank. Fiery green lances from the large pulse laser mounted in the *Black Knight*'s chest nibbled away at more of the left flank armor. The smaller pulse laser shot its ruby shafts through the left flank, burning away the last of the armor and starting on the *Turkina*'s frame.

As the fourth ComStar 'Mech let fly at the *Turkina*, and the *Turkina*'s pilot fired at the *Grim Reaper*, Marthe marveled at the pilot's calm when catching such damage. The *Turkina* had not so much as wavered a centimeter despite the pounding it was taking. Though the armor on the left side of its body had been sorely fragmented and stripped away, the pilot made no attempt to retreat or shield that side. *That pilot, Arimas, allowed himself to be captured on Coventry and begged to join this Star so he could redeem himself from such humiliation. He is a Malthus, and if he survives this, I shall press the leaders of his House to let him fight for a bloodname.*

The ComStar *Quickdraw* shot all four of its medium lasers at the *Turkina*. One missed, and one blackened more armor over the 'Mech's chest. The other two lased away the last of the armor on the right arm, then nipped through the shoulder joint, sending the *Turkina*'s arm and its two large lasers crashing to the ground. The pilot successfully fought to regain balance after losing the limb, and though an armor fog clung to his 'Mech, the *Turkina* appeared unconquerable.

One of the large lasers sent out a stuttering barrage of green needles that flayed the last of the armor off the *Grim Reaper*'s right arm and fused the shoulder joint. The other one laced more fire into the naked right leg, picking away at the muscles and skeleton, leaving it a tattered wreck. One of the two large lasers missed completely, but the other took the right arm clean off. One of the medium pulse lasers sent a ruby hail that devoured the *Grim Reaper*'s right leg, while the other one chewed through more of the midline structural support members. The *Grim Reaper*, missing the right half of its body, spun around and slammed into the ground, face down, trapping the pilot in the cockpit.

Another *Night Gyr* oriented on the untouched *Black Knight* and fired. The Gauss rifles built into each arm spat out silver balls that smashed into the *Black Knight*. One pulverized armor on the right flank while the other blasted away over half the armor on its right arm. The ComStar 'Mech retained its feet, but the assault staggered it back several steps.

The second *Summoner* in Marthe's Star targeted the *Quickdraw*. The heavy ultra-autocannon fired two volleys. One drilled through the armor on the *Quickdraw*'s right flank. A silvery explosion heralded the death of a jump jet, while a splash of green smoke indicated a heat sink had been destroyed. The other blast of shells ripped all the armor from the 'Mech's right arm and all but severed it. The large laser that shot from the *Summoner*'s right arm finished the job, slicing off the *Quickdraw*'s right arm completely.

The last *Black Lanner* again exchanged fire with the *Shootist* it had been targeting since the forces first engaged each other. The pilot hit with all five of the medium lasers he triggered. One carved armor from the *Shootist*'s right arm, while the next concentrated on the right leg. Two more bored into and through the armor on the right flank, evaporating a heat sink. The last sizzled armor from the 'Mech's left arm.

The *Shootist* remained upright and gave as good as it got from the Clan 'Mech. The autocannon stitched fire over the left leg, stripping away all but a few fragments of armor. A pulse laser finished the last of the armor on the 'Mech's left flank while the other one burned away the last of the left arm's protection and crisped muscles and bones. The large laser did the most serious damage when it swept over the armorless right leg. The beam of coherent light dissipated everything it touched, amputating the limb at the hip. The *Black Lanner* wavered, then fell to the ground.

The twin ComStar *Spartan*s engaged the last unattacked Clan 'Mech, the third *Summoner* in Marthe's Star. The first hit with all its beam weapons. A PPC and pulse laser liquefied the armor on the 'Mech's left flank, while another pulse laser burned a line of black dots along the left arm. The last pulse laser concentrated its fire near the *Summoner*'s right hip, but failed to core through the armor and do damage.

The second *Spartan* likewise fired all its beam weapons. A pulse laser carved up more armor on the right leg, while the other two bubbled armor over the 'Mech's midline. The PPC's cerulean lightning stabbed into the 'Mech's left arm, dropping armor in steaming goblets to the ground. More important, the brutality of the twin assaults dropped the *Summoner,* but not before it opened fire at one of its tormentors.

The stricken *Summoner* was equipped entirely with missiles, both long and short range, with which it hammered away at one of the *Spartans.* Missiles peppered the ComStar 'Mech, blasting armor from all over. The 'Mech lost the most armor off its right arm and left flank, but a quintet of missiles smashed into the head and ground down the armor there. The *Spartan* staggered for a step, but didn't go down.

With grudging respect, Marthe spitted the *Excalibur* on her cross hairs and again tightened up on her triggers. The LRM salvo lost a lot of missiles to the *Excalibur*'s missile defense, but the five that did make it through blew the last of the armor off the ComStar 'Mech's right leg and started to work on the limb itself. Marthe cursed when her autocannon shells slammed into the 'Mech's left flank, but the PPC's man-made lightning electrified the 'Mech's right leg. The myomer muscles burst into flame, and the bones glowed white-hot a second before they vanished in a gout of smoke.

As the one-legged *Excalibur* went down, the pilot fired his LRMs and Gauss rifle. The silver ball streaked past Marthe's cockpit, missing by bare centimeters, but the LRMs caught her *Summoner* full on in the chest. A wave of heat washed up over her as one of them cored her armor and hit her engine. The heat monitor spiked her 'Mech up into the red zone while the heat sinks labored to dissipate as much of the heat as possible.

Samantha Clees, in her *Nova,* pumped more fire into the *Black Knight* she'd been fighting since the start. The majority of the laser fire came from the left-arm medium lasers, but finally one of the lasers on the right arm hit as well. The seven medium lasers sent a full phalanx of laser spears to skewer the *Black Knight*. They stripped the last of the armor from the right leg and burned away more over the left arm, but the key damage was done by those that struck the *Black Knight* in the chest. The left flank had all its support structures vaporized, sending the left arm tumbling to the ground, and fire against the midline pierced the armor and nailed the engine, causing the IR sensor profile of the 'Mech to glow.

The *Black Knight*'s pilot fought back valiantly, firing the weapons Clees had not yet destroyed. The PPC mounted in the right arm melted away the last of the armor on the *Nova*'s left arm, then reduced the upper arm actuator to a bubbling, tarry mass. The large laser's verdant beam shriveled the last of the armor on the 'Mech's right arm, but the assault failed to put the *Nova* down.

Arimas' battered *Turkina* targeted the *Shootist* that had killed a *Black Lanner*. The large pulse lasers in the *Turkina*'s left arm ablated armor over the 'Mech's centerline and right flank. The two medium lasers mounted in the left and right flanks flensed more armor off the *Shootist*'s legs, while the pulse lasers rained darts over the 'Mech's head and centerline.

The *Shootist*'s pilot earned Marthe's respect when the 'Mech remained standing and returned Arimas' fire. The heavy autocannon and one pulse laser tore into the armor over the 'Mech's right leg, while the large laser lit up the *Turkina*'s remaining arm, burning it clean off. The last laser nibbled away at the armor on the *Turkina*'s right flank, scorching the only pristine patch on the 'Mech's body.

And yet he does not go down! Marthe felt a shiver run through her. *Arimas is truly a Jade Falcon.*

Marthe looked at the status display in her cockpit and shook her head. She had three untouched 'Mechs to the one unblemished *Spartan* on the ComStar side. Even if Arimas' 'Mech was classed as destroyed—though it still had weapons to fire—she only had three 'Mechs down compared to the five ComStar had lost. *And of those they have remaining, two are seriously damaged and three are in trouble.*

The outcome of the battle was not in doubt. Part of her wanted to press the attack and completely crush the ComStar light company, but another part of her saw no honor in doing that. *Their objective was to take the lake from us, and their attack has been repulsed. Utterly destroying them would be what I would do with bandits, but these people are not bandits. While they are not Clan, they do know how to fight.*

A thin-lipped smile twisted her mouth. She keyed her radio to a frequency that allowed for a wide-beam broadcast. "ComStar, the battle is over. We will allow you to withdraw and will consider your honor intact."

Static crackled through her helmet's speakers, then a weary voice replied to her. "I am Precentor Harvison. You've beaten us fairly and soundly. We will withdraw, and will consider your honor enhanced by your generosity."

"Well bargained and done, Precentor." Marthe switched her radio over to her own tactical frequency. "Falcons, stand down. They are going home and we have successfully defended ours."

=== 12 ===

Wolf Clan Defensive Zone, Kawlm District
Strana Mechty
Kerensky Cluster, Clan Space
23 April 3060

Who is this impudent annoyance? Vlad's snarl echoed inside his neurohelmet as he watched the *Stormcrow* race past him and off toward his own staging area. His own secondary monitors showed the estimated damage to this Lancer 'Mech—the right arm was all but gone and that whole flank was ready to fall off. He started to turn his *Timber Wolf* to track the *Stormcrow*'s flight, but as he did so the rest of the battlefield moved to the margins of his holographic display.

As bad as the damage was to the *Stormcrow*, Vlad knew his *Timber Wolf* had been hurt too. Another shot from the autocannon could take his left leg off or crush the right side of his 'Mech and destroy that arm along with it. Unlike the *Stormcrow*, Vlad had no pristine side to present to the enemy. If he tried to protect his right side, he exposed his left leg and vice versa. There was simply no easy solution to how to deal with the *Stormcrow*.

"Damn you, Lincoln Osis, for losing Huntress and turning its treasures over to these vermin."

Out on the battlefield things were going a bit worse than he had expected. His lighter 'Mechs were indeed faster than the Lancer machines, but the enemy's greater shielding meant they took a longer time to kill. While his 'Mechs' speed should have made them harder to hit, the Lancer pilots seemed to have been chosen for their marksmanship. He already had one *Nova* on the ground and several other enemy 'Mechs with damage. Most of the rest were holding their own, which was not quite good enough for him.

He started to snap orders, but the *Stormcrow* had executed a smart little turn and had come back, angling in on the *Timber Wolf*'s right side. Vlad turned his 'Mech, putting his back to the rest of the battlefield, and settled his cross hairs on the smaller 'Mech. A dot pulsed in the center of them and Vlad hit his triggers.

The LRM launchers spouted smoke and fire. The missiles wreathed the *Stormcrow* with explosions, blasting armor from its left arm, left flank, midline, and even pouring fire into the open rent on its right flank. Even as the *Stormcrow* fired back at the *Timber Wolf,* one of the two large lasers Vlad fired sliced into and through the right flank, collapsing it and spinning the arm off across the battlefield.

Three of the *Stormcrow*'s lasers fired before the 'Mech lost the limb. The scarlet beams sliced into the *Timber Wolf*'s right arm and leg, with the third stabbing into the open right flank. It melted more support structures, and the wave of heat that coursed up into the cockpit told Vlad his engine had lost some of its shielding. The *Stormcrow*'s autocannon let loose with another double burst. The first stripped almost every shred of armor from the *Timber Wolf*'s left arm. The second one gouged into the armor on the 'Mech's centerline and burrowed through to score internal damage. The *Timber Wolf* shuddered and stumbled, then started to go down.

Gyro hit! The *Timber Wolf* crashed down on its right arm and flopped over onto its belly. Vlad's body jerked against the restraining straps, and sparks shot through the cockpit. Panic jolted through him as he saw the *Stormcrow* loom up past the mound of earth the *Timber Wolf*'s nose had pushed up when it fell. *One clean shot to the cockpit and I die.*

He heard the whine of the *Stormcrow*'s autocannon and felt it ripsaw through the armor over his 'Mech's spine. The grinding sound came from behind the cockpit, and the monitors reported severe damage to the *Timber Wolf*'s skeletal structure. He braced for a second blast, but when none came, he saw his chance and tried to scramble the 'Mech to its feet. The damaged gyro defied him, and the *Timber Wolf* crashed down on its right flank.

"I will not die in the mud like this!" Vlad reared back in his command console and all but willed the *Timber Wolf* upright. Dirt fell away from the cockpit canopy as the 'Mech righted itself, revealing a battered and smoking *Stormcrow* standing right before it. The *Stormcrow*'s only remaining weapon, the autocannon, swung into line with the *Timber Wolf,* and Vlad brought his weapons to bear at the same time on his enemy.

The large laser in the *Timber Wolf*'s left arm seared armor on the Lancer 'Mech's right leg, while the companion medium laser burned armor from the midline. The right arm's large laser missed wide, passing through where the 'Mech's right flank would have been, while the red beam from the medium laser in that arm melted yet more armor from the *Stormcrow*'s right leg.

The autocannon's double burst slammed into the *Timber Wolf*'s midline with enough force to tip the cockpit skyward. The depleted-uranium slugs ravaged the last of the forward armor, then ripped away the rest of the internal support structures. Vlad heard the agonized shriek of tortured metal behind his cockpit, then all of his instruments went dead. Through the canopy he saw the sky, then the ground and the sky again, confirming visually what his guts had already told him: his cockpit had been blasted free and sent spinning through the air.

Armor cracked and the cockpit canopy exploded outward when it hit the ground the first time. The jarring impact drove Vlad deep into the padding of his command couch. He slammed against one of the couch's arms, crunching a rib, as the cockpit began to roll right, then it bounced a few more times and spun to a stop on its side in a grassy depression.

Vlad hit the release on his restraining straps and dove out of the canopy opening. He scrambled away from the battered shell that had protected him, and clawed his way up a little incline. He tore off his neurohelmet and tossed it aside, then threw himself down on his belly to watch the battle. The cool grasses sent a chill through him, a chill amplified by what he saw.

One of the *Pillager*s continued battering a *Man O' War* that had already lost its right arm and flank and whose left arm hung on by a thin thread of myomer fibers. Smoke pouring from the *Man O' War*'s open right flank betokened engine damage. The *Pillager* had substantial armor damage, but Vlad could see no breaches in it.

The *Pillager*'s two Gauss rifle slugs shattered the armor over the *Man O' War*'s left leg, then ripped away the myomer fibers covering the thigh. The large laser mounted in the *Pillager*'s right arm amputated the Clan 'Mech's left arm, then melted away some of the flank structures and further crumbled the shielding on the fusion reactor at its heart. Then three of the *Pillager*'s four medium lasers speared the Clan 'Mech with ruby shafts. One that pierced the midline conjured a brilliant explosion. Golden fire jetted out both ruined flanks, and the pilot ejected nanoseconds before the reactor's explosion consumed the cockpit.

Vlad felt the detonation ripple through the ground and into his chest. *That 'Mech gone without his foe going down. He failed, as did I.*

Elsewhere, smoking 'Mechs on both sides stalked over the battlefield. The *Stormcrow* that had killed his *Timber Wolf* targeted the second Wolf *Man O' War*. The 'Mech had already been hammered in its duel with a *Pillager,* so when the *Stormcrow*'s double shot hit it in the legs, egg-shell thin armor vaporized, allowing the projectiles to gnaw through the myomer muscles. The shells clipped one leg off at the knee and wrenched the other one so severely around in the socket that the *Man O' War* spun around, then crashed down on its back.

Even before it went down, though, the *Man O' War*'s pilot clipped off a shot with a PPC that struck the *Pillager* in the head. In an eyeblink all the armor evaporated, then the cockpit exploded. Trailing smoke from where the head had been, the *Pillager* toppled over onto its back.

One of the Lancer *Cataphract*s was down, along with a second *Pillager,* two of the *Blackjack*s, and one of the *Raven*s. The *Fenrise*s and *Nova*s fell back to regroup, warily staying away from the *Stormcrow,* the remaining *Pillager,* and the *Blackjack*s. By using their superior speed the black Clan Wolf 'Mechs could make grazing attacks against the larger Inner Shere 'Mechs, but picking them apart would take a long time.

Conversely, the Lancers arrayed themselves so their fields of fire overlapped, allowing them to concentrate their attacks on a single target. Any Wolf 'Mech that ventured too close faced a withering mixture of beams and Gauss rifle projectiles that could reduce it to slag and rubble in a heartbeat. Because the Lancer 'Mechs were so slow, any move to scatter the Wolves would leave the attacking 'Mech vulnerable to the sort of slashing attacks the Wolves wanted to employ.

Vlad stood and raised a hand to shield his eyes from the sun. He watched a couple of charges at the Lancers start, then stop abruptly. The Inner Sphere 'Mechs remained grouped together in good order and moved around in a circle that kept them firmly in the center of the battlefield. The Wolves were able to circle around them, but any aggression or mistake by either party would end up a disaster for the group that made that first move.

One of the *Fenrises* broke off and ran over to where Vlad stood. The humanoid 'Mech dropped to one knee, and the pilot keyed an external speaker. "My Khan, we are at a standoff."

Vlad nodded slowly. "So it would appear."

"The freebirth scum have offered us a truce. They say we have not lost the field, but neither do we command it. They offer a draw." The disdain in the pilot's voice warred with an undertone of frustration. "Give the order and we will attack and shatter them."

Muscles bunched at the corners of Vlad's jaw. Part of him wanted to issue that order and have his warriors blast the Lancers from the field. He wanted no trace left of these Lancers, and he knew his people would go to any lengths to destroy them, even if it meant the attacks were suicidal. Bravery here would guarantee a warrior's genetic material entering the Clan breeding program, giving her or him all the immortality anyone was entitled to.

Vlad inhaled, planning on issuing that order, but he stopped. His fury with the Lancers was really his anger at himself. The force he had assembled would have been appropriate for battle against an enemy who held the Clans in awe. Had his warriors been facing troops from Rasalhague or the Lyran Alliance, they would have picked them apart. Those Inner Sphere troops had seen the Clans in action before and knew to fear them.

But these St. Ives Lancers, they do not know the Wolves. They had certainly faced the Clans before, but in the form of the Smoke Jaguars. The Lancers had never been broken by the Clans. Of the Clans all they knew was victory. Here they had met a force they out-gunned and out-massed, and *they* were offering a draw.

And a draw it is. Vlad looked up toward the *Fenris'* cockpit. "Tell their commander a draw is acceptable. And convey my compliments to the *Stormcrow* pilot."

"Are you certain, my Khan, *quineg*?"

"Did I sound uncertain, Star Captain?" The Khan snorted angrily. "That pilot reminded me of something that will save our Clan. Killing him or the rest of you in a futile fight will not change that fact. Relay the message now."

A light breeze came up, swirling the smoke rising from broken 'Mechs. Vlad caught the scent of burning plastics mixed with grass smoke and wrinkled his nose against it. The faceplate on the most recently downed *Man O' War* popped up and a pilot climbed out. She started trotting toward him, then slowed to a walk as she looked about and saw she was no longer in the middle of a battlefield.

The *Fenris* pilot spoke. "Message sent and reply received, my Khan. The *Stormcrow*'s pilot offers you his compliments as well."

"Who is he?"

"He is Kai Allard-Liao."

Vlad nodded slowly. He dimly recalled the name from the invasion. This Kai had evaded a Jade Falcon garrison force, then worked with them to defeat ComStar forces on that world. By all accounts he would have made a splendid bondsman, but the Jade Falcons accepted him as an ally instead.

"For them he won a planet." Vlad smiled. "For us, he provides salvation." He gazed at the smoking *Stormcrow* and allowed himself a laugh. "And if he knew that, he'd come here and finish the job he left undone on the battlefield."

=== 13 ===

Coldrill Valley, Neegdye District
Strana Mechty
Kerensky Cluster, Clan Space
23 April 3060

Khan Karianna Schmitt's joy at seeing a Combine *No-Dachi* pitch forward into the muddy stream at the ravine bottom died as the *Kingfisher* to her left fell backward. Sheer surprise at that outcome ate up her elation, then outrage devoured her surprise. The Combine 'Mechs had been attacked honorably, with one of the Blood Spirits engaging each, yet three of the enemy had turned their weapons on a single foe. Such a cowardly act made her blood run cold, crystallizing a desire to see all those before her dead.

She knew, however, her outrage was not simply born of the Combine's craven action. She would have expected no less from people who had banded together to create a sham Star League in the vain hopes it would scare the Clans into repudiating their mission to retake the Inner Sphere. The Combine troops had clearly debased themselves—even on

Strana Mechty she had heard of how common criminals and anyone else who could pilot a 'Mech had been made into warriors. Ganging up on one target really should have been expected.

What fueled her cold fury was the fact that they had not chosen *her* as their initial target. Jason Keller, the fallen *Kingfisher*'s pilot, was a competent warrior, but he was nothing in comparison to her. And while she realized it was irrational to expect the Combine to recognize that *she,* the Blood Spirits' supreme commander, had deigned to fight against them, she was determined they would pay for the effrontery of not spotting her immediately as their most deadly enemy.

Back to the west, the *Battle Cobra* and *Akuma* exchanged fire. Again one of the *Battle Cobra*'s PPCs failed to hit its target, incinerating another tree. The blue beam that did hit mauled the armor on the larger 'Mech's right leg. Despite a cascade of smoking armor plates hissing as they dropped into the stream, the *Akuma*'s leg had plenty of protection left on it.

The gray *Akuma* attacked the *Battle Cobra* with every weapons system it had save the PPC. A medium pulse laser stippled the *Battle Cobra*'s chest with a half-dozen ruby needles. The red beam from the laser built into the right arm likewise scored the armor over the Clan 'Mech's chest. A burst from the *Akuma*'s autocannon shattered the last of the brittle armor on the right flank, raining fragments down to the ground. The MRMs finished the last of the armor on the 'Mech's right arm and ripped away at the myomer muscles they exposed. Others nailed the *Battle Cobra*'s left hip and flank, reducing armor to a glittering hail of dust.

The *Akuma*'s SRMs finished what the other weapons had begun. Black smoke curled up through great cracks in the armor over the 'Mech's heart. The last of the armor on the left arm fell away, and an exploding SRM blasted armor from the *Battle Cobra*'s cockpit area. Finally one of the missiles snapped the 'Mech's right arm off, whirling its blackened skeleton and the sparking remnant of a PPC back out of sight.

Across the ravine the *Crossbow* rained fire down on the *No-Dachi* climbing up the hill toward it. The *Crossbow*'s SRMs all locked on target and gouged armor from the *No-Dachi*'s arm, legs, and especially the already damaged right flank. A spray of LRMs flaked armor off the left flank and midline, but failed to open any holes. The twin pulse lasers raked armor away from the 'Mech's right arm and pierced the right flank, melting cross-members of the *No-Dachi*'s frame.

The paired MRM launchers in the *No-Dachi*'s shoulders disgorged fire and smoke. The rockets streaked up at the *Crossbow*, blasting away at its prow-shaped chest. Most destroyed armor, but at least one got through, starting a black tendril of smoke rising. The others laced into the left leg, left arm, and right flank, chipping away at armor. The left arm came up and the PPC spat cerulean lightning that coursed up the *Crossbow*'s left leg from ankle to knee, stripping it of armor.

The *Crossbow* kicked out with its right foot at the *No-Dachi*, catching it in the left arm. The 'Mech's flat foot slammed into the Combine 'Mech's left arm, crushing all but the last of the armor on that limb. The *No-Dachi* twisted around to the right, absorbing the damage from that blow, then brought its sword around and caught the Clan 'Mech behind the right knee. Armor shards flew as the blade bit deep. The *Crossbow* pilot tried to get the 'Mech's left foot down to maintain the machine's balance, but the heel plowed a furrow through the loam and got no purchase. The *Crossbow* pitched to the left and crashed to the earth.

Mud clung to Jason Keller's *Kingfisher* as the 'Mech lumbered to its feet again. The branches and leaves stuck on it transformed the 'Mech into some primordial monster. The *Kingfisher* oriented itself again on the *Daishi* and fired, but Karianna knew something more than engine trouble was amiss when Keller didn't use the autocannon.

It must have been damaged or jammed when first fired. Without it that 'Mech ceases to be much of a threat.

Despite her assessment, the *Kingfisher* lit the *Daishi* up with its beam weapons. The touch of a large laser evaporated armor from the *Daishi*'s right leg. The quartet of medium lasers splashed their beams across the Combine 'Mech's chest, nearly opening it up completely, as well as dissipating armor on its left breast and right arm. The *Daishi* pilot kept his 'Mech under control and did not so much as take a step back despite the devastation Keller's attack wrought.

The *Daishi* lit back into the *Kingfisher* with a vengeance. The Combine 'Mech's large lasers drove green shafts into the *Kingfisher*'s right leg and through the armor on its right flank. Flame lipped from the autocannons as they tracked shells over the right leg and into the right flank. Green steam boiled out, heralding the destruction of a heat sink, and unfired shells for the autocannon started toppling out through a hole in the armor. The quartet of medium pulse lasers compounded the damage to the right flank and finished the last of the armor on the *Kingfisher*'s right arm. Two of them sent their energy volley against the 'Mech's broad chest, evaporating enough armor to leave the chest's protection transparently thin.

The rising *No-Dachi* brought its weapons to bear on the brutalized *Kingfisher*. The PPC's jagged line of azure energy rippled along the 'Mech's right arm, leaving it a shriveled smoking collection of metal rods. The MRM canisters coughed out fire and munitions, peppering the Clan 'Mech with dozens of explosions. The 'Mech's right arm vanished amid a bouquet of fiery detonations that spread to consume the *Kingfisher*'s right flank and the last of the armor over its heart. Bits and pieces of the 'Mech frame cascaded out of its hollowed middle, and more explosions chewed into the left side of the 'Mech's chest.

Karianna considered it a testament to Keller's skill as a pilot that his 'Mech remained upright, but she knew its combat effectiveness was nearly at an end. *After this battling, even if he dies here, his progeny will be highly prized.*

The other *Kingfisher* laid waste to the *No-Dachi*. Twin PPC beams effaced all the armor from the smaller 'Mech's chest and left flank. A quartet of medium lasers stabbed out from the *Kingfisher* to hit the Combine 'Mech. Two of the red shafts dissolved the armor on the right leg and roasted the myomers they uncovered. The third beam flensed more armor from the 'Mech's right flank, but the fourth cored through the center of the *No-Dachi*'s chest. Smoke belched from the SRM launcher there, then thick black smoke began to pour out. Incredibly, the *No-Dachi* did not go down, but started to make its way up the hillside.

Part of Karianna wanted to disbelieve what she was seeing. She knew the Clans produced warriors superior to anything the Inner Sphere had to offer in terms of skills and abilities, talent and genetic makeup, and her warriors were acquitting themselves admirably. Though the Inner Sphere force did possess an OmniMech, one piloted by someone who clearly knew how to use it, they were standing up to an equal Clan force. All the stories she had heard, all the battle analysis she had performed had indicated that they should have broken when confronted, but here was one of them in a holed 'Mech, rushing up against them.

She quelled the spark of panic in her guts by dropping her golden cross hairs on the *Dragon Fire*. Her large lasers swept across the left side of the Combine 'Mech, coming up sharply toward its head. Armor melted over the *Dragon Fire*'s left arm and flank, then poured in rivulets from the cockpit assembly. Heat washed up into her cockpit as she released two flights of LRMs. They blasted more armor from the 'Mech's left arm and compounded the damage to its left flank, but failed to strike the *Dragon Fire*'s head and kill the pilot.

Karianna did note, however, with some satisfaction, that her attack had gotten the attention of the *Dragon Fire*'s pilot. The squat 'Mech turned its weapons on her *Blood Kite*. The autocannon peeled armor off her 'Mech's right hip, while the Gauss rifle bounced a shot off the *Blood Kite*'s chest. The

Dragon Fire's large laser melted a nasty gash up the *Kite*'s left forearm, causing half-melted armor to ooze down and around to drip off at the elbow. The smaller pulse lasers the *Dragon Fire* packed sent a flurry of red darts that nibbled armor from each of the *Blood Kite*'s flanks.

Keller's *Kingfisher* fired its large laser once more at the *Daishi*, this time hitting it in the right leg. A trio of medium lasers coruscated out and hit the OmniMech, but likewise only took armor off the left leg and left arm. *With the chest armor in tatters, he shoots the limbs. Perhaps his line is not that strong after all.*

The charging *No-Dachi* fired its weapons at Keller's *Kingfisher*. The MRM barrage ringed the Clan 'Mech with fire, collapsing the left side of the chest. The left arm fell to the ground, then careened down the slope toward the stream. The frozen azure lightning of the *No-Dachi*'s PPC carved up through the gaping hole in the 'Mech's left flank and arced from the frame. The Clan 'Mech shuddered, then the pristine cockpit assembly sagged back, as if the pilot were lifting the 'Mech's throat so it could be cut by the *No-Dachi*'s sword. Before the *No-Dachi* could deliver that blow, the Blood Spirit 'Mech tottered, then fell backward, smashing down trees as it went.

The other *Kingfisher* avenged Keller's destruction. The blue beams whiplashed the *No-Dachi*'s arms, flaying armor from the right one and laying bare the left. The tendril of lightning playing along the left arm melted the upper set of myomer muscles controlling the arm, and ripped apart the SRM launcher in the forearm. The *Kingfisher*'s medium lasers vaporized the Combine 'Mech's left arm, then started in on the left flank, while others stabbed deep into the un-armored chest.

And, beyond Karianna's ability to comprehend, the *No-Dachi* did not go down, and continued up the slope.

To the west the *Battle Cobra* hit the *Akuma* with a PPC bolt that bubbled armor off the Combine 'Mech's leg, but the Inner Sphere pilot shifted his aim away from the 'Mech that had attacked him. As the demonic 'Mech's shoulder squared around to face her *Blood Kite,* Karianna realized she was his new target.

The MRM launcher spat out a flight of missiles that sent a shudder through her 'Mech when they hit. Her monitor showed armor being carved off the left and right flanks, as well as the chest, then a second jolt ran through the *Blood Kite.* A warning siren went off and Karianna had to stagger the 'Mech back a half-step to rebalance it. *Gyro hit. This cannot be happening.*

Two lasers, one in a solid beam and the other in a stuttered series of bolts, lashed the *Blood Kite.* The pulse laser dug into the armor on the 'Mech's right arm, while the beam slashed away at its right thigh. The *Akuma*'s autocannon delivered another staggering shot to the *Blood Kite*'s midline, then swarms of SRMs spiraled in at the Blood Spirit war machine. They pulverized armor all over the 'Mech, including the increasingly vulnerable centerline armor.

The *Dragon Fire* that had been her foe throughout the battle again leveled its weapons at her. The autocannon's depleted-uranium shells scarified the armor on the *Blood Kite*'s right forearm. Yellow-green mist exploded as the Gauss rifle's ball crushed the last of the armor on the *Blood Kite*'s left arm and destroyed a heat sink. The *Dragon Fire*'s large laser missed to the left, and one of the two pulse lasers danced its bolts over the Clan 'Mech's right flank. The last pulse laser drilled its needles into the *Blood Kite*'s head, shriveling yet more of the cockpit armor.

Karianna cried out involuntarily as the ruby light spiked the heat in her cockpit, and the dread she had tried to smother earlier started her stomach acid burbling up into her throat. *No, I am Blood Spirit. I do not know fear.*

Then the *Daishi* brought its weapons up and focused them on the *Blood Kite.* One of the autocannons hammered through the last of the armor on the right flank, splashing a heat sink.

The other blew armor scales from the right leg. The paired large lasers drove their beams through the flimsy armor left on the chest and the gaping hole on the right flank, melting yet more of the *Blood Kite*'s frame. The *Daishi*'s four pulse lasers plastered their energy over the *Blood Kite*'s chest, disintegrating what little of the 'Mech's right flank that still existed. The *Blood Kite*'s right arm fell away, carrying with it heat sinks and missile launchers.

The singular shock of losing the right side of the 'Mech unbalanced the whole machine. Karianna fought her controls, trying to keep the *Blood Kite* on its feet and fighting, but with the damaged gyro, there was no way she could accomplish that feat. The 'Mech stumbled back, then careened to the right and flopped over onto its front. It slid down the hill, mud washing up over the cockpit, entombing Khan Karianna Schmitt in a hot dark hole where she would have lots of time to consider how truly badly she had underestimated the warriors of the Inner Sphere.

14

Bloody Basin, Lechenka District
Strana Mechty
Kerensky Cluster, Clan Space
23 April 3060

Off to Victor's right, Danai Centrella's *Falconer* struggled to regain its feet. Only as the 'Mech sagged to the ground again did Victor realize that she had taken a shot to the gyro, giving her the same control over the machine that a drunk has over his own body. Armor plates popped off the *Falconer*'s left leg and arm as it went down. A second unsuccessful attempt did even more damage to the armor.

The *Masakari* righted itself and brought its weapons to bear on the stricken *Falconer*. Victor started turning Prometheus around, bringing the Clan 'Mech into his forward firing arc, but he couldn't shoot fast enough to stop the Clanner from getting his own shots off. A trio of PPC beams lashed out, flaying the downed 'Mech. One hellish blue bolt melted the *Falconer*'s left arm completely away, while another stabbed through the remaining armor over the 'Mech's breast, earning a belching gout of night-black smoke.

The third beam linked the *Masakari*'s right arm with the *Falconer*'s head. Cobalt energy tentacles wrapped themselves around the cockpit, then sank black lines through melting armor. Sheets of ferro-ceramics dissolved like sand in a stream, and in their wake Victor could see nothing. In a heartbeat, all of Danai Centrella's heartbeats had been stilled forever.

Victor went cold inside. He'd not known Danai at all well—they had barely spoken with each other before she came to him with her request to fight against the Smoke Jaguars. He could recall her bright amber eyes, her full mouth and the smile it displayed when he granted her request. Both of them had known they could die in the battle, but neither of them would acknowledge that the risk was that great. *We trick ourselves into believing we are immortal because to think anything less would make us run screaming at the thought of combat.*

The golden cross hairs on his display centered themselves over the *Masakari,* and Victor tugged his triggers tight to the joystick. The Gauss rifle drove its ball through the last of the midline armor and bounced it around, smashing internal structures. One pulse laser delivered its needles in the Gauss slug's wake, tearing away at the engine's shielding. The other two pulse lasers blistered the last of the armor over the left flank and likewise melted bits of the engine's shielding.

Two flights of SRM Streak missiles spiraled in at the *Masakari.* A half-dozen sowed explosions over the left side of the 'Mech, tearing at the myomer muscles in the naked left arm and scoring the armor over the 'Mech's left hip. Almost as many poured through the gaping hole in the *Masakari*'s chest and shredded the last of the skeleton there. The cockpit flipped forward as the arms collapsed in and the whole 'Mech sagged to the left, its slagged middle oozing out over the ground like quicksilver.

Cranston's *Devastator* targeted the lone *Nova* on the northern flank. The twin Gauss rifles flashed, sending both their projectiles ripping into and through the Clan 'Mech's chest. A PPC bolt cored in there after them, liquefying what little they had left intact. The cockpit faceplate exploded outward as the pilot ejected, then the fusion engine's uncontrolled reaction blossomed. In a brilliantly incandescent ball of plasma, the upper half of the Clan 'Mech vanished, leaving two intact legs tumbling across the red rocks.

The missile and laser barrages that had so devastated the *Cauldron-Born* now pounded the last two *Stormcrow*s to the north. The *Rakshasa*s took down the *Stormcrow* Victor had hit previously, while the *Longbow*s combined to attack the previously untouched Smoke Jaguar. At the closer-in range, their fire became far more accurate, wreathing the *Stormcrow* with strings of explosions. The Clan 'Mech careened around as each wave pummeled it and the lasers skewered it, then it finally crashed to the ground and lay there a smoking ruin. The *Rakshasa*s transfixed the *Stormcrow* with their large and pulse lasers, boring through torso and flank armor, then carving up the 'Mech's insides. It crashed down on its chest and rolled, coming to rest upside down with its feet leaning against a slender red pillar of stone.

Off to the south Applegarth's *Penetrator* and the two *Jackal*s had mauled the *Hankyu*s. One *Jackal* had lost an arm and the other looked beat-up, but the withering fire from the *Penetrator* had blown the middle out of one Clan 'Mech and cut one of the legs out from under one of the others. The *Jackal*s had apparently hounded the third and dropped it, because it lay on the ground smoking from the back.

Victor turned his *Daishi* toward where Osis stood and started off across the battlefield. He saw the Smoke Jaguar Elementals moving to intercept him. "General Redburn, I have elementals incoming. Would you mind scattering them?"

Another salvo from the missile 'Mechs ripped across the landscape. Victor saw little armored figures silhouetted against the explosions or tossed about. Some of them landed hard and lay still, while others just disintegrated. Some got back up, their armor broken, but their spirit still intact. Those who were still able came toward his 'Mech in long bounding strides.

From his vantage point high in the *Daishi,* with the rest of his unit closing in, the Elementals looked like toy soldiers waiting to be battered aside by the feet of children. He refused to let himself think of them that way. *They* are *living people, and they deserve a chance at continuing their lives.*

Victor flipped his communications gear over to the *Daishi*'s external speakers. "Stop now and you won't be killed."

The Elementals kept coming. One of them launched the two SRMs in his backpack, but the OmniMech's anti-missile system blasted them out of the air.

"Stop now." Victor let the edge in his voice soften. "The battle is over. Please. You are no longer Smoke Jaguars. Accept it. Stop now."

Applegarth fired both his large lasers along a line between the Elementals and Prometheus, slowing their advance. Victor drove the *Daishi* forward, opening its arms wide. The Elementals backed out of his way, parting for him, and let him lumber toward where the ilKhan waited.

Osis leaped down from his watchtower and landed awkwardly, clearly favoring his left leg. He limped down the slope toward the *Daishi,* then stopped with his arms held wide. "Is this how you come to face me, Victor Davion? You have stolen our technology, aped our ways, and now you come to squash me like a bug you've discovered in your garden? Is that what this comes to?"

Victor blinked. "How did you expect it to end? The Clans lived in isolation for three hundred years, refining combat and military technology while the Inner Sphere nearly blasted itself back to the Stone Age. Then you decided it was time for your return, for you to reclaim a birthright your ancestors had willingly abandoned. What did you think you would do? Take

Terra and send us all eviction notices? Did you think we wouldn't fight back?"

"Not only are you stupid, Victor, but you are vulgar."

"Oh, yes, indeed, vulgar because I use contractions. Vulgar because I don't fight a war the way you would like it fought." Victor's nostrils flared. "Vulgar because I find you to be silly and hidebound and a people who have divorced themselves from mortality and warfare."

Osis extended the claw on his battle armor's left hand and snapped it shut. "You talk of mortality and warfare, but you know nothing of it really. I am Lincoln Osis. I can trace my bloodline back to Charissa Osis, one of those who left the Inner Sphere with General Kerensky. Her daughter, Terrisa, fought with Nicholas Kerensky and established the Clans. From her loins have come warriors and Khans who have brought glory to the Smoke Jaguars. We are a line renowned among the Clans for our courage. Generation upon generation we improve. Leo Showers' sire was an Osis, and Leo Showers was the ilKhan who initiated our return."

A seam appeared around the chest plate and neck on Osis' armor. He reached up with the claw and pried the helmet and front panel of the armored suit loose. It dropped onto the ground before him, revealing the ilKhan's head and well-muscled ebon chest.

"I was bred to be a warrior, Victor, to fear nothing and no one. Only through acts of bravery and tactical superiority could I expect to lead my people to victory. You have seen how easy it is to destroy Elementals when 'Mechs dominate the battlefield—imagine how difficult it is to rise to command among them."

Osis pulled his left arm free, allowing the armored sleeve to drop to the ground. He slipped his right arm from its shell, letting the small laser that capped the arm fall away. The man flexed his arms and chest, then tore away the flank armor and allowed the SRM launcher assembly to crash to the ground.

"Do you know how I won my bloodname, Victor? I met

and broke MechWarriors like you in single combat. Luck was with me because my first battles were fought unenhanced, but not so the last round. To win this bloodname, to become an Osis, I had to destroy a MechWarrior who, like you, sat safely locked away in the cockpit of a BattleMech. We fought in territory not unlike this, in a place on Huntress. He thought he was stalking me, but I stalked him. From a cliff I leaped down and landed on his *Adder*. He could hear me there, blasting away, burrowing into his 'Mech and there was nothing he could do to stop me. He knew it, so he crawled from the cockpit and tried to kill me. He failed, and his genetic heritage was discarded."

Victor's eyes narrowed. "You killed a man who clearly had been defeated? Why?"

"He wanted to die. He knew he had failed, knew he was not the sort of material the Osis House would want to pass on to future generations." The ilKhan sat on the missile launcher pack and pulled his legs from the armor. Wearing only a pair of shorts, Osis stood and made no attempt to hide the hideous wound on his left leg. Victor punched up magnification on his holographic display and clearly saw sutures. *And there's blood oozing from the wound.*

Osis opened his arms. "I am the last of the Smoke Jaguars, Victor Davion. I invite you now to face me, man to man. Face me and earn the honor you think you deserve. Only a coward would not face me. Come to me, Victor, and I will teach you things in seconds that men study lifetimes to learn."

Jerry Cranston's voice echoed through Victor's helmet. "Don't even dream it, Victor. His daughter kicked your ass. Hell, back on Trellwan, *I* kicked your ass."

"Message received, Jerry." Victor shook his head. "What makes you think, Lincoln Osis, that I want to learn the lessons you could teach?"

Osis' mouth opened slowly and his shoulders sagged a bit. "You are a warrior, *quiaff*? As am I. Our business is death.

Here I offer you the chance to face death and see which of us it will claim."

Victor hit the release on his restraining straps, then punched a button that popped the *Daishi*'s canopy open.

"Victor, what are you doing?"

"Easy, Jerry. I know what I'm doing."

"Care to give me a clue?"

"I'd rather ask you to trust me." Victor slipped off his helmet and didn't hear Jerry's reply to his request. He climbed from the command couch and untied the string securing a small rope ladder at the cockpit edge. He tossed it out and let it unroll its way to the ground. He turned to climb down, then saw sunlight glinting from the crossguard of the katana he'd been given upon his arrival on Luthien. Smiling grimly, he slid it from the bracket that secured it to his command couch and carried it with him to the ground.

Osis folded his arms across his chest and glared at him. "Even that sword will not prevent me from killing you."

"Not the reason I brought it." Victor slipped it through the gunbelt he wore, positioning the blade in its proper place over his left hip. His fingers went to the clasps on his cooling vest. He unfastened them and shrugged the bulky garment off. His pasty white chest proved a perfect contrast to Osis' physique and won him a scornful look from the Elemental.

Victor snorted and traced his left hand over the twin scars on his chest. "I wanted you to see these. I had a katana very much like this one shoved through my chest. Why? Because someone thought, by virtue of my birth, that I was his inferior. He thought my very existence in some way sullied the world he imagined existed. The way he saw things, the way his master saw things, demanded my death, and this man, he came to take my life."

"Clearly he failed."

"He did. I killed him with this sword I now wear. It was given to me as a matter of courtesy, to make a statement, but the night I killed my assassin, I earned the right to wear it."

Victor frowned. "And that night I killed him, I died as well. I've felt death's touch, but I came back. I came back with one specific purpose in mind—defeating you and putting an end to your invasion."

Osis waved the comment away contemptuously. "This story might frighten a Nova Cat, but not a Smoke Jaguar. Kill me if you dare."

"No."

"No?"

Victor shook his head. "No. There's been too much killing here, and you must have known that."

"What do you mean?"

Victor jerked a thumb at the battlefield behind him. "The 'Mechs you sent against us, you had to have known that force was inadequate. There was no way it could have stopped me or any of our Inner Sphere forces. You must have thought to preserve some of your warriors, spare them the humiliation."

Osis swallowed hard, then glanced down. "You are wrong." He hesitated for a moment. "They were all I had left."

A cold droplet of sweat ran down Victor's spine. *We really have broken them.* "You're left. Your pilots here."

"You'll destroy them the way you did the rest of the Smoke Jaguars."

"Yes, we will erase all traces of your Clan, but that does not mean the people will die. You may think us inferiors, but we are not murderers."

Osis slowly sank to his knees, his mouth open but mute. His eyes flicked back and forth, as if he were watching the events of the invasion pass before him. His hands, which had been balled into fists, slowly opened. "What in the name of Kerensky have we done?"

The pain in his voice squeezed Victor's heart. "You tried to breed into men a talent for warfare, when perhaps you needed to breed out the stupidity that lets us think the last battle can be fought, the last victory can be won, and that *then* there will be peace."

Osis gave him a weak smile. "But that was the impetus behind your crusade here, *quiaff*?"

"The irony isn't lost on me, but at least I *want* to stop."

The ilKhan's voice lightened a bit. "That will never happen, you know. You will never know peace."

"With the invasion stopped, at least some people will know peace."

Osis lifted his chin and looked up at Victor. "I will never be your bondsman."

"I don't want to make you my bondsman."

"I am finished, Victor Davion. Take your blade. Kill me."

"No. We're not murderers."

Osis reached out to him. "Please, as one warrior to another. My people have been destroyed. Do not make me outlive them."

"No." Victor's eyes tightened. "You've lost. You know it. It is over. For me to kill you now would be murder. I won't do it. Your reward is to live. The Smoke Jaguar warriors are no more, but that does not mean you still do not have a life."

"No warrior can live if he is no longer a warrior."

"So, then you face a new battle, living as something other than a warrior." Victor turned away from the ilKhan. "The last Smoke Jaguar warrior died here today."

Though he heard the scrape of bare feet on the rock, and saw the shadow loom up over him, Victor had felt Osis' move before the sensory input reached his conscious mind. The Prince pivoted on his right foot and came around by reflex. His katana slid noiselessly from its scabbard and golden sunlight skittered along the sharpened edge as the blade came up in a high arc. Without thinking, Victor slashed the blade back down. It met resistance for a second, then swung free again.

Victor stood there, Strana Mechty's sun hot on his back, staring down into the lifeless eyes of Lincoln Osis. The ilKhan's blood dripped from the katana's blade, forming a little stream tracing a path down the rocks to where the Smoke Jaguar's head rested.

The Prince slowly shook his head, surprised to taste tears on his lips. "The invasion started with a Smoke Jaguar, and now it has ended with one. The last Smoke Jaguar warrior *did* die here today. May he rest in peace."

15

Hall of the Khans, Warrior Quarter
Strana Mechty
Kerensky Cluster, Clan Space
25 April 3060

Prince Victor Ian Steiner-Davion tapped his foot nervously as he waited. The clicking echoed up and down the corridor outside the Grand Council chamber, sounding like the ticking of a crude time bomb. He smiled, knowing that what he had to say to the Clan Khans would undoubtedly explode among them like a bomb. *Just have to hope it's a shaped charge that takes out key structures and doesn't bring the whole thing crashing down.*

The battling in the Trial of Refusal had gone well for the Inner Sphere. The draw between the Wolves and the St. Ives Lancers had surprised Victor when he first heard of it, but a review of gun-camera holovids and battle roms showed that things could very easily have gone much worse for the Inner Sphere. Everyone who looked over the after-action data credited Kai with having taken control of the battle and eliminating one of the Wolves' most potent weapons. Kai, with his usual humility, credited luck for his success. Victor had told him, "Yes, it's better to be lucky than good, but you're very lucky and excellent which is very tough to beat."

The Jade Falcon victory over ComStar had disappointed everyone, but the Falcons had chosen an excellent defensive position, had deployed their 'Mechs well, and had used tactics that maximized their ability to deal damage while minimizing losses. Victor and his other advisors told Focht that none of the forces that had come from the Inner Sphere could have won that battle. Despite that reassurance, the loss seemed to take the edge off the Precentor Martial who, for the first time in all the years Victor had known him, finally seemed tired.

The only other Clan win came in the battle between the Star Adders and the First Free Worlds Guards. The Guards had entered a swampy area to fight the Star Adders and re-acted over-enthusiastically when they first ran into a couple of light 'Mechs and a Point of Elementals that they assumed was a formation scouting for the Clan main body. In fact, they were bait. As the Guards started pounding on the easy targets, the Star Adders blasted into their right flank and rolled it up. One Guards lance did manage to escape, but all the 'Mechs were damaged and five of the other pilots died.

The Inner Sphere won the rest of the battles. The Nova Cats thrashed the Ice Hellions. Khan Severen Leroux was credited with bringing down Asa Taney's *Visigoth* fighter. The two Nova Cat Khans took upon themselves the brunt of the fighting and were both slain, but none of the Nova Cats seemed upset about that fact. As nearly as Victor could make out, the Nova Cats viewed the deaths of their leaders as a point of transition for their Clan, and the deaths just fit pieces into a larger puzzle that gave them comfort and direction.

The Capellan Confederation's Red Lancers severely beat the Fire Mandrills. That Clan, while wholly Crusader in control, had political subdivisions including Wardens that meant the two Stars in their force did not work at all well together.

Using tactics that owed more to Napoleon than Sun-Tzu, the Lancers managed to hold one Star off while pounding the other, then they mopped up what was left of the second Star. Only Victor's win over the Smoke Jaguars resulted in more destruction of the Clan opposition, but the Red Lancers' commander wisely allowed the last Mandrills to surrender, then confiscated all the 'Mechs on the battlefield.

In perhaps the biggest and certainly the most pleasant surprise, the Free Rasalhague Republic's Third Drakøns defeated the Hell's Horses. The Clan deployed armored vehicles and tanks, as well as infantry, to support their 'Mech forces, and initially turned back the Drakøns. The Hell's Horses tried to exploit their advantage, then Overstë Dahlstrom rallied her troops. Her crisply shouted commands galvanized her people and got them moving. The accuracy of their shots spiked to where it seemed as if she had a whole company of Kai Allard-Liaos fighting for her. Their withering fire stopped the Hell's Horse advance and sent them reeling back. While the Drakøns did take a beating, they obtained their objective and even held off one last desperate attempt by the Clanners to liberate it.

Victor drew in a deep breath, then slowly exhaled. Of eight battles, they won five, which gave them victory in the Trial of Refusal. *The invasion is over.* For the last eleven years he had waited for this day to come, but could never have imagined that he would find himself here, dictating terms of the peace. Looking back he had assumed this role would fall to his father, or Morgan Hasek-Davion or Takashi Kurita.

Here I am, thirty years old, the man who led the largest military operation the Inner Sphere has seen since the fall of the old Star League. By my age Alexander the Great had become King of Macedonia and had spread an empire over much of the known world. I've beaten an invader back from whole worlds, tracked them to their haven, and defeated them here. Am I, like Alexander, at the pinnacle? Will I die in three years, my greatest victories behind me?

The door to the Grand Council chamber opened and an un-armored Elemental looked at Victor and nodded. Victor tugged at the hem of his Star League Defense Force jacket, then strode through the door and toward the high bench. In front of it sat a misshapen man—more metal than flesh, it seemed—who glared at him. Victor ignored the poisonous glance and mounted the steps to the high bench. Once there, he turned to face the assembly and hesitated.

The room itself was magnificent. The amphitheater's tiers, desks, and seats had been fashioned from black granite streaked with white. Red cushions had been set on the benches for the Khans, and Victor could see them because of the absences among the assembled Clan leaders. A banner with the Clan crest hung over the appropriate seats and Victor counted fourteen of them. He double-checked and saw none for the Smoke Jaguars or Nova Cats.

He pressed his hands to the cold stone surface of the high bench. The Clan Khans all wore their ceremonial garb and hid their faces behind ornate enameled masks. The masks looked truly fearsome, but Victor found them to be brittle and a sham. He had no doubt many of the Khans used them to conceal their fear.

"I bring you greetings from the First Lords of the Star League, and I thank you for receiving me here. I have been told I am the first person who is not a Clansman to address the assembled Khans and, despite the circumstances, I consider this an honor. For over a decade I have learned to fear you, and now, looking at you here, I know this assembly to be the wellspring from which the Clans have drawn their strength."

Victor kept his voice even and a bit low, forcing the Khans to listen to him carefully. He saw a few of them shift in their seats and wanted to interpret this as an easing of their tension, but without being able to look at their faces, he had trouble reading them at all. Their culture is alien to me. Can I even trust what I think I see?

"As you know, a week ago the Star League Expeditionary Force challenged your ilKhan to a Trial of Refusal concerning your invasion of the Inner Sphere. Two days ago we fought against the eight Crusader Clans. We lost to two, achieved a draw with one, and defeated five. Your invasion is over."

He let that comment sink in for a moment, then continued. "There are those among you who have interpreted this Trial of Refusal to be about more than your invasion. It has been seen as a test of your culture, your ways, your history, and your right to continue living the way you do. *That* was never part of our intention in coming here, in issuing the challenge or in defeating your forces. We came here not to impose our way of life upon you, but to stop you from attempting to impose your way of life on us."

The Wolf Khan stood and removed his helmet. "You successfully imposed a new way of life on the Smoke Jaguars."

"Your point, Khan Vlad, is a good one, but not entirely on target. We knew, when we came after you, that the only way you would take us seriously was if we managed to do what only the Clans have done before: annihilate a Clan, erase its identity. We chose the Smoke Jaguars and we brought war to Huntress. I am certain all of you know how brutal things were there." The Prince glanced down for a second. "Your way of life hid from you the reality of warfare and we needed to remind you of it—the way your attacks on our worlds brought it home to us. The fact remains, however, that we do not want to change the way you want to live.

"The invasion is ended, but not so our contact and our futures. While there are countless individuals in the Inner Sphere who have learned to hate you, we do not intend to prosecute a war against you—at least, not as the Star League. As the Star League we would invite you back to the Inner Sphere, to allow your people and ours to become acquainted. We have things to offer you, as you have to offer us. Beneath this umbrella of peace, there are many new possibilities. We invite you to explore them."

"You invite us to our death, Victor Davion." Vlad moved from his desk in the first rank, to the open floor before the high bench. "In fighting against the St. Ives troops I realized I had made a mistake. I let your Kai Allard-Liao get too close to me and, in doing so, I allowed myself to be hurt. As I crawled from my 'Mech's shattered cockpit and watched my troops fight, I realized that my error was a small piece of the larger error we all made."

Vlad addressed the other Khans but pointed his finger at Victor. "The Inner Sphere is a breeding ground of discontent from which our isolation had saved us. They are diseased and we were pure and healthy before we invaded them. Our prolonged association with them has hurt us, it has weakened us. It has allowed them to defeat us. And even now, with this invitation, the Inner Sphere seeks to absorb us."

Bjorn Jorgensson of the Ghost Bears stood and removed his helmet. "It strikes me, Khan Vlad, that your assessment of Prince Davion's invitation is wrong. He has not asked us to abandon who we are."

"No, not yet, but that will come." Vlad shook his head. "These people have a world where combats are staged for entertainment."

Victor smiled. "And the champion fighter on that world is the one who took you out of the fight. You can't denigrate the quality of the Solaris warriors like that."

"Immaterial, Victor, and beside my point." Vlad opened his arms to the other Khans. "These are a people who use as spectacle contests where people die, not to prove who is worthy of passing their genetic potential on, but for money. They sell soap and crackers, sugar-water and cosmetics. They mock what we do, they mock that which defines us, and they will turn us into clowns.

"You all know the history of the Inner Sphere, especially since the Exodus of the great Kerensky. The Wolf Dragoons were sent to them to determine what sort of people they were, and how were they employed? As *mercenaries*. They fought and shed their blood as proxies for their employers' people, and this will be our fate. Our technology will be sold to the highest bidder, our culture will become rootstock for trends. Clans will be franchised, merchandise will be sold, and our traditions will be tarnished."

The passion in Vlad's voice astonished Victor. He'd always seen the Clans as implacable warriors, and yet here was a man, one of their premier warriors, who had a very real fear about how his way of life would vanish. While Victor had learned to be afraid of the Clans, he also respected them and truly did not wish to see their way of life disappear. Worse yet, he could see everything Vlad predicted coming true.

The Prince leaned forward, supporting himself on his arms. "Khans of the Clans, the Wolf's fears are based on a false assumption—the assumption that I am here to dictate terms of peace. One advantage to your methods of waging war is simply that I need not dictate terms. We bargained and fought for a cessation of hostilities. We are at peace. My invitation to you is simply that of one neighbor to another. How you choose to react to that invitation is your own decision.

"I should note, however, that further adventurism on your part will be met with swift and devastating retribution. Enough blood has been spilled here and on Huntress to sate any warrior's fantasy. As a reminder of that, the Star League has declared the area on Huntress surrounding Lootera and Mount Szabo to be an open and neutral zone, held in trust, for the survivors who wish to live in peace on that world. Some of the city will be rehabilitated, but not all. We want the scars to remain in place so no one can mistake the consequences of moving against the Star League again. We *will* retain possession of the genetic repository in that area, keeping it functional and not destroying it. We will also, of course, send an ambassador there to take up residence and facilitate any communication you wish to have with the Star League."

Khan Jorgensson nodded. "Speaking for at least half my brethren, we appreciate the Star League's consideration. We all have had our eyes opened. Because of your victories, the matter of the invasion is closed. All who are here are bound by the Trial of Refusal."

Vlad laughed coldly. "Not so quickly, Khan Ghost Bear. You will recall that the Wolves abstained from the vote, and we were not defeated by the Inner Sphere. This matter is not binding on us."

Prince Victor's eyes narrowed. "If you wish, Khan Wolf, I will reassemble my forces in the Free Rasalhague Republic and we can drive you from the Inner Sphere."

"I am quite certain, Victor, that such an exercise would entertain you no end, but I am a warrior and am not concerned with your amusement. Fear not, I am still bound by the Tukayyid truce. I would not dream of crossing the border before the seven remaining years are up. You may decide you want to gather your warriors and attack me now, but I doubt the Star League will back that play."

Something in Vlad's voice sent a shiver down Victor's spine. Because his forces had traveled to the Clan home-worlds on a covert mission to rescue another force on a covert mission, they had not had any communications with the Inner Sphere for many months. In fact, if their disinformation efforts were holding true, the First Lord of the Star League actually did not know exactly where they were or exactly what they were doing.

The Clans, on the other hand, could have been getting news from the Inner Sphere and relaying it to Strana Mechty. Victor had long known of Clan ships entering a system, soaking up as much media as their databanks could hold, and fleeing to analyze the data. *Could it be he knows something about the Inner Sphere that I don't?* Victor saw the hint of a smug smile on Vlad's face. *Not a question of* if *but* what.

"You could be correct, Khan Wolf. Seven years may be seen as an eternity by many, but it is an eyeblink to me. If you decide to come after us in seven years, or sooner, I will be ready for you."

"If I choose to come for you, Victor Davion, you will never guess when or why, and you will forever regret seeing me again." Vlad turned and looked at the rest of the Khans. "You have chosen to be bound by this Trial. So be it. My Wolves and I will leave you to your fate. We shall remain true to the Kerensky vision and one day, when I have reclaimed Terra, you will come to me and beg forgiveness for your timidity."

He reached up and plucked his helmet from his desk, then turned and stalked out of the room. The Wolves' female saKhan trailed in his wake, with the other Khans watching. Only the Ghost Bear Khan had bared his face, and on it Victor saw a variety of warring emotions. Horror and amusement seemed to balance out somehow, and Victor found that more scary than either extreme.

Jorgensson kept his voice low. "The Wolves, or a portion of them anyway, are known for their volatility."

Victor nodded. "Is this a trait shared by the other Clans, or shall I load my people on their ships and prepare for a long journey home?"

Jorgensson smiled. "There is no need for threats, subtle or otherwise, Prince Davion. You challenged us and defeated us. That is enough. Peace you want, peace you have."

"No, my Khans," Victor said and smiled, "peace *we* have. That difference, though minor, is one I am certain you will come to treasure as time goes by."

16

Star League Expeditionary Force Command Center
Lootera Enclave, Huntress
Kerensky Cluster, Clan Space
18 July 3060

With Tiaret Nevversan following a shadowlength behind
him, Victor strode through the streets of Lootera with Sir Paul
Masters of the Knights of the Inner Sphere. Autumn had begun on Huntress, with the leaves on the few deciduous trees
remaining starting to turn gold and red. Aside from the leaves
that had already fallen, the city's streets were clean and surprisingly empty under the gray sky.

Victor looked over at the taller man. "You've done good
work here, Sir Paul."

"I enjoyed the chance to help rebuild some of what we destroyed." The blond, blue-eyed man frowned slightly. "I
understand why you're leaving some of the ruins as memori-
als, but so much has been laid waste. There is much more we
could do here."

The Prince looked through the hole in the cityscape where

the Smoke Jaguar command center had once stood. In front of it lay some buildings that had been half-crushed when the headquarters building sagged and spilled into the parade ground. "I agree, there likely is more you could do here. The fact is, though, I don't want it done. Human beings, as you are well aware, are capable of blocking their worst fears and memories. Even looking upon something like this will become mundane. I want things left as they were so that the people here, and the people who come here to our enclave, will always have reminders. Even if it is the inconvenience of having to drive out of their way to avoid a blocked street, or having to sit in a restaurant and look at ruins, I don't want them to be able to forget."

"After all we have done to them here, you think they will forget?" Masters' voice dripped with scornful disbelief. "Their way of life has been completely and radically altered. Before our coming here, the lower castes lived to serve and provide for the warriors. While they may have had many modern conveniences, they were in thrall to the warriors. Now they have their freedom from that prison. If we give them the chance they will rebuild their society to reflect this freedom."

"Perhaps." A flash of anger flickered over Victor's face. "Then again, they could find themselves free to repeat the mistake their forebears made."

Masters shook his head. "You don't know these people, Prince Victor."

Victor's head came up. "Perhaps not, but I *do* know people."

"What do you mean by that?"

"Let's assume your assessment is correct." Victor looked further down the street where some children played on the front steps of a brick rowhouse. "If those kids grow up and learn the lesson we've taught their parents, they will eschew war and we won't ever face them as a problem."

Masters nodded and stepped off the curb to cross the street.

"We are putting programs into place to educate all the youngsters here about the Inner Sphere, so they feel reconnected with the history their ancestors abandoned. They will end up thinking of themselves as being part of us. We're teaching them that the original Kerensky mission, the re-establishment of the Star League, has been accomplished and they're responsible for it."

"That's good, and I'm sure it's a plan that will bear fruit in the long run." Victor shrugged. "However, let's look at their parents, at the adults here. They've known one way of life only and we've radically changed that. Now, instead of doing work that, ultimately, maintains a military society, they're going to have to shift into a more open economy. Some won't adapt, some can't adapt. They will be the core of a reactionary element that will pine for the old days and old ways. I know this, I've seen it. That's the sentiment that allowed my sister Katherine to split the Lyran Alliance off from the Federated Commonwealth.

"If I'm right, and we've sanitized and removed the brutal traces of the war, they might trick themselves into thinking it was an aberration." Victor pointed off toward the north. "We have that whole repository of their warriors' genetic material there just waiting to be exploited."

"We can't destroy it."

"I know, and I agree, we can't destroy it without infuriating the rest of the Clans and giving them a new excuse to go to war with us. We'll leave it there and, for some of these people, it will be a holy grail through which their hurts can be soothed."

Paul Masters nodded at a woman in a window watching the two of them walk along the street. "I don't think your assessment of these people is correct, Prince Victor. While you have been helping our forces here rebuild and getting our casualties stabilized for transport home, I have been working closely with the ordinary people of Huntress. The scientist and merchant castes are very sophisticated and have adapted particularly well to the absence of the warriors."

"It's never the sophisticated folks who swell the ranks of a revolution, Sir Paul. An intellectual may lead them, but it's the desire of the common man for change that fuels things."

"If I might make an observation, Highness, it sounds as if you view your citizens as rivals for your power."

Victor laughed. "Hardly. They are my strength, but you know as well as I do that the grand political play that determines the course of the Inner Sphere really affects them very little. When a planet changes hands, very often the only difference the citizens notice is a shift in tax forms or a new face on currency. I love my people, which is why I'm willing to be here to make sure they will be safe from the Clan threat."

Masters' eyes half-closed. "But that's not the only reason you're here."

"No?" Victor stooped and picked up a ball some kids had been playing with. He arced it back to them with an easy throw. "Now it's my turn: what do you mean by that?"

"You're a warrior. You live to make war."

"Ouch." The Prince frowned. "I would have hoped the experience on Coventry would have convinced you otherwise."

"Your condoning of the tactics used by Task Force Serpent influenced my thinking."

"Ah, I see." Victor's blue-flecked gray eyes narrowed. "Sir Paul, the Knights of the Inner Sphere were formed around you. You and your warriors view warfare through a lens called chivalry. You try to do the most honorable things you can, grant quarter when asked, and keep warfare as far as possible from having an effect on non-warriors."

"Agreed."

"You want to keep warfare clean, but the truth of the matter is that warfare is anything but clean. It's nice to assume a foe who's been battered will see he's going to lose and surrender so you won't have to take his life." Victor shook his head. "It's a nice fantasy, but few, if any, humans in the chaos of warfare take the time to think about what is logical and proper. If any of them did, they wouldn't be involved in war in the first place."

Masters face closed. "Are you suggesting we are fools?"

"Not at all. What I am suggesting is that your position means that you look down on others who do not cling to so stringent a set of guidelines as you have imposed on yourselves." Victor opened his arms. "I'm as proud as can be that we've stopped the invasion. I'm not entirely proud of the things we had to do to stop it."

Paul Masters snorted a laugh. "This from the man who dismounted from his 'Mech and beheaded the ilKhan with a sword."

That stopped Victor cold. "You weren't there, you don't know what transpired."

"Come now, Prince Victor, your champions are legion. I've seen gun-camera holovid of the incident. Osis is there on his knees. You turn away from him. He rises and you wheel and strike his head off. Your swordsmanship was flawless." Masters stopped and turned to face Victor. "Do you deny that's what happened?"

"You've seen the holovid, how can I?" Victor shuddered. One of the *Jackal*s had caught his confrontation with Osis on holovid, but no sound came with it, and the range was too far even for a person accomplished in lip-reading to make out what was said. It was very easy for someone to view that evidence and characterize things exactly the way Masters had.

Victor lowered his voice and let it turn cold. "If you are disposed to think the worst of me, for whatever reason, then what I will tell you won't make a difference. Lincoln Osis realized there, on his knees, what a mistake the invasion was. He begged me to kill him because he didn't want to live life if he could no longer be a warrior. I refused. I said killing him would be murder. I turned away. He rose to attack me, again assuming the role of warrior so he would die a warrior. I don't regret defending myself, but I'm sorry he had to die."

Masters listened without reaction. "I imagine that story will play well in your memoirs of the Clan Invasion. It has a very storybook ring to it. If they make a holovid I am certain it will be a most illuminating scene."

Victor forced his hands to remain unclenched. "If I choose to write memoirs, you're likely correct. You seem to be saying that you think I did all this for self-aggrandizement."

"No, I think your motives were pure in the beginning, or as pure as you can attain." The taller man shrugged. "Still, you are a political animal, Prince Victor. You must see the advantage of returning home as the conqueror of the Clans."

Victor started walking again. "Of course I do. That doesn't mean I want to exploit it."

"Really? You're not going to use your new power and prestige to reunite your realm?"

The Prince sighed. "How? I can't do it without a war and, truth be told, I'm rather sick of war at the moment. What I really want right now is to go home, see my friends, and do nothing."

Masters shook his head. "That won't happen."

"No?"

"No. You have the matter of Morgan Hasek-Davion's death to deal with, remember?"

"His murder, you mean."

"Indeed, his murder." Masters shot Victor a sidelong glance. "On whom will you pin the blame?"

They turned a corner and descended some steps into a green valley two blocks long and one wide. Row upon row of simple white markers stood like soldiers on parade. The stark white against the background of green made Victor pause. The graveyard looked very peaceful, and its being sunk below street level somehow made it far more conducive to contemplation.

"Blame will fall upon the guilty." Victor shook his head. "I really haven't thought about it."

"But yours will be a long trip home."

"Indeed." Victor looked over at him. "Do I take it by the way you said that, that you have given my offer more thought?"

"Your offer?" Irritation washed over Masters' face. "How can I refuse the honor of being appointed Star League Enclave Governor and the first ambassador to the Clans?"

"I chose you, Sir Paul, because I think your warrior philosophy gives you insights into the Clans that will allow you to be very effective, especially now, during this difficult initial period."

"And it's not to prevent me from coming back to the Inner Sphere to tell my impressions of this whole business?"

Victor gave Masters a sharp look. "You're more than welcome to send any messages you want back with us."

"But no direct contact with the Inner Sphere until you relay a message here announcing your return?"

Victor sighed. "I believe, Sir Paul, it was you who suggested there might be pockets of Smoke Jaguar resistance on worlds between here and the Inner Sphere. It is because of that suggestion that our return will be conducted slowly and under radio silence. We'll check out the most likely planets and deal with any problems we encounter. And to clear up the sort of problem we had coming out, we're bringing extra DropShips and JumpShips so we can relay any survivors back here for repatriation on Huntress.

"I really am not a bloody-handed murderer, Sir Paul. You may not like things I'm doing or that I've done, but I've only done what seemed necessary."

"Forgive me, Prince Victor, but I think you worship death."

"Excuse me?"

"If you don't, why are you bringing a dead man back to the Inner Sphere with you?" Masters waved a hand toward the cemetery. "Morgan Hasek-Davion should rest here with his people."

Victor frowned. "As little as you liked Morgan, I would hardly think you would want him here in this place."

Masters made to reply, but Victor cut him off.

"Besides, Sir Paul, I'm taking him home so his family has a chance to grieve for him. You have interred your dead here, and many other groups have done the same."

"Including Morgan's First Kathil Uhlans."

"True, but Morgan was different."

"He was murdered, but without a body, proving it would be politically difficult, wouldn't it?"

Victor folded his arms over his chest. "Again you impart motives to me that I don't have. I loved my cousin and I love his family. I'm taking him home for a hero's burial. That in no way diminishes the sacrifices of all the others here, from General Winston on down to the lowest trooper who died.

"But, look, if you want to head back to the Inner Sphere and tell everyone how horrid this war was, you're more than welcome to leave with us tonight. If you don't want to oversee the work you started here, I'll find someone else to do it. You may not trust me, Sir Paul, but I trust you. I trust you to do everything you can to normalize our relations with the Clans, and to lay the foundation for continuing and amicable relations between us. I don't think I have anyone here who can do a better job than you can, which is why I'm asking you to do it."

Masters arched an eyebrow. "Not even yourself?"

Victor looked him straight in the eye. "Most assuredly not."

Masters blinked. "Really?"

"Really." Victor watched the other man's face closely. "I do know my own limitations. You may think I hold myself above humanity, that I consider myself a law unto myself, but it's just not true. I'm just like everyone else—a man who was given a job to do, and now it's time to move on. I have responsibilities elsewhere that demand I move on as quickly as I can, but I will make sure this job was done right. And that means I leave a responsible, thoughtful, and competent person in charge of this piece of Huntress. That's you."

Masters frowned. "Just when I think I've got you figured out, you do something to force a change."

"That's because I'm changing. This whole expedition has wrought changes in us all." Victor shrugged. "And just like you, I'm hoping these changes are for the better."

"I see." Masters slowly nodded. "Then, yes, I will remain here and govern Huntress for you. Do tell them to send an ambassador to replace me—diplomacy is an occupation with too little chivalry in it."

Victor smiled. "An ancient Terran pundit once defined diplomacy as the art of saying 'Good dog,' while you search for a big rock. I hope you find it to be a bit better than that."

"I'm certain I will." Masters smiled and offered Victor his hand. "Have a safe journey home and make sure whoever they send out here has a sweet voice and a supply of big rocks."

17

**State of the Art Gallery and Café, Crescent Harbor
New Exford
Arc-Royal Defense Cordon
15 August 3060**

Francesca Jenkins felt her heart skip a beat as she entered the gallery and caught sight of Reginald Starling. The tall, lean man had dyed his hair and eyebrows a bright, unnatural scarlet and had his fingernails elongated and painted a frightful incarnadine shade. As she drew closer, she saw the hint of fang-like dental implants lengthening his canines and saw blood-red contacts that hid his normally blue eyes. His black clothes, cut conservatively and severely, emphasized just how slender he was and definitely cast him as a creature of the night.

She'd heard he'd taken to this undead persona, and admired his ability to tap into the zeitgeist of the Lyran Alliance. The stunning victories the Star League Defense Force had won against the Jaguars in the Combine had surprised everyone and buoyed their spirits. What everyone had thought would be a long, difficult war had become a walkover that was greeted initially with great joy.

Then the SLDF moved into the Periphery to deal with Smoke Jaguar resistance, and reported progress came less quickly. This left people wondering if their earlier optimism wasn't born in haste. The Jade Falcons remained on the Lyran Alliance border and, even though no Falcons had crossed into the Arc-Royal Defense Cordon area, tomorrow could always herald an attack. People began to think the Clans were not as finished as the Star League liked to report, and they waited for the Clanners to rise from the grave and wreak havoc once more.

Starling looked up over the ice-blue coiffure of a diminutive patron and clapped his hands to his breastbone when he saw Francesca. His feral grin broadened, giving her a better look at his teeth. He immediately sidestepped the woman he had been speaking to and strode over to her. "Ah, Fiona, you are a vision."

"You are too kind, Reg." Francesca smiled carefully. She'd chosen to wear a red-sequined, sleeveless dress with hemline that fell almost to mid-thigh. It had a high collar that fastened tight to her throat, but a slender diamond cut-out that ran from the hollow of her throat to her navel, revealing the soft curves of her breasts and showing the bullet-wound scar right below her breastbone. That scar had always fascinated Starling, and she knew showing it off so boldly would excite him.

"I am so glad you came."

Francesca slipped her hand through his arm. "Are you, Reg? I was surprised to get an invitation to this opening. I'd ignored the others, assuming you wanted to gloat."

"Just as well you didn't come to the others, because I *would* have gloated." Starling led her deeper into the gallery, past the coffee bar, to a smaller room. "Your absence at first enraged me but, then, upon reflection, I found you inspiring."

"Did you? How so?"

Reg slipped his arm from hers and spread his hands wide. "Very inspiring, my dear. This work is all from you."

Francesca looked around the room and swallowed hard to force her heart back into its proper place. The paintings in the room varied in size, but all shared a style and color scheme. Starling had used a fairly primitive and impressionistic style to paint them, relying on a palette of mostly black and green, with red as an accent color. She recognized parts of her own body in many of the images, including the scar on her chest and the one over her hip. Her face, when it appeared at all, had been abstracted and rendered huge in comparison to other figures, as if she were some uber-deity constantly aware of what the other figures were doing.

The paintings had titles like *Honesty I, Trust IV,* and *No Secrets VIII*. She did some quick mental calculations and, assuming Starling wasn't lying about the series numbers, he'd done nearly two dozen in the three months since their breakup, which was a pace that, for him, exceeded all expectations.

She looked over at him, eyes wide. "I don't know what to say."

"You don't need to say anything, my dear." Starling glared at a patron about to enter the small room, but that person shied off quickly. "You have never heard me say this before, but I'm sorry and I thank you."

"Reg, are you well?"

The man threw his head back and laughed. "Do you remember when we first met?"

"At the spa? Yes. You took me to an opening like this that night."

"Yes. You said something to me at that first meeting—that your condition of friendship was having no secrets from your friends. You suggested that if I couldn't handle that, perhaps we shouldn't be friends. I thought I could, at the time, and we became involved."

She reached out and stroked the side of his face. "We became lovers."

"We did. I shared an intimacy with you I don't think I've ever shared with anyone else, and that frightened me. That's why I had that liaison with the model I was painting. When you found out, your reaction was partly what I expected and wanted."

"You wanted me to throw you out." Fiona let a little smile twist her lips. "And I did what you wanted."

"Yes, darling, but not for the reason I expected. I thought you would throw me out because I had been unfaithful to you. You told me that my infidelity was not the issue, but the fact that I had lied to you about it." Reg shook his head. "After you left me, I sat and thought for the longest time. I wanted you to come to those other openings so I could humiliate you, but then I realized I had made the mistake. You had operated openly and had set up simple conditions for our friendship. I had violated those rules and paid the consequences."

He sneered and pointed back out the doorway toward the gaily dressed patrons. "You are not like them, Fiona. They come here to own a piece of me, as if mere money could buy my spirit and command my loyalty. If I go out there and insult them, they lap it up. It's a mark of prestige that I would deign to insult them. If I refuse to sell them a piece because I say their home is not worthy of it, they will find an agent to buy it so they can say they've tricked me, not knowing that the agent will buy it at a hyperinflated price."

"What are you telling me, Reg?" Francesca looked around the room. "Are you going to sell pieces of me to these people?"

"Well, yes, of course." Reg smiled impishly, then walked over to a small painting showing a human heart rendered in green, surrounded by black, with tiny red cracks in it. "But this represents my heart, envious as it is of the peace you know. This painting, *No Secrets X*, is for you. It is a piece of me that knows no price, though I would hope to redeem our friendship through it."

Francesca peered more closely at the painting, then turned

back and stood on tiptoe to give him a kiss on the lips. "Consider it a down payment, shall we?"

Reg smiled. "A better bargain than I expected."

"Oh, you'll pay, Reg. You'll pay dearly." She smiled at him. "But I think it's time you make your patrons pay even more dearly."

"Indeed, my dear." Reg leaned down and kissed her. "Perhaps I will sell the pieces in this room for a fortune and a secret from each buyer. That should be fun."

"And you'll share the secrets with me?"

"With pleasure, Fiona Jensen, great pleasure indeed."

Francesca was introduced to Mr. Archie, the owner of the gallery—a man trying studiously to appear younger than he was and who fawned all over her—then presided over the ceremony of having *No Secrets X*'s display tag altered to read "From the Private Collection of Fiona Jensen." After that the gallery owner insisted on naming some absurd coffee drink after her, which was an honor she bore only because it actually didn't taste that bad despite being only twenty percent coffee when all was said and done. She listened to Starling give a brief lecture about the "Full Disclosure" series of paintings in that room, linking its production to a demand that the government tell everyone what was really going on with the Clan war. In less than five minutes Starling turned owning a piece of his work from an investment into political protest, which spiked the prices and encouraged brisk sales.

She begged off on joining Reg and Mr. Archie for a late dinner, but promised she would stop by another time to discuss the possibility of signing prints of the "Full Disclosure" series works along with Reg. She knew that offer was an attempt on Reg's part to give her money and to bind her more closely to him.

This was fine with her. Her mission all along had been to get as close as she could to him and learn all his secrets. Knowing as many of them as she already did—and had known before she met him—she had a simple gauge by which to measure her progress. So far, that progress had not been great.

Reginald Starling was really Sven Newmark, former aide to Ryan Steiner. Ryan Steiner and Katherine Steiner, current ruler of the Lyran Alliance, had conspired together to assassinate Melissa Steiner-Davion, Katherine's mother and the previous ruler of the Federated Commonwealth. Katherine had engineered things so it appeared as if her brother Victor had killed Melissa, then had used the resulting civil unrest to split the Federated Commonwealth in half.

Sven Newmark had dropped out of sight shortly after Ryan's assassination. Various and sundry pundits had pointed to the fact that Newmark had been alone with Ryan at the time of his death. Because the older man had died of a through and through gunshot wound to the head, self-appointed experts suggested that Newmark had, in fact, been the assassin, not some sniper shooting from a half a kilometer away, as official reports suggested. Newmark's disappearance made a lot of sense, given how well-loved Ryan had been in some quarters, and only through a lot of hard work had Francesca been able to track him down to New Exford.

Newmark was, as nearly as she knew, the only man who could link Katherine with the plot to murder Melissa Steiner-Davion. Not even the assassin who had done the job—who, as far as Francesca knew, had never been apprehended—might know of the connection between mother and daughter in this case. If Newmark could implicate Katherine in her mother's death, she would become known as the woman who murdered her own mother as well as one of the Inner Sphere's most beloved figures. And if the news ever got out, Katherine's days in power would surely be over.

Francesca returned to her apartment, checking for telltale signs of covert entry. She pulled a keyring from her clutch and used the flashlight attached to it to provide enough illumination for her to select the proper key. Then, as she prepared to insert the key in the lock, she hit a second button on the flashlight, which played out an ultraviolet beam that swept over the floor in front of her door.

A single set of footprints made by the high-heeled shoes she wore glowed purple for a second, then returned to invisibility when she shut off the light. The carpet just inside her door had been liberally dusted with a powder that clung to the soles of shoes and phosphoresced under the ultraviolet light. Anyone who had gone in and come out of the apartment would have left footprints, or would have swept them away, obscuring her prints as well.

She opened the door and stepped inside, locking the door behind her. Flicking on a light, she took a quick visual inventory of the room, noticing if the pile of diskzines was still correctly aligned with the edge of the coffee table, or if the chair at the end of her dining table had been re-seated in the divots in the carpet, or if the legs were still offset by two centimeters, the way she'd left them when going out.

Everything seemed in order, so she went to her bedroom, kicked off her shoes and slipped out of the dress. She hung it up, then pulled on a warm, terry cloth robe and sat down at her computer. She flicked it on, did a hardware reset, then interrupted the normal init process. She called up a program named Scramble, which, if loaded after a normal init process, would fill the screen with a children's puzzle game.

In its present form it allowed her to encrypt and decrypt messages. She typed in a brief message. "Contact made. Target is receptive. Mission hot again." She glanced over it once, quickly, then set the program to encrypting it.

The encryption scheme functioned in two ways. The first thing it did was to pull out of memory the contents of a book and locate each of the message's words in that book. Those words then became reduced to a three-number code indicating page, paragraph, and word number. Contact, for example, was found on page seventy-seven, the second paragraph, fifth word, making it 77-2-5 in the encrypted message.

The second half of the encryption worked similarly, but had been designed to work with Francesca's cover occupation. She had told Newmark she was a researcher who compiled bibliographies for scholars doing research. The Scramble program sorted through the indices of countless volumes, looking for similar subject cites, which could be expressed in terms of edition, volume, and page number. Each coded word of the message, then, would be rendered into a book cite and even if the lot of them were pulled and read, they would make a certain amount of sense. The indices searched were highly technical, so even if codebreakers looked up the cites, they wouldn't have a clue as to what they meant.

The cites were then packaged up into a simple email that went to any of a dozen cover identities Francesca's control agent, Curaitis, used to recover data. The cover identity was chosen to be consistent with the nature of the data used to create the cites. Similarly, messages back to Francesca would contain cites, travel ticket prices, or other data that could be expressed in numbers, and the program would pull them apart and present her with the message. All messages were kept short to minimize the ability of others to decode them, and the books from which the words were chosen were changed on a regular schedule.

Francesca sent the message, then sat back and smiled. When she had first come to New Exford it hadn't been difficult to befriend and seduce Newmark, but getting deep enough into him to win his trust had been much harder. Just when she thought she'd made some headway, he betrayed her. She had been tempted then to take him back, but decided at the last moment that rejecting him would work better. Since everyone loved him on the surface and despised him behind his back—and he knew it—having someone who cared for him at heart seem to hate him on the surface was different, and Reginald Starling lived for different.

As a covert operative for the Federated Commonwealth's Intelligence Secretariat, Francesca Jenkins knew her mission was vital and that speed was of the essence. The initial stage of the operation had been to let Katherine know that her brother knew of her complicity in Melissa's death. It was a move meant to unsettle Katherine and had been effective, but it also meant Katherine would want to tie up any loose ends that might implicate her directly. Sven Newmark was such a loose end and, even though Francesca had used computer viruses to destroy the information that led her to Reginald Starling, she knew that her Lyran intelligence counterparts wouldn't be far behind her.

She stretched, shut off the computer, lay her robe across the foot of her bed, then crawled under the covers. "Doesn't matter how close they are now, though. I'm closer and soon, very soon, I'll have the information I came for."

18

DropShip Josephine, *Nadir Recharge Station*
Skye, Isle of Skye
Lyran Alliance
30 September 3060

Archon Katrina Steiner studied a holographic projection of
the Inner Sphere and allowed herself a moment to luxuriate in
anticipation of controlling it all. There were, she admitted to
herself, a few obstacles to her taking power everywhere, but
obstacles were meant to be overcome. *And overcome I shall.*

The first barrier between her and success was her brother
Victor. Though no one in the Inner Sphere had yet learned of
the success of his strike at the Clan homeworlds, Katrina already knew all that had transpired during her brother's year-
long absence from the Inner Sphere. *Little automaton that he
is, he went, he saw, and he conquered. Damn that Lincoln
Osis to a dozen hells for not having twisted off Victor's head
when he had the chance.*

Her information came from the Wolves, relayed by a net-
work of spies that, to my delight, wormed its way through the

Arc-Royal Defense Cordon. She knew the Kells would be furious if they knew Wolf spies lurked among their people, and she meant to scourge them with that fact once she had crushed their pitifully small realm. The Kells had long played on their relationship to the Steiner household, but it was a relation by marriage only and Katrina was determined that they would be eliminated, too.

She got up from behind her desk and ran her fingers back through her long, golden blonde hair. It rippled like a silky curtain from her fingers and fell softly against her white sweater. A white woolen skirt and white leather boots completed the outfit, which had been cut along vaguely military lines. The skirt was not wholly practical for times when the lack of acceleration left the ship weightless, but whenever she planned to be seen during those times, she dressed more appropriately.

She circled around her desk, studying the cloud of light pinpoints that made up the map of the Inner Sphere. Having been warned that her brother was returning triumphant, she continued with the plan she'd initiated almost immediately upon his departure for the Periphery. The results, so far, had been staggeringly successful. So much so that when and if Victor returned, the surprise she'd have waiting for him would be rather rude indeed, from his point of view.

And most delightful from mine. Katrina smiled coldly and focused on the other realms of the Inner Sphere. The large red area on the map sandwiched between Victor's Federated Commonwealth and the Clan conquests was the Draconis Combine. Once her people's greatest rival, it seemed no more than a minor consideration at the current point in time. The previous year's war effort had indeed liberated most of the worlds the Clans had taken from the Combine, but the process of reintegrating them into the Kurita regime was not going to be easy. People who had formed resistance cells to throw off the Clans were having trouble with the re-establishment of civilian authorities not drawn from their own ranks. And the

Combine's repressive politics now curtailed some freedoms the people had won in their struggle against the Clans.

Below her realm, all outlined in shades of dark purple, lay the Free Worlds League. That state had always been something of a weakling, primarily because internecine fighting among members of the Marik family had repeatedly split the realm. That fighting had taken its toll and, luckily for the League, had killed off a fair number of claimants to the throne. Thomas Marik, the current ruler, had survived an assassination attempt, and his new wife, Sherryl Halas, had borne him a son, Janos, four months ago. This solidified his succession, but left his legitimized daughter Isis not nearly as powerful a player as before. *Not that she ever was more than a prize to hold Sun-Tzu Liao at bay.*

The Free Worlds League's newfound solidarity presented Katrina with a bit of a problem because it was a strong realm that had not been ravaged by the Clans. Prior to Thomas' marriage to the Halas woman, he had been eyeing a liaison with Katrina herself. It certainly would have been to his benefit and even to hers, as the League's military could have bolstered her own in case of a renewed Clan offensive. The Inner Sphere's decision to go after the Clans lessened the urgency for such a union, and the opportunity slipped past.

As a result, Thomas had to be thinking about what it would cost to take by force what he would have hoped to gain by marrying Katrina. *His troops have made no moves toward my border, but I think he is being cautious while Victor is still away. Thomas believes enough in the sanctity of the Star League that he would do nothing to shatter it.*

Not so Sun-Tzu Liao, current First Lord of the Star League and Chancellor of the Capellan Confederation. His election had come at her brother's instigation. Katrina had nominated him for the post, expecting that her brother's vehement objection to Sun-Tzu would be sufficiently irrational that no one would turn around and vote in Victor's favor on a subsequent ballot. That would leave her the only logical compromise candidate, and she would have reluctantly agreed to serve in that post. Instead of taking the bait the way, Victor had backed Sun-Tzu. *It is his fault that the Capellan weasel is in power.*

Sun-Tzu Liao had made good use of his power. He had stepped up operations in the Disputed Territories as well as in the area popularly known as the Chaos March. His progress in the Chaos March had been stopped cold, but he'd been extremely successful in reclaiming worlds in the Disputed Territories. Neither Katrina nor Thomas had objected because Sun-Tzu's adventurism gave him something to do. His determination to win back previously lost Capellan worlds continued to tie up his resources, for which Katrina was thankful.

Her first move would be against her brother. Once she'd eliminated Victor, rolling over Sun-Tzu would be simple. She wasn't certain if she would conquer his realm, or simply offer to marry him and absorb it. *War would be so costly, but so, too, would be my wedding.*

After dealing with Sun-Tzu, Thomas Marik would find himself trapped. The problem with the League was that external threats did bind it together, so she couldn't look at direct military conquest there. *No, with Thomas what I would offer him is a union of realms, much as my father accomplished in the alliance with grandmother. I could promise my first-born daughter to his son, Janos, to further seal the bargain. That might well work.*

The holovid projection plate on her desk buzzed. She returned to her chair and hit a button. The starfield vanished in favor of a static head-and-shoulders shot of a man in uniform. Below his image was a legend that identified him, noted when the message had been sent, what stations it had been relayed through, when it had been received by the ship's code room, and when it had been decrypted and passed on to her. She glanced at all that information casually, then sat back and used a remote control to start the message playing.

"Highness, I have word of Operation Fray. We have a

line on the target. It came out of a normal survey of anti-government activity. The man believed to be the target was noted to have made very anti-government remarks at an art show opening. He was calling for complete disclosure of facts concerning the Clan war and other matters, including your mother's murder. We have located a catalog for the show and are now in the process of analyzing the works to determine their subversive content. I have authorized surveillance and covert entry if further study of the actual works is indicated. Colonel Lentard, out."

As the Message End light started blinking in the upper right corner, Katrina froze the image and slowly shook her head. Operation Fray had only one purpose—killing Sven Newmark. Newmark was the only person who could possibly link her to her mother's assassination. The other individual who had been in Ryan's employ and had helped set up Melissa's death had died in a freak accident on Poulsbo in April. She had even sent a handwritten note of condolence to the man's widow.

Using the remote she started recording a reply to the intelligence operative. "Colonel Lentard, I appreciate your caution in this matter of Operation Fray, and all efforts should be made to ascertain whether your individual is our target. Bear in mind, however, that he is not a threat for subversive activities, but a criminal who is in possession of material of a highly sensitive nature. Consider him a plague-carrier, if you will. The longer he survives, the more damage he can do. If you are certain of your identification of him, eliminate him. Immediately. Archon Katrina Steiner, out."

She hit another button on the remote to route the message back to Lentard, then tossed the remote onto her desk with a clatter. She supposed it made sense that Lentard wanted to be careful where civil liberties were at stake, and Katrina appreciated his caution. That was the difference between Lentard, say, and the assassin who killed her mother. The assassin had fashioned a bomb that killed Melissa, but had slain other people as well, including Morgan Kell's wife, Salome. It had also maimed Morgan Kell and made him into Katrina's mortal enemy. *If only he had used a bit more explosive, I'd now be rid of the Kells.*

Katrina sighed, knowing that wasn't entirely true. Caitlin Kell she'd always liked and considered a friend. *Naive, but a friend.* Caitlin had been poisoned against her by Morgan, and Morgan's own shift of attitude had come about through Victor's influence. And though Morgan's death in the bomb blast that had killed her mother might have eliminated one problem, Morgan had also served to hold in check Phelan Kell, newly returned from the Clans and bringing a huge chunk of Clan Wolf with him.

She stroked her throat and could still feel Phelan's grip on it a year later. Katrina had, she admitted to herself, overstepped her bounds by threatening Morgan Kell when last they had met. Phelan had been there too and had made it very clear to her that if either he or his father died, he had a world teeming with Wolves who would delight in destroying her. Luckily for her, the Kell Hounds and Phelan's Wolves had traveled to the Draconis Combine to fight the Smoke Jaguars, which had kept them out of her hair. It had also kept them from guessing what she was up to.

The Kells presented an interesting problem for her. Their Arc-Royal Defense Cordon was, in essence, an autonomous region within her Lyran Alliance. While the Hounds and Wolves were off fighting the Jaguars, the Kells had hired mercenary units like the Legion of the Rising Sun, Group W, and the Wild Bunch to keep the Jade Falcons on their side of the border. Those mercenaries were certainly not strong enough to threaten her realm, but they were tough enough that she couldn't see wasting troops on trying to conquer the ARDC.

Doing just that had initially been one of her plans, but she had reconsidered in light of the amazing successes on the Combine border. Phelan's Wolves had absorbed enough

Smoke Jaguar forces to actually make them stronger than before, so not providing them with an excuse to return home to oppose her was a good thing. She also knew Morgan would never act against her unless the move was in concert with something Victor was doing, so anything she did to forestall action by her brother also insulated her against the Kells.

Which brought her back around to Operation Fray. Her only real vulnerability was possible implication in her mother's death. Revelation of such facts could easily sway public opinion against her and set the stage for a popular revolt that would sweep her from power. *Given how much the people loved my mother, I'd be torn limb from limb. I cannot and will not let that happen.*

She fingered a slender gold bracelet on her right wrist and smiled. *My secret weapon.* As much as Morgan and Victor hated the idea that she had slain her mother, they would be even more horrified to learn that she'd secretly traveled to Clan space and allied herself with Vlad Ward of the Wolves. Katrina and Vlad's mutual hatred of Phelan Kell had solidified the bond between them—a bond born of a strong physical attraction.

With Vlad poised to strike into the Lyran Alliance—he had been fairly certain crossing the Jade Falcon Occupation Zone would present no problem for his troops—any move by the Kells to unseat her would be rewarded by the destruction of the ARDC. That would involve them in fighting against their old foes, weakening them at a time when Katrina would be rallying loyal soldiers to oppose their treasonous attack on her. Mere saber-rattling by the Wolves or Jade Falcons could forestall Kell action and provide her plenty of time to destroy them.

Katrina smiled. "So, Colonel Lentard, you deal with Sven Newmark and eliminate that problem for me, and I shall deal with Victor. When he gets home, he'll have a nasty surprise waiting for him, but will have no surprises for me. And that is just the way I want it." She clapped her hands once. "Oh, dear brother, you have won much for the Inner Sphere, just to lose everything for yourself. One must truly pity the hero who lives long enough to see his victory tarnish."

19

DropShip Barbarossa
Landing Zone Alpha Tango III, Unnamed Planetoid
Deep Space
1 November 3060

Victor Davion looked at the image of Kai Allard-Liao on the holovid screen in his office. "Roger that, Kai. None of the other teams have reported contacts either. It looks as if there are no Jags hidden here."

"Probably true, Victor, but I want to take my lance into a valley about a klick and a half north of here. The iron content in the rocks is giving me weird readings. Probably nothing, but worth checking."

"Agreed. Be careful and report directly to me if you find anything."

Kai's smile, though largely hidden by his neurohelmet, showed in his eyes. "Wilco, Victor. Kai Allard-Liao out."

The image faded, and Victor glanced over at the trio of individuals in his office. "Looks like another possible haven isn't working out."

Tiaret turned from the DropShip's external viewpoint. "I do not think any of my old brethren would choose this place as a hideaway."

The planetoid she'd been looking at was hardly hospitable. Cold and barren, the only indication that it might have been a place where fleeing Smoke Jaguars would take refuge was the thin atmosphere whose winds stirred up the dust. The survey teams had found some signs of ancient mining efforts, likely started by Kerensky's people when they first fled the Inner Sphere. The holes they did inspect yielded no signs of recent life and Victor suspected Kai's valley would prove to be empty, too.

Andrew Redburn nodded slowly in agreement. "This is the kind of rock one has to be sentenced to."

The Precentor Martial adjusted his eyepatch. "It might look wonderful to someone fleeing for his life, but the Clans have never struck me as the fleeing type."

"No, and our intel analysis of their records and battle reports seems to indicate we've accounted for pretty much all of the Smoke Jaguar warriors. The discrepancies are minor. I think our mission is accomplished." Victor sighed. "But, as much as I'd like to be home *today,* we'll keep searching likely sites."

"Leaving no asteroid unturned, as it were?" Redburn smiled. "I wish we'd been able to do that with the investigation of Morgan's murder."

Victor tapped a data disk on his desktop. "I've read the preliminary report that was put together, and your annotations to it, Andrew. I think you did as thorough a job as possible, given the resources you had. We're not much better off here—I didn't bring a full criminal forensics team with us—but I want to go over the details because there's something in the conclusion you've reached that's bothering me. I also think we need to figure out a story to give the rest of the task force so that by the time we get to the Inner Sphere this thing doesn't explode like a bomb."

Redburn frowned, his brown eyes growing hard. "The conclusion is fairly cut and dried, Highness. Your dear sister Katherine had Morgan assassinated."

A cold chill ran through Victor. He knew his sister had been behind the murder of their mother, so it was not a difficult stretch to imagine her plotting Morgan's death. Part of him very much wanted to believe she'd done just that, but some details just didn't jibe in his mind.

"Believe me, Andrew, I'd love to take your conclusion as gospel, but I don't have a smoking gun or, in this case, a vial of fugu poison that got slipped into Morgan's scotch nightcap." Victor hesitated. *I gave that case of Glengarry Black Label, Special Reserve, to Morgan for Christmas, so he could take it with him. I wonder if the assassin knew that? I wonder if my sister knew that and demanded it be used against him?* "Whoever was behind this took great care to leave no traces back to him or her."

Victor sat back in his chair. "Andrew, please correct me where I'm wrong, but this is my take on the report. Morgan was in the habit of having a drink of scotch before bed in the evening. On this particular night he takes a drink from a bottle that's been laced with a type of pufferfish toxin—highly deadly and, because of cultural biases, indicative of a Combine hit. It was determined that a highly special piece of lock-breaking equipment had been used to capture the keycode to Morgan's door, admitting the assassin."

Redburn raised a hand. "Actually, I was talking to a tech who had to crack some locks on Huntress. I commented that the sort of device he used was probably what got the assassin into Morgan's room. He disagreed. He says spook types always assume folks have the latest in high-tech equipment, but with the time and access the assassin had crewing on the ship, what he probably did was just open the lock and clip onto it a small combination stealer. As the electrical impulses from someone punching the combination in to the keypad traveled to the lock mechanism, the little clipped device, which isn't much more than a chip, a battery, and some wires, just pulled them in and recorded them. The assassin returned, pulls the chip out and plugs it into a reader and he has the combination. With the right adapter, he could have used any number of trideo players other crew members had to view the combination."

"I'm glad you pointed that out, Andrew." Victor smiled. "I was thinking it also would have been possible for the assassin to do some computer code-morphing and not pull out Morgan's combination, but just insert another one that would allow him access when he wanted it. No one checked that, according to the report."

The Precentor Martial frowned. "I'll put people on it just to double-check. And, I must say, I'm rather pleased you have a job, Highness, because I'm not liking the ease with which you're finding holes in security."

Victor smiled. "Spend your life trying to duck your security people and you learn a few tricks."

Tiaret interlaced her fingers, then twisted her palms outward and stretched, cracking her knuckles. "You will not find me so easy to shuck, Prince Victor."

"No, I don't suppose I will." The Prince sighed. "The assassin introduced the poison into the scotch, then Morgan drank it, lay down, and died. A subsequent search of the ship produced no poison or special devices for stealing the combination to the cabin. A check of personnel records did, however, turn up a number of people who had no real past history before their recruitment by and admission into ComStar. One of them was a man named Lucas Penrose. When they tried to take him for questioning, he killed his guards and almost killed General Winston before she shot him out herself."

Focht leaned forward in his chair. "In reading over General Winston's statement about Penrose's rantings, he seemed to indicate that upon his return to the Inner Sphere he could escape prosecution for the murder because one of the Great Houses was behind it."

Redburn hammered a fist against the arm of his chair. "The Lyran Alliance. All the evidence points in that direction, including the message Ariana got."

"Yes, the message." Victor sat back in his chair. "General Winston gets a call from a nekekami named Talisen . . ."

Tiaret frowned. "Nekekami?"

"Japanese for 'spirit cats,' " Redburn told her. "They comprise an elite and highly secret corps of assassins. Apparently Theodore Kurita sent them along and told Morgan about them. General Winston only found out about them when she opened Morgan's safe and read its contents after his death. I found out about them the same way when I took over for her."

"Right, even I didn't know about them until you mentioned them on Huntress." Victor hesitated. "I wonder if Theodore sent any with us, too? I'll have to ask Hohiro about that, I suppose. In any event, this Talisen told Winston that Penrose was a Loki agent who'd engaged in wetwork for both the Federated Commonwealth and the Lyran Alliance. Talisen ID'd the guy because he knew of him back in the Inner Sphere. He also asked for the release from custody of another suspect who, it would seem, was a member of his team—that conclusion being drawn from the fact that he'd have no other reason to want her freed."

Focht glanced at the Prince. "You don't seem to put much weight on this Talisen's statement. Do you think he was lying?"

Victor shifted his shoulders uneasily. "Not entirely, but I think the truth was hedged. First off, the identification was made well *after* Penrose's death, and Talisen likely had a good idea that the task force did not have the resources to verify his identification of the man. Talisen said Penrose had worked alone, which would have been enough to call off further investigation, and the current investigation had already snared one of his people. Moreover, identifying Penrose as a Loki agent saddles Katherine with the murder, taking the pressure off the Combine's troops. Talisen traded on the trust

Morgan and Winston had in him and his mission to free his own team member and to put the end to an investigation that might have torn the task force apart.

"What I think is this: Penrose likely is or was a Loki operative on some level or another. I do think he worked alone. The question is, for whom."

The Elemental folded her arms across her chest. "You said he worked for Loki. This answers your question, *quiaff*?"

"Not exactly." Victor pressed his hands together, fingertip to fingertip. "Look, I'm willing to grant that Katherine could well have wanted Morgan Hasek-Davion dead, if for no other reason than Morgan supported me and brought with him the whole of the Capellan March of the Federated Commonwealth. Without him I'm . . ."

Victor's voice failed him as a lump rose in his throat. He closed his eyes, remembering all the times he and Morgan had spent together. *Morgan was mentor and friend, big brother and ardent loyalist. He forced me to face decisions I didn't want to have to make, and he forced me to work hard. If not for him I'd not have formed the Revenants and Hohiro would have died on Teniente. But for Morgan I'd not have agreed that the task force should go to Huntress. I may have led the people who defeated the Clans, but Morgan put everything in position to make that victory possible.*

"Dammit, I will miss him." Victor's nostrils flared for a second, then he pressed his hands flat to his desktop. "Killing Morgan would further isolate me, and Katherine is fully capable of manipulating public opinion to make it appear as if I had Morgan killed to keep from having to share the limelight of victory with anyone. In fact, I expect that."

Focht nodded. "She is a venomous snake, your sister."

"Agreed," snarled Redburn, "and all the more reason to bring her to justice for killing Morgan."

"Venomous my sister may be, but she's not stupid."

Tiaret nodded slowly. "Ah, I see the problem. Very subtle."

Redburn sat back and frowned. "What are you talking about?"

"It is simple, General Andrew. The timing of the murder is all wrong." Tiaret posted her fists on her hips. "You all say this Katherine has ample motive to want Morgan dead, but she also had motive to want him alive. He was leading the task force that would strike a blow directly at the Jaguar's heart. His value as Prince Victor's rival increases after he succeeds. If he is successful, it also pulls pressure from her realm. If she meant to have Morgan dead, she would have slain him *after* the strike on Huntress, not before. Killing him before put the success of that strike in jeopardy. No slight intended, General."

"None taken. General Winston did all the hard work. I was just there at the end." Andrew Redburn smoothed his beard with his right hand. "I had an answer so I didn't look to motive. But, then, I have to ask who would want Morgan dead before the strike against Huntress?"

The Prince drew in a deep breath and exhaled noisily. "That's what I've been trying to figure. Look at the act on two levels. First, it takes Morgan out and causes friction between portions of our force. That's clearly designed to lessen our effectiveness as a fighting force and put the success of the strike in jeopardy. Who benefits from that but the Clans, or someone who benefits from the Clans still posing a threat to us. On the second level, the use of a Loki agent means suspicion falls on my sister very clearly. This increases tensions between my realm and hers, which others can exploit."

The Precentor Martial rubbed at his forehead with a hand. "Even Sun-Tzu Liao couldn't be this mad. Besides, I can't believe the Maskirovka could have successfully planted a sleeper agent in Loki, who then slipped into ComStar's service. Not possible."

"I agree. Sun-Tzu would benefit to a certain extent, but being First Lord of the Star League during the time the Clans are defeated is a much bigger benefit to him." Victor shook his head. "I know I didn't do it, I'm sure Theodore Kurita didn't, and Thomas Marik's motives are weak. While Marik's benefiting from selling 'Mechs and munitions to everyone in the Inner Sphere, his philosophical bent is one that abhors war. He wants an end to the Clans as much as any of us. I'd rule him out."

Redburn frowned. "That doesn't leave much. None of the Periphery states would have anything to gain and, like the Capellan Confederation, they couldn't plant someone that deeply."

Focht shook his head. "In Loki, maybe. In ComStar, never."

Victor looked over at him. "That was the sticking point for me, too. And, truth be told, I don't think Loki could insert anyone into ComStar. I know my father tried on numerous occasions, but it never worked. Even with the schism after Tukayyid I don't think a Loki effort would have gone unnoticed. In fact, I think there is only one entity in the Inner Sphere who could have accomplished the insertion."

Focht's face drained of color. "Word of Blake."

"Agreed."

The Word of Blake faction of ComStar had split off when the Precentor Martial and current Primus, Sharilar Mori, had secularized the organization. The Blakists clung to the superstitions that had long driven ComStar. Victor suspected that Word of Blake had plenty of sleeper agents in ComStar, and that not a few of ComStar's own security personnel had slipped into Word of Blake to keep tabs on it. Despite ComStar's efforts to keep track of its splinter group, the Blakists had recently succeeded in covertly attacking and taking Terra away from ComStar.

The Elemental scratched at the back of her neck. "This Word of Blake, why would it benefit from a continuation of the war?"

Focht shrugged wearily. "The Blakists have ties to the Free Worlds League and might be benefiting from the war economy, but that would make them far more cold-blooded than I would have thought possible. They also still believe that war will destroy civilization, and that Jerome Blake's vision for humanity reborn through the Word of Blake is a matter of destiny. By prolonging the war and sowing discord among enemies, they bring the collapse of civilization closer. As with most misguided cults, when the apocalypse they predict fails to come true, they take actions that are far more dangerous than anyone could imagine."

Victor looked over at Andrew Redburn. "You can see now, Andrew, why I can't blame my sister for Morgan's death, even though I would love to. Since we have no smoking gun to implicate her, there is no purpose served by even letting a rumor of her involvement slip out. And, *if* the Blakists are behind this, shutting down the discord within our returning forces will frustrate them."

"I can see that, Highness, and I agree." Worry furrowed Redburn's brow. "But what are we going to say about Penrose? Everyone knows he did it. Now we're just waiting for the why."

Victor allowed himself a careful smile. "Back in the war of 3039, the First Kathil Uhlans did some fighting on Quentin, then were pulled off and the Combine took the world. Turns out Penrose was from Quentin—or will be once his files are morphed—and lost his mother, father, and the rest of his family there. He blamed Morgan Hasek-Davion for the death of his family and planned revenge. He moved to the Lyran half of the Commonwealth and, being an orphan, Loki welcomed him in. He hoped to get close to Morgan soon thereafter, but the Clan invasion kind of killed those plans. He'd given up hope, left the service, joined ComStar and, as his luck would have it, got assigned to the task force. There his training came in handy and he got his revenge."

The Elemental smiled. "I have never before heard a lie more smoothly constructed."

Focht laughed. "It also explains why he wanted to implicate the Combine in the murder, since it was their conquest that killed his family. It will work and our files will be adjusted to show his personality profile did show him to be a borderline paranoid, but who isn't these days, with the Clans and all?"

The Prince glanced over at Focht. "That could hold ComStar up to some heat for Morgan's death."

"It is a storm we will weather."

Victor looked to Redburn and Tiaret. "Any objections to that story?"

Tiaret shook her head, but Redburn hesitated. "You're not going to be forgetting to get to the bottom of the mystery just because you've got a cover story, are you?"

Victor swallowed hard against the lump that materialized again in his throat. "You have my word, Andrew, that Morgan's death will not go unavenged. When we find out who did it and get him, if you want to pull the trigger, you've got the job."

"A gun, highness?" Redburn smiled. "I'd be preferring to use a knife. A dull one, so it would go slow."

"I'll remember that." Victor smiled. "I'll make a statement to the task force so we can put the difficulties to rest and hopefully have this story fully circulated by the time we get home. I think news of our success should be the most important thing we bring back, and I don't want anything to tarnish it."

20

Crescent Harbor, New Exford
Arc-Royal Defense Cordon
27 November 3060

Francesca Jenkins had wanted to laugh at Reg Starling's paranoia, but his paranoia saved her life. After the show had closed, successfully selling all but two of Starling's older pieces and *No Secrets X,* the time had come for her to take possession of his gift to her. Though Reg had been to her apartment before, and had spent more than a few nights there, he looked it over with new eyes when he realized it would house a piece of his work. He insisted she get an alarm system put in and split the cost of doing so with her, taking her half of the cost out of the money earned on the print sales.

What had struck her as funny was that she knew more about security devices than the eclectic crew Reg had found to wire her apartment. They put small maglocks on the windows, but she knew those could be defeated by the use of a simple electromagnet that kept the circuit closed while the windows were opened. The new lock they put on her front door required a special key with a microchip in it, but those locks fell prey to relatively sophisticated but available random code-generator keys or, in a pinch, a five-kilogram sledgehammer. They wired everything into her phone line, but the snip of two wires down in the basement's junction box would eliminate any alarm calls to the local constabulary.

It turned out to be the oddest device Reg had bankrolled that saved her. Because he was concerned about the theft of *No Secrets X,* Reg had ordered the installation of an alarm trigger the workmen called "the devil's fork." The hook that would hold the painting had two tines, well separated and implanted in the wall through a plastic insulating plug. To the back of that plug was attached a set of wires that led to the alarm system. The actual picture wire completed a circuit, so while the picture hung in place, no alarm went off. If the picture was moved, the alarm would ring at the local constabulary.

This was insufficient for Reg, however. He had attached to the wire an auxiliary unit that made a low-frequency radio broadcast within the immediate area that would trigger a vibrating sensor in a beautiful gold and platinum watch he gave Francesca. He insisted she wear it at all times, so that if thieves broke in while she was sleeping, the theft of the picture would wake her and allow her to get a good look at the thieves so they could be apprehended later.

Francesca figured she'd just grab a gun and shoot the robbers, but she never mentioned this to Reg, as he thought she abhorred guns and violence. That certainly was in keeping with her cover story. She often wondered what his reaction would be if he discovered who she really was, but deep down she knew without a doubt. *My being an agent of the Intelligence Secretariat would just confirm all of his paranoia.*

His reaction would be violent and perhaps even self-destructive, which is why she never gave any hints as to her true purpose on New Exford. She'd crawled inside Reg's world, eschewing news of the Inner Sphere in favor of the microcosm that was New Exford society. She found it just as treacherous as the Inner Sphere, but a bit more comic, especially with Reg and his antics stirring things up. She found Reg to be Chaos incarnate and even admired his ability to manipulate those who sought to control him.

Though part of her remained hidden behind the Fiona Jensen identity, she did come to like Reg Starling. Francesca found it amusing that she could like the identity Newmark had assumed, while he clearly liked the identity *she* had assumed, but that their true identities would be mortal enemies. Still, it seemed to her that Sven Newmark had almost completely been submerged in Reg Starling and that Reg believed Newmark was just another fictional background he'd made up for himself.

The sun had all but set, painting the skies a bright blue, while layering pink into the clouds. She looked up as she walked from where she'd parked her hovercar toward her apartment house. She found the sky beautiful, but she knew Reg would have decried such a clichéd use of color.

"Nature is, after all, the justification truly mediocre talents use for not pushing themselves. They seek to capture reality, while I seek to create it," he had explained to her. She accused him of having delusions of godhood. Reg replied, "As a creator, God is overrated. He worked six days and has done little since. Crediting him with all this would be like crediting the man who mixes my paints with my genius."

She shook her head and smiled, then felt her watch begin to vibrate. The smile froze on her face, but she continued across the street and into her building's foyer. She punched in the security code to let herself in, then paused to let the door close behind her. She saw nothing behind the little decorative grating in her phys-mail box, so she mounted the stairs. She could have taken the lobby lift up to the third floor, but it was far too easy for someone to wire something into the controls that would slow or stop the lift from accessing that floor.

Her right hand went into her purse and pulled out her keys, which she transferred to her left hand. Her hand dipped into the leather bag again and came out with a slender little black needler—a pistol that fired plastic flechettes instead of bullets. It wouldn't be much use in shooting through a door or wall, but would make a mess of any person she shot with it.

She reached the third-floor landing and took a quick glance through the small glass window. She saw her front door, but it was closed and nothing appeared to be out of the ordinary. She twisted the doorknob and opened the door just a hair. She looked for any monofilament line or wires that might have been connected to an alarm or explosive devise, but saw none. She cracked the door a bit more, double-checked what she'd seen before, then opened it enough to let her slip through.

Francesca eased the door shut behind her. She knew she was probably overreacting because, like as not, thieves had broken in to steal *No Secrets X*. The fact that the watch was vibrating proved the painting had been disturbed. On New Exford she was no one important—her connection to Reg Starling the only claim to fame she had. The sort of thieves who would come after that painting would not be sophisticated enough to rig the stairwell door.

Then again, the alarm has been tripped, but no constabulary, which means they cut my phone lines. They aren't complete amateurs. That meant they were also likely long gone from her place. That conclusion should have reassured her, but as she got closer to her door, she could feel the hairs rising on the back of her neck.

She crossed in front of her door, then crouched low to the right side. Opposite her on the other wall was a thick, oaken cabinet that would offer her a little protection against anyone shooting through the wall. She used her flashlight to check for powder residue and saw only her own footprints. They had been smeared, however, by someone walking in over them, and the lack of exit prints meant the thief was still in there, or had gone out through a window.

Francesca slipped her shoes off. Though they were only

small heels, they would be difficult to run in, and her martial arts training hadn't included balancing on a high heel while kicking. Her toes gripped the nap of the carpet outside her door as she reached up and, jingling her keys, inserted the key into her lock and slid back the dead bolt. She twisted the knob, then gave it a hearty shove.

Still crouching, she scuttled around the corner and jammed her back against the cabinet. The door rebounded off the wall and slammed shut behind her, cutting off the light from the hallway. She waited, holding her breath, her ears straining for any sound of an intruder. She heard nothing, so she played the ultraviolet light along the carpet and saw a quartet of foot-prints track their way in. From the nature of the shoes and their size she assumed two men had entered the apartment.

She shut off the light and left it with her keys on the carpet. She reached up to the cabinet's top and felt around on the right corner. She always left a twenty-kroner bill on the cabinet, knowing that a thief would steal it. Had the alarm not been ringing, the missing bill would have tipped her right at the doorway that her place had been broken into.

Had the bill still been there it would have indicated that the two men had come to covertly toss her apartment. They wouldn't touch the money, but had tripped the alarm they didn't know about. *Of course, if they wanted to toss the place and make it look like a simple theft . . .*

Francesca started to work her way down the narrow hall-way, keeping the needler pistol pointed deeper into the apartment. The living room opened off to the right and took up that whole side of the apartment. Closer to the door was her small kitchenette, and beyond it was the doorway to her bedroom. As she advanced into the apartment she encountered one of the couch's pillows slashed open and tossed onto the floor. She shifted it out of the way and found a few diskzines scattered beneath it.

She slowly straightened up and reached around to flick on the kitchenette light. In its yellow illumination she saw that the whole apartment had been tossed. Everything had been scattered, and her computer smashed against the fireplace over which *No Secrets X* hung at a weird angle. She finished a quick check of the rest of the place and found herself alone.

She double-checked the door, recovered her keys and set the dead bolt, then began a more complete search of the apartment. Piles of her personal computer disks had been stolen, as well as jewelry. She checked the remains of her computer and saw that the hard drive had been ripped out of it. She checked the keyboard, and though the case had been cracked, the special chip that allowed her to encrypt and decrypt messages still remained intact. Without it there was no way anyone could resurrect and crack the messages there.

Aside from a few other small items of value that could be easily concealed, the thieves had taken nothing. She was actually surprised they'd not added *No Secrets X* to their booty, and took their leaving it behind as a mark of contempt. In an instant she knew that it wasn't thieves who'd hit her place, but agents in someone's employ. Anyone from New Exford would have demanded their agents get Starling's painting, which meant these folks were from off-world.

Francesca began to shiver. *Lyran Intelligence, probably Loki. They don't know who I am, but the computer stuff they took suggests they think I might have information they want. The info I could have would be about or from Reg.* Her mouth went sour. She immediately turned and checked the phone, but the line remained dead.

She took a last look around her apartment, then gathered up the keyboard and *No Secrets X*. She shoved them and some clothes into a nylon bag that she set by the door. She then went to the window in her bedroom, opened the left side of the shades and tugged the strings of the blinds so the bottom slanted up on the left side. That odd configuration would let Curaitis know she had abandoned her digs and cover. They would meet, but the next emergency site and time wasn't until the following afternoon.

She left the apartment with her handbag and satchel and took the stairs down. She came out of the apartment house, looked around, then crossed quickly to her hovercar. She tossed the satchel into the rear boot, then pulled away from the curb.

She started driving in a seemingly aimless pattern and constantly checked her rear-view mirror for signs of anyone following her. She saw no pursuit, so spun the wheel and headed straight for Reg Starling's studio, hoping she wouldn't be too late.

When she saw the open door, she knew she was.

Gun drawn, she made her way into the studio. Reg had taken over an old hovercar repair shop and had converted the offices in the back into an apartment. The service bays had been left pretty much alone and were covered with paint that had been sprayed and splattered. Around the base of the walls a layer of canvases, all properly stretched and most covered with paint, stood in ranks. She recalled having looked through them once, early one morning, before Reg had awakened. When he found her looking at them, he referred to them as his "retirement fund." He said he'd sell them for a fortune someday, then wander off to some quiet and tropical world to relax.

Not going to happen now. Francesca moved quickly through the studio to the apartment. The bottom floor, which boasted a small kitchen, bathroom, and auxiliary bedroom, was empty, but had been ransacked. She mounted the stairs to his private quarters. When she reached the top, she heard water draining from a tub. She passed through the bedroom to the master bath and froze in the doorway.

Reg had insisted on a bathroom done in white marble, and he had kept it spotless. He always said it was his sanctuary from paint and color. It had been quite opulent, with a double vanity and wide mirrors, a shower stall, and a huge bathtub suitable for soaking and relaxing. Reg had loved spending time in the tub and had ended up spending the rest of his life there.

But the room was no longer absent of color.

Completely clothed, Reg Starling sat in a full tub of pink water. His wrists had been slashed open and his blood splashed about. Across the mirror, in his blood, had been written, "I'm sorry. I did it. I killed Ryan. Now I must die."

Francesca slumped against the door jamb. "Oh, Reg, she got to you. And I was so close. That last secret, what you knew about Melissa's death . . . I know I would have had it from you soon. And now . . ."

She'd been about to say she'd never know, but something about his expression stopped her. He had died with the hint of a smile on his lips. *He must have concentrated so hard to be able to do that. But then, it would have been easy. They were here to silence Sven Newmark, but they were killing Reg Starling. And Reg Starling never let anyone get anything over on him.*

She crossed into the bathroom and crouched down to kiss him on the forehead. "You made sure that whoever was after you wouldn't win. That was a secret and now I know it. And between us, Reg Starling, she won't win."

═══ 21 ═══

State of the Art Gallery and Café, Crescent Harbor
New Exford
Arc-Royal Defense Cordon
27 November 3060

The stern expression on Francesca's face melted the plastic smile Mr. Archie wore. The little man with slicked-back black hair and a pencil-thin moustache had opened his arms to welcome her, but he stopped with his lips pursed for an air-kiss. His brown eyes widened as she drew closer, and a couple of patrons noticed his surprise.

Francesca ignored them. "Your office, Arch." Her growl widened his eyes further, and brought secret smiles to the faces of those among the staff and regulars who heard her. Mr. Archie, as the self-appointed judge of what was artistic and not on New Exford, ruled supreme in his gallery. He did not tolerate such familiarity from anyone save Reg Starling, and Francesca was treading perilously on her connection with Starling.

Mr. Archie sniffed and half closed his eyes. "I'm afraid I have things I must be doing out here."

"It wasn't a request." With her nylon satchel over her shoulder, Francesca brushed passed him and mounted the red, cast-iron circular stairway that led up to the gallery's office.

The little man clutched at her arm. "You can't . . ."

Francesca let molten fury pour through her eyes. "Now, Arch."

Her footsteps echoed alone from the steps until she was almost to the top, then she heard Mr. Archie begin to follow her. She reached his office before he did and had already slid behind his desk by the time he caught up. The light from a single desk lamp provided all the illumination for the cluttered room. Every flat surface had small bits and pieces of sculpture on it, and many of those flat surfaces were formed by canvases stacked against the walls.

"Fiona Jensen, I don't know what you think you're doing . . ."

Francesca unclipped the keyboard from the computer on the desk and tossed it to Mr. Archie. He caught it and clutched it to his chest like a virgin raising a sheet to protect her modesty. Francesca clipped her keyboard into the machine, then started it up.

As the machine churned through its startup routine, she glanced above the monitor at the gallery's red-faced owner. "Get one of those agent sheets you sign that authorizes you to sell art for an artist showing here."

"What? Why?"

"You're going to become Starling's agent forever and all time."

The man blinked his eyes. "What? How is that possible?"

"I'm going to forge his signature and then you'll sign the contract and I'll witness it."

"But that's fraud . . ."

She hit the reset switch and sent the machine into startup mode again. "Brace yourself: Reg is dead."

The keyboard clattered to the ground, keys popping off to skitter over the floor. "Dead? How?" Mr. Archie's eyes grew wide. "You murdered him . . ."

"No, but I know who did, and I can prove to you that I didn't do it."

The owner's face took on an expression of smug superiority. "Oh, and how will you do that?"

"You'll be told that Reg Starling committed suicide."

"He talked about it often enough."

"Right, I know, but remember what he said. Remember how he said he wanted to go out."

Mr. Archie smiled carefully. "Always the showman. Reg said he'd step in front of a speeding hovertruck, one of those white ones that cruises the streets selling ice cream to children."

"Right. He wanted the blood to show and to give the kids something to remember." Francesca hesitated as the bathroom scene came to mind. "Reg slit his wrists, scrawled a message on a mirror in his blood, and then sat in a warm tub to die."

Mr. Archie shivered. "Oh, no, not Reg. That's so . . . so Elvis, dying in the bathroom. Whoever did it might as well have scattered doughnuts around and copies of *Modern Mercenary Monthly*. Not Reg at all."

The little man's eyes sharpened. "And you, you would have staged it so he made a big splash. Not that I would have blamed you for wanting to murder him. We all did."

"Yeah, but not recently." She glanced at the computer screen, then back at Mr. Archie. "Get that agent agreement out, will you?"

He frowned. "No one would believe he signed it."

"That's wrong because the signature will match over half of the certificates of authenticity and signatures on the prints you've been selling." Francesca smiled in spite of herself. "Reg thought it was the ultimate joke to have him signing my name and me signing his. We practiced until we could forge each other's signatures perfectly. If anyone is inclined to contest it, it will pass muster with experts."

Greed sparked highlights in Mr. Archie's eyes. "And what will you want out of what I make?"

"Nothing more than what I have coming out of the deals we've already made. I might need a little help before that, but the money is all yours. In fact, I doubt you'll ever see me again after I walk out of here."

"Oh, that's unfortunate." The mock sympathy in Mr. Archie's voice was not lost upon Francesca.

"One thing, though, I need whatever it was that Reg gave you to hold in the event of his death."

Mr. Archie blinked again, then his right hand rose to cover his mouth. "In the shock, I had forgotten. Yes, just a moment." He sidled over to the corner of the room and knelt in front of an old safe. "I put it in here."

As the gallery owner worked on the safe, Francesca encrypted a short message to Curaitis. Because she no longer had access to the books on her hard drive, the encryption routine used the onboard computer software help files to encrypt things. She typed in several of Curaitis' cover addresses and sent the message. *If he gets it soon, great. If not, I meet him tomorrow.*

She shut off the computer and unplugged her keyboard as Mr. Archie turned and handed her a plasticine envelope. She tore it open and poured a safety-deposit box key and a notecard into her hand. The key had the bank's stamp on it, and she figured it was the branch where she and Reg had opened the account to handle the funds from the print sales.

The notecard was covered with Reg's crabbed handwriting.

Fiona, love,

   No tears and no secrets. You hold the key to my last secret and since you alone know what it is, it will be up to you to make people pay for its having been transferred to you. You're my friend and, now, my last work. Make a big splash, baby.

Love,
Reg

Francesca sighed. "You didn't let me down, Reg."

"Good news?" Mr. Archie hesitated and glanced down. "I mean, given the circumstances . . ."

"The best that can be expected." Francesca held the key up. "Now I just have to wait for the bank to open tomorrow and finish things off. Can't go home, though."

Mr. Archie's eyes suddenly hardened and the priggish air he wore like flesh seemed to drop away. "You'll come downstairs, we'll eat something, then I will find you a place to stay . . ."

"Thanks, but anything connected with Reg might be a bit dangerous."

The small man waved away her objection. "My dear Fiona, I supply artwork for this world's elite. Half the leading executives here have hideaways they use for clandestine meetings, and I've seen them all. I'll make a call or two and we'll have you a place to stay. It's the least I can do."

Francesca smiled. "Thanks. And I'm sure Reg would thank you, too."

"And ruin his image?" Mr. Archie shook his head as he waved her toward the door. "A little early to be making a saint of Reg Starling, Fiona. It *will* happen. I'll see to that, but not quite so quickly as this, I think."

Over dinner with Mr. Archie, which they ate in a back booth that afforded them privacy from being overheard, but let everyone see them together, a bit of his cattiness returned. Reg was free to spurn anyone while Mr. Archie had to pick up the pieces to make sales. Archie himself had to be courted by patrons and those who wished to be put on his primary lists for special sales and openings. He knew quite a bit about the local comings and goings, and shared Reg's delight in dissecting the faults and foibles of the rich.

He did make good on his promise to find Francesca a place to stay. She spent an uneventful night in a fairly sterile corporate apartment, then woke early and made her way to the First Bank of New Exford's downtown branch. She flashed the key to the safe deposit box to the assistant manager, who took her over to the vault and had her sign in on the box log. She was not surprised to find that the bank had a digitized copy of her signature already on file for the box, and she knew by looking at it that Reg had forged it.

The assistant manager led her into the vault and together they keyed the box open. Francesca slipped the long, slender metal box from the vault and took it to a private examining room. She opened it carefully and raised an eyebrow at the contents. "Oh, Reg, you really did pile all of your secrets in here, didn't you?"

A chunk of the space in the box was taken up by 100,000 kroner in ten stacks of 100-kroner bills. It was not an insubstantial amount of money and certainly enough to get off New Exford and to another world if Reg had needed to run. In addition to the money, there were three sets of official documents. Two were in Sven Newmark's name—one issued by the Free Rasalhague Republic and the other by the Federated Commonwealth. The third was in the name Stefan Kresescu and had been issued by the Free Worlds League. Francesca couldn't tell at first glance, but she was fairly certain the League documents were forgeries. *Very good ones, though.*

Reg had hidden away copies of diskzines that had said good things about his work and a small penknife with his initials on it. She picked up the sterling silver knife and smiled. She'd given it to him as a present and he later claimed he'd lost it. *He didn't want me to know he could be sentimental. Not the image he wanted at all.*

The final thing in the box was a key and an attached tag with an address. It came with no message, but that didn't surprise her. The note that had gotten her this far had said everything Reg wanted to say. Even though he was counting on her to be his instrument of revenge, he didn't want to make it too easy. *Even now he wants me to prove myself worthy of his trust.*

She pocketed the key and knife, then slipped the money into her handbag. She closed the box and returned it to the assistant manager, then got her box key back and left the bank. The address on the key's tag was only a few blocks away, toward Crescent Harbor's waterfront, so she darted across the street, dodging a couple of hovercars, and walked to it.

The building at that address was known in Crescent Harbor as The Plinth. It looked very much as if a jagged lightning bolt had been frozen in gray granite and shoved up from the center of the earth. The stone had been polished to a mirror-like finish and had windows spaced irregularly. At night the lit windows seemed to stagger across the sky—"a Morse code distress signal from the sun," Reg had once commented to her when they had seen it after dark.

She entered the lobby and stopped at the building directory. She keyed in some search parameters and took three tries before she hit what had to be the right one. Mark Newson and Associates, Limited, had its offices on the twenty-fifth floor. She walked over to a bank of elevators, picked out one that serviced the middle range of floors, and started her ascent.

The firm's name clearly pointed to Sven Newmark, but not so obviously that anyone would make a connection if they weren't already certain there was one. As she rode upward, Francesca hoped Reg had been clever about paying the rent and obtaining the lease because a computer check of either could forge a link between Reg Starling and the firm; and the Loki agents who killed him certainly had been checking out his connections, which was how they had come to ransack her apartment.

The elevator slid to a silent stop on the twenty-fifth floor. She found the Newson offices over on the west side of the building, meaning the offices would have a wonderful view of the harbor. *An office in a building he hated, giving him a view of something he considered suitable only as a subject for the "starving artist factory fabrication" school of art. Just a study in contrasts, isn't this, Reg?*

She opened the office and took comfort in the fact that the room seemed stuffy. A thin layer of dust had accumulated on the secretary's desk nearest the door. Francesca closed the door behind her, then made directly for the half-open office with Mark Newson's name on it. She slipped into the inner office and paused because the harbor's view was indeed breathtaking.

The office's huge mahogany desk had been oriented so anyone sitting in its leather chair would have his back to the view. That was typical Reg, but it made Francesca focus on the art on the wall facing the desk. All reds and blacks, with a hint of green, she recognized as something from the Honesty series. The other pieces on the walls, save one, had come from Reg's retirement fund piles and did not clash with the decor terribly. They looked almost a perfect fit for the place.

The other picture in the room definitely was a perfect match for the office. It had been rendered in bright colors, using an impressionistic stipple technique where everything was created out of carefully placed color dots. It showed a view of Crescent Harbor that could have easily been painted by looking out the window in that officee.

The harbor picture immediately drew her to it. Even before she'd come within two meters of it she knew Reg had not painted it. Getting closer she tapped it with a fingernail and heard a sharp click. The art had been painted on a hard, pressed-fiber illustration board—material Reg only used to make secure packing cases for some of his canvasses. The frame, while perfectly suitable for the picture, was the sort of thing that made Reg grit his teeth whenever someone had slapped one around one of his pieces.

All in all, that simple harbor view was something that

would have caused Reg to go ballistic if he saw it. *Another contradiction here, Reg.* Setting her purse on the desk, Francesca pulled the piece down off the wall and looked at the back of it. The frame had a small tag from a local frame shop Reg loathed, but the painting itself had nothing on the back. That struck her as odd because once, when Reg had descended on a "starving artist exhibition and sale" because he heard some of the works were reminiscent of his style, he'd made a show of turning several pieces over and pointing to the price being boldly scrawled on the back, along with a stock number. As he had explained, firms had hundreds of artists grinding out the same piece over and over again, allowing just about everyone to own an original copy of artwork usually found in cheap motels.

She hooked one edge of the frame on the desk and yanked down, popping it free. She glanced at the picture edge and found it actually consisted of a double thickness of the fiberboard. She stripped away the rest of the frame, then pulled out Reg's penknife, extended a blade and worked at the adhesive holding the two layers together. She nibbled away at the seam with the knife, then slid the blade in and twisted.

The two layers parted with a dull crackling sound. The back layer slid off, revealing two carefully milled circular depressions. A single CD-ROM had been sealed beneath a plastic membrane into each of the holes. Though they were not labeled, she knew, beyond a shadow of a doubt, they contained records that would implicate Katherine Steiner in her mother's murder.

"We'll take those," said the first of the two Loki agents who entered the office. Both wore black business suits, but had pulled on balaclavas to hide their features. The first man extended a gloved hand toward her. His partner, who slid to the left and faced the window, held a rather nasty looking slug-thrower on her.

Francesca let her mouth open with surprise. "Look, you

can take what you want. I just want the pictures. Reg said they were mine."

"Just give us the disks."

She turned toward her purse. "Look, I have money."

"The disks." The man's voice became more adamant. "Don't make this more trouble than it's worth, Ms. Jensen."

"How do you know me? How did you find me?"

The leader rolled his eyes and nodded toward his partner. The second man fished into his pocket and took out a cylinder that he started to screw onto the front of his pistol.

Now or never. Francesca flipped the fiberboard at the lead Loki agent, letting it scythe through the air at him. She dove across the desk, hooking her purse with her left hand. She heard a quick cough and felt splinters gouged up from the desk hit her in the legs, but then she fell below the desk's firm top. She hit the ground hard, then rolled on to her back and snaked her needler pistol from her purse.

She didn't bother to pop up to fire, but instead shot the lead man's feet from beneath the desk. She heard him cry out, then saw him land on his chest on the carpet. Two more shots shredded his mask and shirtfront, but his body blocked her view of the second man. She remained hunkered down, waiting for any sign of him, but she saw and heard nothing more than a languid sigh.

Then the stink of burned flesh hit her nose. She snorted it back out again, then said, "Clear."

"I'm coming in."

Francesca pulled herself to her feet and smiled as Curaitis entered the room, a laser pistol in his right hand. Tall and muscular, with coal-black hair and icy blue eyes, the intelligence agent glanced at her, then dropped to one knee and felt the neck of the man she'd shot for a pulse. The second gunman lay on the floor, his jacket still smoldering from the shot that had roasted his heart and lungs.

"They're dead."

She nodded. "Thanks for the save. Where did they pick me up?"

"The bank. Computer check probably showed Starling's box there. You got it and cleaned it out before they could. They spotted you leaving and followed you. I trailed them. Give me your pistol."

She tossed him the needler, which he put into the hands of the man who'd been shot with the laser after he stripped the man of his mask and gloves. The laser went into the hands of the man she'd killed, and he retained his mask and gloves. The obvious impression would be of a robbery that had been interrupted. Francesca knew that with the bullets in the desk, and the traces of her blood from the little splinter wounds, the sham wouldn't hold up under close inspection, but the local constabulary wasn't much on close inspection.

Curaitis picked up the fiberboard with the disks in it. "You think this is it?"

She nodded. "Reg knew this day would come, and he planned to strike back from the grave at those who killed him. I'm sure that stuff will be explosive."

Curaitis smiled slightly, which was the first time she'd ever seen him do such a thing. "Good. With Katherine's latest antics, the bigger the explosion, the better."

22

Takashi Kurita Memorial Spaceport
Imperial City, Luthien
Pesht Military District, Draconis Combine
15 March 3061

Though he knew the occasion was a most solemn one, Victor Davion found it impossible to keep a smile from his face. He waited with Kai Allard-Liao, Hohiro Kurita, the Precentor Martial, and General Andrew Redburn for the mobile transfer gantry vehicle to roll up to the DropShip *Tengu*'s egress hatch. The normally opaque shell on the vehicle had been stripped away, leaving the platform open. As it approached, he saw Theodore Kurita standing there, along with various officials and Theodore's daughter, Omi.

Though the sight of her filled him with joy, it was just icing on the cake of being back from the Clan worlds and actually touching down on an Inner Sphere world. His task force had gone out toward the Kerensky Cluster from Combine space, and reentered the Inner Sphere through it as well. They first stopped at Richmond and were told to proceed immediately with all due diligence and haste to Luthien. They were also asked to do so under a complete communications blackout.

That request had come close to sparking a mutiny among some of the Lyran, League, and Capellan troops, but Victor quickly quelled it by pointing out that while they had been hunting for Smoke Jaguar stragglers—and had found a few along the way—the Ghost Bears or Wolves or another Clan could have made moves in the Inner Sphere in the meantime. If that were true, keeping their return a secret would be a powerful weapon. Victor said he'd refrained from sending messages home and, since none of the others had as pressing a reason as he did to contact their capitals, he expected they would keep quiet.

The fear that something horrible had happened in his absence grew in his gut and had him eating very little as they traveled to Luthien. Then, when the fleet jumped in at the nadir recharge station, Theodore Kurita himself addressed the task force and reassured them that nothing was amiss. He said that the people of the Combine wanted to pay homage to the returning heroes first and best, and the request for communications silence had been a selfish one by him. He asked that they observe it until they reached Luthien. After their welcome, they would have all the facilities of the Combine government put at their disposal.

Victor shook his head. Normally the request to keep silent longer would have sparked grousing, but the promise of a party seemed to quell more complaints. Most of the folks in the task force just wanted to get dirt under their feet, and nearly ninety percent of them never figured that dirt would be from Luthien, so they were game. During the eight-day journey in from the recharge point. Luthien Aerospace Control dictated landing sites, patterns, and times, and anticipation grew within the fleet.

The *Leopard* Class DropShip *Tengu* had been the first allowed to land, and its passenger list had been very carefully specified. Victor recalled well the ceremony surrounding his first arrival, so having the five of them being the first warriors from the task force to set foot on Luthien made perfect sense to him. From what he had seen of the plans for the rest of the landings, he knew the Kurita talent for symbolism and ceremony had been pushed to the limit by their return.

The hatch hissed open as the gantry vehicle bumped the side of the ship. Hohiro emerged first, resplendent in the First Genyosha's black uniform tunic, its right arm splashed with embroidered gold stars. Hohiro wore two swords in the manner of a Kurita warrior. He paused on the edge of the gantry to bow deeply to his father, and Theodore, wearing a simple black suit, returned the bow and held it respectfully.

Both men straightened up at the same time, then Theodore's mouth tightened into a hint of a smile. He pulled his son into a hug and Victor heard distant cheers. Hohiro then worked his way down the line of dignitaries, bowing and shaking hands as he went.

Andrew Redburn followed next and bowed crisply. Redburn had maintained on the way down that hell would be freezing over the second he stepped on Luthien, but his arrival came without any supernatural fanfare. He and Theodore exchanged bows, then shook hands. The Combine's Coordinator whispered something in Andrew's ear that brought a smile to the man's face, then he, too, began moving down the line of dignitaries.

Kai went next, also wearing two swords. The swords had been a gift from the Coordinator on Kai's first arrival on Luthien. Theodore greeted Kai warmly and had a whispered message for him as well. Kai retreated a step and bowed again to the Coordinator, then moved off, allowing the Precentor Martial to step onto the gantry. Focht once again adopted the simple robe of a ComStar adept, but there was no mistaking his warrior background in his bearing and the crisp precision of his bow.

Victor swallowed against the acid bubbling up in his stomach and made sure his swords were tucked properly into his sash. He composed his face solemnly and followed the Precentor Martial onto the gantry. He paused where Hohiro had and bowed to Theodore. Straightening up again he stood stock still as Theodore returned the courtesy of a low and long bow, then they stepped together and shook hands.

Theodore smiled at him and spoke in English. "It has been a long time you have been away. You cannot know the joy I feel at your return."

Victor smiled and replied in Japanese. "All of us are just as happy to be here. Thank you for hosting our return."

The Coordinator's eyes widened. "You have been studying while you were away."

"Your son has been an excellent tutor."

"A sensei's skill can be measured by the advancement of his students." Theodore pressed his right hand on the back of Victor's left shoulder. "You will want to meet our friends here, so you may take your place in the line. You will be there, next to my daughter."

"*Domo arigato.*"

"I was once a soldier, too, Victor."

The Prince moved down the line of officials, bowing, shaking hands and exchanging pleasantries, then he reached Omi. He bowed deeply to her, then accepted her bow. Without saying a word to her—but fully catching all that could be communicated from her glance—Victor took his place at her side.

The gantry vehicle moved away from the DropShip and started on a slow circuit toward the terminal building. As it left the DropShip's shadow, Victor got a chance to see, for the first time, the throng at the spaceport. People lined the windows and rooftops, and were being held back by makeshift fences and riot police. The gantry vehicle moved toward a raised platform behind which waited a fleet of convertible limousines. Several smaller platforms bristled with holovid cameras from the Combine's Information Agency, and Victor was certain their return was being beamed throughout the Combine. Light towers had been erected to illuminate the platform, with the lights blazing to life as the gantry vehicle came to a stop at the platform.

Theodore stepped onto the raised platform first and the crowd roared their approval. The other dignitaries filed off and stood along the platform's back edge. Hohiro led the others into a rank behind his father, with Omi retaining her place at Victor's right hand. As each of them moved onto the platform, a new cheer went up to echo off into the growing twilight.

The Coordinator stepped up to a microphone and opened his arms. "Rejoice, my people, for the day we have awaited is here. Over a year and a half ago the liberation of our worlds from the Clans was begun. These men here, and the valiant troops they led, swept the Smoke Jaguars from our nation. Then these brave warriors tracked the Smoke Jaguars back to their lair, where another task force had already ventured. Together they finished the Jaguars and defeated the combined might of the Clans. Through their efforts, we need never again fear tyranny at the hands of the Clans."

Applause erupted spontaneously and washed over them. Victor found himself blushing. He was proud of what he and his people had accomplished, but usually lavished all his praise on the soldiers and leaders who had fought for him. The heartfelt appreciation the Combine's people were expressing overwhelmed him. *I know we did this for them, but it was so easy to forget that fact while fighting. The mind can't possibly quantify the impact our victory will have on trillions of people, and I have no way to handle their thanks.*

The Coordinator raised his hands again and the applause faded slowly. "People of Luthien, I want you all to look to the skies. You will see above you a shifting of constellations as stars move in the heavens and grow bright. These stars are the DropShips that are bringing to us the victorious warriors who have saved our realm and our homes. Once was a time when the movement of stars like this would have heralded a catastrophe, an invasion from which we would never recover. Now it betokens the return of friends, good friends, who are heroes all. Into your care I entrust them. You will make them welcome and show them the full depth of your appreciation for their sacrifices on your behalf."

With everyone else, Victor looked up and saw the vault of the sky crawling with bright lights. Dozens of DropShips began their descent to Luthien. Several from each nation were headed toward Imperial City itself, but most of the rest would be scattered around the larger cities on the world. Combine troops would land in the more rural areas on the simple assumption that the more metropolitan districts would find it easier to deal with people from other nations.

Theodore nodded solemnly toward the crowd and the holovision cameras. "Luthien, this is no less a great day than when the Smoke Jaguars and Nova Cats were defeated here. Rejoice with all your hearts. You have fulfilled your duty, so these warriors were able to fulfill theirs. This is a victory we all share, and shall celebrate together."

Another burst of applause thundered through Victor's chest as the Coordinator turned away from the microphone. He waved everyone toward the stairway at the far end of the platform and they descended to the hovercars. Hohiro and Theodore were shown to the first one, and the Precentor Martial, Kai, and Andrew Redburn to the second. Omi and Victor got the third one, and had just gotten settled when the engine roared to life and the driver started out after the first two vehicles.

Victor smiled at Omi, brushing the back of her hand with a finger. "I have missed you so much."

She glanced down for a moment, then caught his finger between two of her own. "My garden has flourished. It has been watered with so many tears. You were gone a lifetime and, I am certain, it seemed like many lifetimes to you. All I had to do was wait."

"We both waited. I just had different things to occupy my mind."

She searched his face with her blue-eyed gaze. "You are very kind to equate what I had to do with what you were doing. Your task was much more important than mine. There is so much of what I endured I would share with you, but I cannot and will not."

Victor frowned slightly. "Why not?"

"You would think me weak. I would not diminish myself in your eyes."

Victor interlaced his fingers in hers. "You could never make me think ill of you, Omiko. Without knowing you waited for me, I never would have finished what I set out to do."

"You cannot know the joy your words pour into me." She gave him a quick smile. "Later we can speak more on this, and I shall show you the depth of my happiness at your return."

The Prince nodded. "I, too, relish a chance to show you how happy I am to be here with you again."

"But, now, we must be who we are for the people." Omi looked away from him as the limo passed through the airport gates and lifted her right hand to wave.

Victor looked to his left and his jaw dropped open. The streets of Imperial City thronged with people. Banners hung from windows and across streets. Most of them had Japanese characters on them, but many also had English and German legends added on. He could read very little of the signs, and found the translations sincere but flawed. Even so, the sentiment that had sparked their creation was readily apparent.

Even without the signs, the joy on the faces could not be mistaken. People, hundreds of thousands of people, young and old, rich and poor, noble and peasant, lined the streets and cheered. Many wore broad white headbands with letters inked on them, others had fashioned uniforms reminiscent of those worn by his Tenth Lyran Guards or the Com Guards or another of the task force's groups. Children stood at the curb and saluted, or waved from their perches atop parents' shoulders.

The crowd bowed and bobbed as the vehicles passed. Some of the people held slender tapers and others whole torches, and these open flames amply lit the procession. Skyrockets crawled up into the sky and exploded in brilliant colors, and the flashes of holovid cameras sparkled like stars in the crowd.

Again the response stunned Victor. He had, more times than he cared to remember, ridden through parades on a variety of state occasions. As a child he had hated it because his arms grew tired from waving. Growing into manhood he understood the need to be seen and to smile and greet others, but it had always seemed something of a game to him. Here, however, the unadulterated love and thanks pouring forth energized him and made him smile and wave all the more, hoping everyone he saw would assume he had been waving at him or her specifically.

Victor lost track of time in the passage from the spaceport to the Palace of Unity. The journey *had* seemed to last forever, but had also passed quickly. He could tell, from the ache in his shoulders, that he had been waving quite a bit, yet he really didn't feel tired. He lowered his hands as the hoverlimo slid through the gates, and when it came to a stop he hopped out and offered Omi his hand to help her alight.

Almost immediately she slipped her hand from his and glanced down. Victor turned and saw the Coordinator approaching. "That was quite a reception, Theodore-*sama*."

"I am glad you were impressed." Theodore's expression darkened a bit. "There are things we must discuss—no, not about my daughter and you—but first there are people here who you should see. Omiko, if you would take Victor to them."

"As you wish, Father."

Victor offered Omi his arm and she took it, slipping her left hand through the crook of his right elbow. "What is your father hinting at?"

"Trust me, Victor, and trust my father." She stopped in the

shadows near the entrance and drew him close. "Do you recall the cheers of the crowds?"

"Just now? How could I forget them?"

"Good, you should never forget them." She smiled and kissed his nose. "And do you recall our last time together in my sanctuary?"

Victor smiled. "Very well, indeed, my love."

"Good." She started toward the Palace of Unity's entrance again.

"What am I missing, Omiko?"

"Nothing, Victor. Trust me."

Omi led him through the doorway and Victor's heart jumped. Standing there in a hallway that emphasized her height, his sister Yvonne smiled weakly at him. She wore a red kimono several shades deeper than her hair, embroidered with tigers of the same gray as her eyes. She started toward him, then hesitated.

Victor smiled at Omi and slipped his arm from hers. He crossed to his sister and hugged her. "Yvonne, you're here. This is great."

"I'm glad to see you, too, Victor. I've been so afraid."

"What?" Her voice had a tremble running through it that surprised him. He pulled back a bit and looked up at her face. *Red rimmed eyes—she's been crying.* "What's the matter, Yvonne? Why weren't you at the spaceport?"

His sister stiffened and stepped back out of his grasp. She folded her arms against her belly and refused to meet his eyes. "I didn't want to spoil your homecoming."

"Huh?" He frowned heavily. "How could you do that?"

"Don't you see, Victor?" Tears spilled down her cheeks. "I've lost your realm."

23

Katrina watched the bubbles stream upward in her champagne. She marveled at how the light amber liquid and the champagne flute conspired to narrow the world she viewed through them. Slowly rotating the glass in the slender fingers of her left hand, she allowed it to capture the whole of what had once been Victor's office. She smiled, realizing she now held everything that had once been her brother's in the palm of her hand.

She sipped the champagne and smiled. *Dry, as dry as the dust Victor tastes now.* Sitting back in the chair that had served both Victor and their father, Hanse Davion, Katrina allowed herself a throaty little laugh. She had not been surprised at Theodore's move to bring the task force to Luthien for a hero's welcome—it was so very Kurita a gesture, after all. There, Theodore would be able to break the news to Victor of how he had lost everything.

But will the Coordinator do it himself or allow Yvonne to atone for her sins? Katrina sipped again, relishing the champagne's faintly fruity flavor and the tickle of bubbles bursting against the back of her throat. She knew Yvonne would have enjoyed the champagne—she'd been the one to lay in the stock of it, in fact. *Too bad she does not see a cause for celebration now.*

Yvonne had fled the Federated Commonwealth soon after the new year, but the strains had been there during the holidays. Katrina had known that Yvonne would be hurt by the transition, but the First Princess had hoped her younger sister would see reason. *After all, I did it for the benefit of our people, and the people of the Inner Sphere.*

Katrina sighed. From the very first she had known her brother Victor would be a poor fit as a ruler of men. Even as a child little Victor had been very proper, a little soldier who all but glowed beneath their father's praise for him. Given a choice, Victor would dress himself in the various uniforms the Federated Commonwealth's units sent as presents. She understood why the military loved him: his birth came at the cessation of the Fourth Succession War in which their father had gobbled up over half of the Capellan Confederation. Victor, born a male heir to Hanse Davion, with that name, became an avatar for their great success.

She lowered her glass and looked around the office that had not changed in her memory. Victor had not altered it after their father had died. *In this chair, in fact, Hanse Davion had his heart attack.* Victor really had been shaped by their father— *forged, more like*—into what he had become. Victor truly had been the man most suited to dealing with the Clans, but his being a weapon meant he could never be a good ruler. *Conflict, for him, involves blood and pain.*

Katrina again smiled, barely able to refrain from shouting for joy. As she began to vie with her brother for power, she had learned that opinion was as good as fact for swaying the minds of many. She had dealt Victor a death-blow in the Lyran Alliance territories by letting it seem as if there truly *was* truth to the rumor that he had murdered Melissa Steiner-Davion. Katrina had easily slipped into the role of being her mother's heir and had won the hearts of her mother's people. When she pulled the Lyran Alliance out of the Federated Commonwealth, the people heralded the move not as treason but salvation.

Her manipulation of the media brought home to her a method for destroying Victor. With him still in power on New Avalon, her efforts had begun slowly, and were meant to cause him internal troubles, but with his venturing forth to slay the Clans, she was able to use Yvonne's innocence to further her plans. *It all was so frighteningly simple.*

Rulers who have to contend with nations spanning hundreds of light years cannot take time to speak to each citizen to learn what they want and need. The reason a feudal system had arisen again was because of the need for direct local governance of worlds. The nobles who controlled those worlds were held accountable by the central government, and looked to that government for help, but they were also powerless to poll a whole planet by themselves.

Enter polling firms who conducted research on opinions. Most such firms conducted polls that asked a variety of questions, including a section for opinions on whatever consumer product was sponsoring the survey. The business got useful data on their consumer base, with political and moral surveys of the populace a byproduct of the process.

Through a variety of corporate shells, Katrina sponsored lots of polls. The questions on them were slanted to elicit specific responses. Instead of asking "Is Prince Victor's leadership of the Star League Expeditionary Force a good thing?", the people being polled were asked, "Does Prince Victor's leadership of the Star League Expeditionary Force distract from his ability to deal with domestic issues?" All but the most staunch militarist would have to answer the latter question with a yes, leading to polls that showed over eighty percent of the populace believing Victor was distracted from his duties as ruler by his Star League activities.

When Victor and his forces left for the Periphery, Katrina stepped up her activities. Questions became more slanted, and dissatisfaction with Yvonne's leadership began to mount. To exacerbate all this, Katrina had produced and distributed a number of documentaries about the Clan war, the departure of Kerensky, the collapse of the original Star League, and the rise of the new one. In these stories Victor was likened to Aleksandr Kerensky. That showed Victor off in a most glowing light, but also played upon the fear that he would abandon the Inner Sphere, just as Kerensky had done. Worse yet, the Clans had been the product of Kerensky's exile, leaving people to wonder what sort of monster Victor's campaign would produce.

In the Draconis March, the stories about the Clan war played up Victor's efforts to save Hohiro Kurita and to liberate Combine worlds—without first seeing to the liberation of the Lyran Alliance worlds that he still nominally claimed as his own. The people of the Draconis March had long feared the Combine, and Victor's actions on behalf of the latter began to polarize the population there.

And dear Arthur was such a help in all that. Her youngest brother was a student at the Battle Academy on Robinson, the capital of the Draconis March. Though a willing and able military man, Arthur was a weathercock that pointed in the direction of the strongest wind, which, in this case, was that being produced by Marcher lords who were afraid their realm would be swallowed up by the Combine now that the Clans were no longer a threat. Arthur pledged that he would not allow that to happen, unknowingly placing himself as a rallying point for those who thought Victor had abandoned them.

Arthur had been easy to manipulate. A couple of short messages to him, encouraging him and praising him for his astute addressing of local concerns guaranteed he would stay that course. Yvonne had not been so easy to play with, largely because Tancred Sandoval proved a shrewd advisor. Sandoval was Yvonne's political tillerman, steering her away from the traps Katrina had set. With him in place, her conquest of New Avalon would have been impossible.

Fortunately for her, Sandoval's family ruled the Draconis March. As that border region became more and more restless, Tancred returned home to Robinson as Yvonne's personal envoy to smooth things out. Arthur and Tancred had a number of direct confrontations in which Tancred showed Arthur to be thinking more with his heart than his brain. This should have settled the situation, but Tancred had not reckoned with Arthur's appeal to many of the March people. As polls soon showed, Tancred came off as a bully in trouncing Arthur, undercutting Tancred's ability to be effective on Yvonne's behalf.

The third and final phase of Katrina's covert war on the Federated Commonwealth kicked in when she learned of Victor's imminent and triumphant return. With hefty bribes being paid to polling company officials and petty bureaucrats, Katrina cooked the data being sent to New Avalon to show unrest spiking. This data also filtered back to the planets, and a few rabble-rousers scattered here and there—aided and abetted by Sun-Tzu's Free Tikonov Movement—were able to stage demonstrations that provided excellent holovid proof of the widespread dissatisfaction in the Federated Commonwealth.

Yvonne's distress was apparent in her personal communications with Katrina. Katrina, in turn, suggested little things that Yvonne could do to win support. These strategies produced immediate and positive results—again thanks to poll manipulation. Unfortunately for Yvonne, a grant going to one world to solve a problem would cause other worlds to wonder why they weren't getting their share of central government assistance, deepening the problems Yvonne had to deal with.

Suddenly the polls began to show a rising sentiment for Katrina. She spiked these by making a journey to border worlds, bringing with her support from the Lyran Alliance, which was much closer to worlds like Addicks and Helen than New Avalon was. Cheering crowds greeted her, and holo-ops provided her with perfect sound bytes. The image of a child crawling into Katrina's lap and saying, "You're pretty. I wish you were our ruler," was sweet enough to crystallize blood, but it received widespread play throughout the Federated Commonwealth.

By the middle of October the debate had been neatly framed and boiled down to a simple question that was asked in barrooms and on holovid political shows. "If Victor died," it went, "wouldn't Katrina be the heir to the Federated Commonwealth throne?" After all, Yvonne had only been placed there as regent, and it was rather clear she was not up to the task. And, for all anyone knew, Victor *was* dead somewhere beyond the Periphery. It could have turned out that Yvonne had been driving the Federated Commonwealth into ruin for nothing since her sister should have already been ruling them.

The debate drove Yvonne to desperation. By the middle of November she sent Katrina a message begging her to come and take over for her. Katrina agreed and accepted the reins of government just in time to preside over the holiday celebrations. She made certain Yvonne was at her side, and praised her sister for her valiant effort in such trying times, but everyone breathed a sigh of relief knowing a seasoned ruler was again at the ship of state's helm.

Katrina put her honeymoon period with the people to good use. The polls showed an immediate spike in confidence, and Katrina initiated reforms that made her appear to be more responsive to the people. She sent Yvonne to Robinson to assure the people of the Draconis March that she would not abandon them, and was not surprised to learn Yvonne and Tancred had vanished and later turned up on Luthien.

She drank more of the champagne and looked around the office again. "Too much old wood and leather. I will have it redone."

A sharp knock at one of the oaken doors brought her out of her reverie. She glanced over and saw an older, solidly built man, clearly of old Asian descent, bow his head and enter her office. "Is there something you need, Mandrinn Liao? Are you here to spoil my mood, or shall I be generous and offer you some of this champagne?

Tormano Liao regarded her carefully with his blue eyes. "I am not certain if what I have to tell you will displease you or not, Highness."

She shrugged. "Then join me for champagne first. We shall have a toast to my brother's newfound life of leisure. Now he will have all the time in the world to cat about with his Drac lover."

Tormano poured himself a glass, tapped it against hers, then drank. "Excellent, as always, Highness."

"Of course. I do deserve the best." She clutched her flute in both hands. "What is it you wish to tell me?"

"I need to resign your service, Highness."

"Curious. Explain please."

The elder Liao set his glass down and clasped his hands behind his back. "My nephew, as First Lord of the Star League, used Star League Defense Force units to occupy the St. Ives Compact, my sister's realm. As you know there has been fighting there and it has not gone well for my sister's people. Moreover, Sun-Tzu has been making gains in the Disputed Territories, reclaiming planets your father liberated before your birth. I have friends on these worlds."

"I know, Mandrinn." Katrina smiled coolly. "As I recall, I have rewarded your loyalty by diverting my own assets into some of your liberation cells. The Free Capella Movement, I think it is called."

"Yes, Highness, you have been most generous. However, at a time like this, leadership is as vital as money. While Cassandra and Kuan-Yin Allard-Liao are doing all they can to oppose their cousin Sun-Tzu, there is need for more leadership there."

"And you would fill that role?"

"I would." Tormano pressed his hands flat against his chest. "I am not the most able warrior anymore, but I do have experience my nieces do not share."

"And you have a lust for power that they also do not share." Katrina laughed lightly and smiled at the forced look of surprise on Tormano's face. "Come now, Tormano, we both know you wish your ass was on the Celestial Throne on Sian."

"I would gladly accept my duty as a Liao."

"I know you would, but there are things you should consider that might get you there sooner than you expect. The first is this: right now Kai is on Luthien and will be hearing about the plight of the St. Ives Compact. I think he will come to fill that leadership role you seek."

Tormano blinked with surprise, then smiled. "Kai will be most effective in that role, yes."

"The second and most important thing to consider is this, however: Sun-Tzu's reign as First Lord of the Star League will end in November. At the Second Whitting Conference, which I will host on Tharkad in eight months, we will choose a new First Lord, and I mean to be chosen."

Tormano frowned. "That is by no means assured."

"Oh, I don't know. I get Sun-Tzu's vote by threatening his realm with complete destruction if he doesn't give it to me. Since little Janos Marik will be Thomas's heir—and I gather the Halas woman is pregnant yet again—Sun-Tzu's sham engagement to Isis Marik means nothing. He has no sanctuary, so he will vote for me. Likewise, Thomas will be mine in order to curry favor with me and to have me keep Sun-Tzu focused on the Federated Commonwealth, not internal League politics."

"Theodore Kurita will oppose you."

"No matter, he is one vote among six. I buy the Free Rasal-hague Republic's vote through trade pacts and win your sister over by providing more aid to her troops." Katrina held her glass out for Tormano to refill it. "And, most important, there is no viable candidate to oppose me. Theodore would be the logical choice, but he is still consolidating the gains from pushing the Clans off his worlds. He can't afford the distraction."

Tormano filled her glass again, then returned the bottle to the silver ice bucket on the desk. "And your brother, who would have been the logical choice, has no standing because he has no realm."

"Exactly."

Tormano nodded carefully. "And when you are First Lord of the Star League, you will rid St. Ives of SLDF troops."

"Using you, Mandrinn, as my personal envoy to engineer the cease-fires and withdrawals."

Tormano smiled and reached for his champagne flute. "Then a toast to you, Highness. Wisdom and success in all things."

"Thank you, Mandrinn Liao." She touched her glass to his and considered the resultant ringing a happy sound. "To our loyal friends go rewards and to our enemies, the obscurity of a life squandered."

24

Palace of Unity
Imperial City, Luthien
Pesht Military District, Draconis Combine
16 March 3061

Victor sat huddled in a chair in the Coordinator's briefing room, staring at the projected starfield that represented the Inner Sphere. Gold slashed across the map, indicating the consolidation of his realm with Katherine's Lyran Alliance. The green of the Capellan Confederation had been overlaid on the St. Ives Compact. The Chaos March had fragmented a little more, but the Confederation had also gobbled up more worlds in the Disputed Territories.

Numb, he looked across the lozenge-shaped black table at the Coordinator. "All the time I was gone I assumed Katherine and Sun-Tzu would make moves. I thought I had left programs in place to deal with them, but I never expected this . . ."

Theodore shook his head. "No one anticipated this. Your sister was most subtle."

Victor closed his eyes and hugged his arms tighter around himself. Yvonne's confession of having lost the Federated Commonwealth had stunned him, and her reportage of how it happened defied logic. There was no reason why his people should have begun to hate Yvonne inside a year. When he'd left the Inner Sphere she was doing just fine. To learn that within a year the populace had decided he had died fighting the Clans and that they wanted Katherine on the throne amazed him.

It crushed Yvonne. She went to pieces as she told him what had happened, as if she'd held herself together just long enough to report to him. He listened to her and hugged her and stroked her hair. He soaked her tears up with his uniform and told her it was all right. He said it wasn't her fault because, even before Theodore had briefed him, he could see Katherine's fine hand in what had happened.

When Theodore had come to take Victor for his briefing, Omi had taken charge of Yvonne. She and Tancred were being housed at Omi's Palace of Serene Sanctuary. With a silent nod Omi assured him that she would take care of Yvonne, so he left with the Coordinator to get himself brought up to speed on the Inner Sphere's current events.

Victor opened his eyes again. "All this through the manipulation of public opinion. I knew she was good, just not how good."

Theodore nodded wearily. "We had no idea either, and might have missed what she was doing save for two things. First, we had a sleeper agent in the Federated Commonwealth who, quite on his own, had become interested in environmental issues on his world. He organized a small group that staged protests—minor annoyances to the realm, really, but he was known as a malcontent. People approached him and offered him funding to step up his protests. He agreed, and accepted direction from them concerning timing of events and the particular slant on the protests. They went from general problems to becoming very pointedly anti-Yvonne. The man deemed this shift serious enough to break cover and report to us."

The Prince nodded. "Have you recovered him yet?"

"Soon."

"Good. If he runs into any trouble, I will do what I can to help." A quick laugh shook Victor. "Well, I guess *that* offer is worth exactly the medium it's been encoded on. What was the other thing that tipped you?"

"Our comparison of economic data on a planetary level with the reported survey results from your people. We noted a divergence, that the media and government were reporting that matters were worse than individuals themselves seem to think. Apparently everyone who heard the news of how difficult things had become under Yvonne assumed that if they were doing well it was because they were in the minority. They had no reason to stand up and say to friends that their lives were just fine. They were happy and just kept quiet so they wouldn't seem to be gloating."

"Not at all like Katherine." Victor shook his head. "Yvonne said Katherine shipped many of my personal belongings here. Is that right?"

Theodore glanced down at the table. "They are at my daughter's palace." He hesitated for a moment. "It is perhaps best that I will say this here, in a soundproofed room, but I would offer you the hospitality of Luthien for as long as you want it or need it. I have no idea what you may have had planned for the future. This news must certainly come as a shock, but it would be best not to act hastily because of it."

"No, no haste." Victor sighed. "I thought Katherine might try something military, which is why I left Phelan behind to keep her honest. Turns out she moved in a way that prevented him from doing anything."

Theodore smiled. "Khan Kell was interested in mounting a campaign to dislodge your sister, but I pointed out to him that he could do no such thing. Worse than the appearance of Combine ships over New Avalon would be the appearance of Clan ships. I told him he had to wait for your return before acting. If you want to go to war to win your realm back, his Wolves and my warriors will gladly go with you."

"I appreciate that more than you know, Theodore, and I will tell Phelan the same thing, but I don't know." Victor opened his hands and looked at them. "On one hand I know my sister murdered my mother and has systematically done all she could to undermine me. She is evil and to leave her on the throne will likely result in untold troubles in the future. The only recourse would seem to be to go to war to end her reign.

"On the other hand, I've just spent two years involved in some of the nastiest fighting I've seen in my career. Using the sword you gave me on my first trip here, I beheaded the ilKhan of the clans. If his is the last blood on my hands, I'll be very happy."

"I should be very happy for you, Victor, if I thought that could possibly be the case." Theodore shook his head sadly. "Warfare is not the only choice here, however. In November the members of the Star League will meet at the second Whitting Conference, to discuss matters of concern and to select a new First Lord. By the way, the Star League Constitution was amended to allow the First Lord's election by a simple majority."

"Interesting, but since there are now only six realms that vote: CapCom, FedCom, League, Compact, Combine, and Free Rasalhague Republic, any majority vote would automatically be the two-thirds vote previously required. Who proposed the change?"

"Thomas Marik, and it passed unanimously." The Coordinator smiled sheepishly. "It was readily apparent to all of us that Sun-Tzu's election occurred because you did something your sister did not expect. No one wants to have the next First

Lord chosen by lot, so a simple majority seemed to make sense."

"And if there's a tie, ComStar casts the tie-breaker."

"True, though, at the time, we had seven states able to vote, so their input wasn't a considered factor." The older man smiled. "I had hopes that you would have been the next First Lord."

Victor nodded. "You know, deep down I guess I hoped I would be, too. Now that seems long ago and very far away."

"At the Whitting meeting I intend to bring up the issue of Katherine's usurpation of your throne. I'm certain she'll claim it is an internal political matter—much as Sun-Tzu will claim when the issue of the St. Ives Compact comes up. I doubt I will get anywhere with her. I know she wants to be First Lord, and there is no way she can allow you to be at the head of a realm because you would be selected before her in a heartbeat."

"Nice to hear, but you're right, we'll have no standing at the conference." He chuckled. "I imagine I won't even be invited to go. I suspect that the moment Sun-Tzu hears I've returned, he'll send me a note of thanks and relieve me of my command duties, and Katherine certainly won't appoint me commander in chief of the Star League Defense Forces after she's elected."

Theodore's head came up. "You do not sound particularly saddened by that prospect."

"No, I guess I don't." Victor shrugged. "I know I'm not tracking emotionally at the moment, and I'm damned tired, but if I never had to issue another order in my life, I could be happy. It's rather funny, actually, because in that final conversation I had with the ilKhan, he asked me to kill him because he said a warrior cannot live without being a warrior. For him, being a warrior was inbred, it was his destiny, and we fought a war to prove to the Clans that warfare was a choice, and one that should be rejected whenever possible.

"Here, now, I have a chance to exercise that choice. I went off with the cream of the warriors in the Inner Sphere. We defeated the Clans. I did my job and now I could easily slip away into obscurity."

Victor leaned forward, resting his elbows on the table. "And, Theodore, believe me, I don't say any of this to denigrate the Combine's warrior tradition. I cherish it and am arrogant enough to think I understand it. One of the things I understand is that sometimes a warrior leaves his vocation behind to adopt a new one. He enters a monastery just as Yorinaga Kurita did."

"Or as your own Morgan Kell did."

"Right."

"Yet both of them returned to the warrior path when needed."

The younger man smiled. "Perhaps I'll do that, too."

"What would you do instead of fighting?"

"Well, you've offered me the hospitality of your world, and Omi has a garden that needs tending." Victor hung his head for a moment. "Does it sound strange that I would like to putter around in a garden, bringing life forth instead of sowing destruction everywhere?"

"Not strange, and decidedly most honorable." Theodore leaned forward on the table as well. "This choice you face, it is not one I ever had a chance to make. You never met my father, but he was much like your own. He pushed me to become the heir he wanted because I was his only child *and* because he knew his realm was in a difficult position. He did not have your mother's influence to temper him.

"Knowing my father, and having known yours, I think they would wonder about this choice you mention, but they would also respect it. Warfare is too horrible a thing for one to approach as a hobby or vocation. That you even realize there is a choice, a chance to choose something else, marks you as being very special."

"Domo arigato." Victor stretched and covered a yawn with his hand. "Forgive me, but this has been something of a draining day."

"Indeed, I can imagine it has." The Coordinator stood and walked to the briefing room's door. "I'll summon a driver to take you to Omi's palace."

"Again, thank you." Victor smiled at Theodore. "And I never did thank you for letting Omi and me be together. Because of your wishes, we had been resigned to living apart. In fact," Victor laughed, "I had once considered the idea of abdicating so politics would no longer separate us."

The Coordinator smiled. "I had opposed your union initially because of the tensions between your nation and mine, but I always assumed that if love existed between you, it would win out."

"Your daughter always was faithful to your wishes."

"I know." Theodore waved Victor through the door and out into a hallway. "I don't know if you are aware of it, but I married my wife in secret, very much against my father's wishes. I am pleased Omi found a way to blend her independence of spirit and her devotion to her duty."

"She's a very special woman. She's the only one I've ever loved, and the only one I can ever imagine loving."

"Then, thank you, Victor. I now know my daughter's future is assured." The Coordinator sketched a brief bow to him. "I'll send a driver for you. Good night. Rest well."

Victor returned the bow and watched Theodore walk away. As the sound of the other man's footsteps faded, Victor suddenly realized he was alone for the first time in forever. This prompted a smile, but it died quickly as a shiver ran up his spine. *I really am alone. My nation is gone.*

The image of Omi waiting for him banished that shiver, but another peculiar sensation rose in its place. He turned and stared at a deep patch of shadow off to his left. He narrowed his eyes and felt certain there was nothing there, but he couldn't shake the sensation of being watched. Just when he thought he'd actually seen through the shadow, to see the corner where wall abutted wall, a piece of the shadow detached itself and moved into the light.

"Komban wa, sensei." Victor bowed toward the man. "I had wondered at your absence."

Minoru Kurita returned the bow. Though he actually stood a few centimeters taller than Victor, his slight build, marginally oversized head, and thick glasses gave an impression of his being smaller than the Prince. Had Victor been shown a picture of him and asked if he could kick his butt in a fight, he'd have answered yes without reservation.

But a holograph cannot convey the power in that body. Prior to his first visit to Luthien, Victor had known little of Omi's younger brother. Intelligence Secretariat files had described and dismissed him as a mystic, a non-player in the Combine's power structure. Victor's attitude toward Minoru changed after his wounding, when the younger Kurita had worked with him to guide and heal him. While Victor's therapy regimen consisted of *t'ai chi chuan* exercises that helped strengthen his body, Minoru supplemented them with chants and other esoteric exercises meant to strengthen his life force. Though initially skeptical, Victor had recovered sooner than his own doctors predicted he could, lending certain weight to Minoru's therapy.

"It is good to see you again, too, Victor." Minoru gave him a slight smile. "I have been about, but I did not wish to be seen. It is good that you saw me now."

"I didn't see you. I felt being seen."

"An even more useful skill to cultivate." The younger Kurita snaked his hands into the opposite sleeves of the red robe he wore. "You have continued your exercises. This pleases me."

"I am glad. You strengthened me."

"No, I merely showed you how to find your strength."

Victor gave him an appreciative nod. "Without your help, I would not have recovered from my wounds, so I am grateful. If there is anything I can do to repay you . . ."

"There is."

"Name it, though, in my present state, I think you'll find my generosity knows very tiny bounds."

"What I want you have coin to pay for." Minoru reached up and adjusted his glasses. "You slew the ilKhan with a sword. Tell me of the stroke."

"The stroke?" Victor's eyes tightened. The ilKhan's death had been a highlight to the news of the task force's return, as if all the malevolence of the Clans had been embodied in one man and destroyed with his death. Victor thought back, peeling away layers of memory. He'd not thought about his fight with Osis for a long time. *Why not?*

He looked up. "I was in a 'Mech and Osis challenged me to meet him as an equal. He offered to acquaint me with death. I left my 'Mech and carried my katana with me. I told him I wasn't going to fight him, that I'd killed before, and that I'd died, and I wanted no more of killing. I told him he was defeated and I saw in his eyes that he knew the whole Crusade had been folly. After he made that realization, he begged me to kill him."

"And this is when you took him, to give him an honorable death?"

Victor shook his head. "No. He was no longer a warrior. He had no honor and no right to make that request. He knew it, but made it anyway. He told me a warrior could not live if not as a warrior, but I told him his sentence was to live as something other than a warrior. Then I turned my back on him and started walking back to my 'Mech.

"I heard the rasp of his feet on the stone, saw his shadow fall over me but, even before that, I knew he was coming for me." Victor felt his heart pound, his breath quicken. "I spun and drew and cut, all without thought. I barely remember the stroke. I recall the sun hot on my back, looking down at his head, watching his blood try to link body and head again."

He focused on Minoru. "I'm sorry I cannot tell you more."

"You have told me enough." Minoru bowed his head. "Listen to me, Victor. You are a weapon of great power. You have destroyed our enemy and, like a sharp sword, have been returned to the scabbard. You may like that safe darkness, and you have earned it. For the man who had everything, as you did, having nothing is the only gift left for you."

Victor smiled. "I'd not thought of it that way. Thank you. You are most kind, as everyone else has been."

Minoru's right hand came out of the left sleeve, his index finger held aloft. "The others, they speak to you from *ninjo*— a sense of compassion. I speak to you from *giri*—the demands of duty. In a scabbard you may rest now, but it will not always be so. Duty will call to you and you will answer."

A chill worked its way up Victor's spine. Minoru's words, though spoken softly, carried the weight of a 'Mech's tread. *It is as if speaking to the Nova Cat Khans.* "I cannot say I understand exactly what you mean . . ."

"Understanding is for the future, Victor." Minoru looked past him, then whirled away.

Theodore came around a corner further down the corridor with a woman dressed in the uniform of the Otomo, his bodyguard unit. "Victor, this is *Tai-i* Lainie Shimazu. She will conduct you to my daughter's home. You may trust her as much as you trust your Smoke Jaguar bodyguard."

Victor gave the woman a quick bow. "I am in good hands, then."

She returned his bow, but said nothing and drifted toward the palace foyer to give him and Theodore a last moment alone.

The Coordinator shook his head. "I apologize for having kept you so long, both in the briefing and here, waiting for me to bring Lainie back to you."

"Not a problem, Theodore." Victor smiled. "Today I've been given a lot to think about, and I was just getting a head start on it all."

25

Musashi House
Imperial City, Luthien
Pesht Military District, Draconis Combine
2 April 3061

Though wearing a uniform had been part of his daily routine for as long as he could remember, Victor felt uneasy in the one he wore now. It no longer seemed to fit him. He wanted to shed it as a snake sheds skin, and he knew, in that analogy, he had mixed feelings. Yes, he had outgrown the uniform and would be well rid of it, yet he felt like a reptile for itching so for the change. *This will be taken as a betrayal by some, and I can't say I blame them.*

Victor stepped to the center of the small stage in Musashi House. The bright lights from the holocameras made it difficult for him to see the audience as much more than silhouettes, but he knew who they were. He'd seen their uniforms as they came in—an officer or enlisted person from every unit that had been in the task force, as well as the commanders of the national contingents. Though the uniforms varied, all the warriors had a Star League Defense Force patch sewn on the shoulder, and a series of tabs below denoting the battles fought in the war against the Clans.

In the two weeks since his arrival, Victor had tried to avoid anything approaching duty and, thankfully, no one had tried to disturb him. Kai's wife and children had come to Luthien to welcome Kai home, and Theodore had made available to them one of the family's vacation palaces on a small island in the southern hemisphere. Victor had spent time with Yvonne and was pleased to see how supportive Tancred was of her. She again apologized and he accepted, though he was sure he'd have to keep on accepting her apologies until Yvonne herself began to believe she'd really been forgiven.

Most of his time had been spent with Omi and she was a delightful salve and tonic for him. Their physical intimacy brought Victor back into himself and made him capable of feeling again. It anchored him in a reality that was pleasant and pleasurable and as diametrically opposed to warfare as it was possible to be. He had spent the last two and a half years in combat, on a constant war footing, and Omi's soft presence, her sweet scent and midnight whispers, returned him to a world that did not have killing as its focus.

Her solicitousness of his needs meant that she anticipated what he wanted in all areas of his life. Until he dressed himself for the speech he would give, he'd not seen a single one of his uniforms. His meals ranged from mundane and very standard Federated Commonwealth fare to exotic dishes that suited him perfectly when he felt adventurous. Omi was nowhere to be seen when he wanted to be alone, and present when he couldn't stand to be alone.

He had no doubt that she truly was his other half, the part of him that had been missing all his life, and without whom he would die. He became convinced of this when, working in her garden, he'd pricked a finger on a rose. Omi, who was seated a few steps away reading, immediately looked up, though he'd not cried out or jerked his hand away nor given any other sign of his injury. She crossed to him on cat's-feet, produced a handkerchief to bind the wound, and kissed his finger to banish the pain.

And the next morning he awoke to find proper gardening attire laid out for him, including a pair of gloves.

As the days passed, Victor's focus sharpened and he knew he would have to make this speech. Now, as he stepped up to the podium and adjusted the microphone's height, all the various versions of the speech flashed through his mind. There had been no clear-cut best way to say what he wanted to say. Some phrases sounded pompous, and others saccharine. He wanted something that would convey what he felt to the warriors he'd led without any hidden messages. *Things are too tense now to allow any misunderstandings.*

"My greetings to all of you, both present in this auditorium and throughout Luthien and in orbit. I apologize for interrupting your holidays, for I know all of you need, deserve, and have well earned your time off. Two and a half years ago the Lords of the Star League authorized our war against the Smoke Jaguars, and all of us predicted it would take years to win. Yes, we said years, plural, but none of us expected it would be just *two* years." Victor smiled broadly. "Had I known how well you would fight, I would have suggested we plan for months, and a low number of them as well."

Mild laughter rippled through the audience, and Victor could imagine beer mugs and sake cups being raised across Luthien.

"As I am certain all of you know by now, the Federated Commonwealth has undergone a change in leadership during the time of our battles against the Clans. My sister, Katherine, was invited to assume control of the Federated Commonwealth for the good of the citizenry. This she did in December of last year and does not seemed inclined to relinquish her position. In fact, the same message of greeting you all got from her here on Luthien also came to me, but it came attached to many of my personal belongings. Apparently she is renting out my rooms on New Avalon, so if any of you need a place to stay, the view is wonderful. . . ."

More laughter filtered through the audience, and Victor flashed a smile that he knew would infuriate his sister. He let the laughter die, then continued.

"In the past two weeks I have heard from many of you . . ." He hesitated for a moment to let the thickening in his throat ease. "Both from Federated Commonwealth units and others, saying you would be ready to fight alongside me to depose her. Your willingness to step back into the hell we have all returned from on my behalf touches me more deeply than you will ever know. That you would again trust me with your lives is the highest praise I can imagine. I had thought there was no way I could be *more* proud of you, and I am happily proved wrong."

Victor lifted his chin, stretching out his throat. "I consider your trust in me to be sacred, and it forces me to make a difficult decision. That decision is simply this: do I have a right to bring war to the Inner Sphere, to involve you and your loved ones and the citizens of countless worlds in a blood orgy that will return me to the leadership of a shattered realm? The answer is clear: I have no such right.

"Some will argue that I have a *duty* to do that, but I would disagree. My duty, *our* duty, is to keep people safe. This was the reason that we fought the Clans, and our commitment to that duty was why we defeated the Clans. To go to war with my sister now would be to mock everything we have done to secure peace for the Inner Sphere. I will not do that to you or to the memories of those we love who have died in this cause."

Victor pulled a water glass from a shelf in the podium and drank a little to ease the dryness in his mouth. "My mandate to lead you ended once we again reached the Inner Sphere. I know you will all soon be receiving orders to return to your homes, to see your families and friends, and I am very glad you have that opportunity. I know some of you are thinking it's a pity I've been robbed of that same joy, but I haven't, really. For the past two years, *you* have been my family. Knowing you are back where you want to be means I recover the joy of a homecoming from each and every one of you. My personal pain will dissolve in the ocean of your happiness."

He stared straight into the holocamera at the back of the hall. "Because our mission is at an end, I have tendered my resignation to the First Lord. I have done this in part because I am tired of war, but more I do this because of all of you. A soldier could never hope to have a greater collection of brave men and women in his command. It has been my distinct honor and a sincere privilege to serve with you. I wish you all peace and godspeed and safe journeys home. You are the heroes of the Clan war, never forget that, no matter what. You won a future for the Inner Sphere. Now that future is yours to shape and live. Go, live it, be happy. That is my final order to you all, and one I expect you to carry out."

Applause, solemn and proper, rippled through the audience. Victor stepped away from the podium and when he looked up again, he saw the soldiers had all risen to their feet. A lump materialized in his throat and he could feel his chest tighten. His heels clicked as he stood at attention and snapped his right hand up in a crisp salute. In an instant the applause died as the assembled soldiers aped him and returned the salute as one.

Victor bowed to them, then retreated to the stage's wings. He slipped out through a side door and into a waiting hover-limo in which he'd expected to find only his driver and Tiaret Nevversan. To his surprise he found three other people waiting for him as well, two of whom he recognized immediately. Seated next to Jerry Cranston was Curaitis, the agent he had sent out two years earlier to find evidence against his sister. Next to Curaitis, across from Victor, sat a petite woman who looked vaguely familiar.

Victor leaned forward, a big smile on his face, and offered Curaitis his hand. "It's good to see you again."

"And you, Highness."

"How did you get here?"

"We got here."

Jerry Cranston laughed easily at Curaitis' taciturn response. "They arrived on a freighter that made planetfall two days ago. They couldn't find a way to reach you, so Curaitis tracked me down in Kubeto and I brought him here. Then I had a devil of a time talking Tiaret into letting us wait for you here."

Victor smiled. "You see, Curaitis, to replace you I had to take on someone from the Clans. You should feel honored."

"Could be a good choice. We'll see."

Jerry shook his head. "Neither of them is sure the other is a suitable guard for you. They're going to find a dojo and work out their differences."

Victor nodded toward the young woman across from him. "Curaitis, who is this?"

"Francesca Jenkins."

That name sparked a memory in Victor's brain. Jenkins had originally been a Free Worlds League sleeper agent in the Federated Commonwealth. She had been the source of information that let Thomas Marik know that his son, Joshua, who had been on New Avalon for treatment of his leukemia, had died. Subsequently she herself almost died preventing assassins from getting to the double Victor had put in Joshua's place. Curaitis and others had been successful in turning Jenkins into a loyal FedCom agent and she had been set on the trail of Sven Newmark.

Victor shook her hand. "It's a pleasure, Ms. Jenkins."

"More so mine, Highness."

The Prince unbuttoned his uniform jacket and sat back as the limo's engine started and the vehicle rose on a cushion of air. "What have you got?"

Curaitis looked at Francesca, so she began her report. "We found Sven Newmark in his identity as Reginald Starling, an avant garde, neo-gothic artist on New Exford. I befriended him and, over the course of fourteen months, managed to get him to trust me. I wanted him to give me his diaries and records of his service with Ryan Steiner of his own free will, and I believe he would have, but Loki agents working for your sister found him and killed him.

"Reg had taken precautions—he was paranoid, with good reason. After his death I recovered two ROM-disks full of information. One contained a vast library of books and the other what appeared to be a dump of information from whatever noteputer he'd used while working for Ryan. I isolated what I thought were likely his diaries and found they were encrypted."

Victor nodded. "Were you able to decipher them?"

Francesca blushed. "Eventually. I should have been able to do it sooner because Reg had given me the key to his cipher, but I wasn't thinking straight at the time. He'd encrypted the diaries using a nearly unbreakable code that matches a word in a message to a page/paragraph/word designation in another book. If you don't have the proper book, you can't crack the code."

"It's an ancient technique, Highness, and one we often use." Cranston smiled. "As she said, without the key book, you can't break the code."

"But, Francesca, you said Newmark left behind a disk full of books, so the key must have been one of them, right?"

"Yes, Highness, that's what I thought as well." She glanced down at her hands for a second. "I ran his coded diaries against every volume on the library ROM and came up with gibberish. Nothing made sense. I couldn't figure out why it didn't work. I thought maybe Reg had gotten into the book files and scrambled pages themselves to encrypt the key book on one level or another, so I sat down and started reading the books to see if they made sense. I even obtained copies of the books from elsewhere to compare them, but computer comparisons showed the text matched identically."

Victor arched an eyebrow. "They were identical?"

"Yes, Highness, the *text* was identical, but the books were not. Though I had two copies of the same book in the computer for comparison purposes, and the text matched, the book parameters themselves did not. The books on Reg's disk were either longer or shorter, and often by a good margin of pages."

"Why?"

"Page count on a book is an illusion, Highness. The length depends on the size of the typeface used and whether or not the type font is proportional or not. Literally the same number of words can be spread out over any number of pages, making a fat book thin or a short book long.

"This got me thinking, and I started to go back through the memory dump disk. I pulled up the various fonts Reg had on the disk and discovered one called *No Secrets*. Now Reg had given me a painting titled *No Secrets X*, which I took to be the tenth in a series by that name, but it also could have been a directive to use *No Secrets* the font, in ten-point size, to reformat his encryption keys. I did that and ran decrypts and we now have everything."

"Everything?"

Jerry Cranston nodded. "Newmark was good. He kept complete records with a key to the codenames they used to defeat listening devices. He has a detailed description of the plan to have your mother killed and how it would be paid for. It checked out perfectly with what we learned five years ago. Newmark directed Sergei Chou to send an assassin after the Archon, and the payment was arranged thanks to your sister. Chou bought worthless wetlands, then a corporation bought them from him for an inflated price, then gave the land to the government of the Federated Commonwealth to become a nature preserve. The corporation got a tax deduction for the donation and the CEO was ennobled and given a land grant at Katherine's suggestion."

"We've got her, we've finally got her." Victor blinked away amazement, then frowned. "But, with Newmark being dead, she'll claim we've manufactured this evidence. And, without a nation to back me, I can't even bring this up before the Lords of the Star League."

He smiled ruefully. "Hell, I don't even pay your salaries anymore. You're really working for her."

Curaitis shook his head. "Think you've got a monopoly on resignations, do you?"

Francesca's eyes sharpened. "I will not work for the woman who murdered her mother and had my friend Reg Starling murdered. Agent Curaitis and I have been talking about a number of things we can do to get more evidence on your sister. We might not be able to get her for killing your mother, but we can gather evidence of her trying to hush up her link. Obstruction of justice doesn't seem like much, but, in this case, it could be enough to trip her up."

The Prince sat back and rubbed a hand along his jaw. "There's a part of me that wants to wash my hands of all of this, of all the trouble, but she murdered my mother. We're the only people who know that for certain—well, outside my sister, that is. If you're going to go after her, it will have to be quiet. When you get enough evidence we can ask her step down or threaten to go public. You'll need a light touch—you're not going to pot her from a rooftop with a rifle, are you?"

"No, Highness." Francesca shook her head. "Your sister, she likes Byzantine plots and all. We've got a gem for her. We'll keep her off balance and get as much proof against her as we can. When we've got her dead to rights, we'll turn it all over to you and you can decide what to do."

"Okay, that works." Victor smiled carefully. "Jerry, do I actually have any money or anything to help them out?"

Francesca shook her head firmly. "Don't worry, Highness. Reg gave me enough to land his killer, or at least to start. We'll get funding as we need it along the way."

Jerry smiled. "Keep receipts."

Curaitis glared at him. "Where we're going to go, and with what we're going to do, there won't be any receipts."

Victor leaned forward. "Then be very careful."

Francesca glanced at Curaitis, then gave Victor a smile. "We will, Highness, as if our very lives depended upon it."

26

Palace of Serene Sanctuary
Imperial City, Luthien
Pesht Military District, Draconis Combine
16 April 3061

Victor Davion straightened up slowly, pressing a gloved hand to the small of his back. He let the muscles of his back stretch out for a second and luxuriated in the pain that slowly faded. Then he rocked back and unfolded his legs, heaving himself to his feet. His thighs protested mightily and he staggered a step backward, spraying white, crushed-marble stones back behind himself.

Smiling, he pulled the glove from his right hand and offered it to Kai. "This is a pleasant surprise."

"Good to see you, too." Kai jerked a thumb at Tiaret's retreating form. "Someone blacked her eye but good. Your work?"

Victor shook his head. "Curaitis. They went best out of five falls and that was his best shot."

"Oh. So how long will he be in the hospital?"

"She took it easy on him. He limped away." Victor tipped his big straw hat back and let it dangle against his shoulder blades by a piece of cord lying against his throat. "How was your time on Komadorishima? Omi says it can be beautiful this time of year."

"It was wonderful. If you don't pay attention to the minimal tech, it would be easy to believe you were vacationing a couple of millennia ago in feudal Japan." Kai frowned. "Aside from lights and some really basic stuff, they've got no electronics there at all. I guess that's why you didn't call me before you resigned. I didn't know about it until I got back to Imperial City, in fact. No holovision receivers or players out there."

The hurt in Kai's voice stabbed deep into Victor. "I wanted to talk to you about that, Kai, but I didn't want to spoil your time with Deirdre and David and Melissa. How are they, by the way."

"Fine, Victor. Thanks for asking. Don't change the subject."

"Right, sorry." Victor waved Kai a bit deeper into the garden, toward a stone bench, and waited until his friend had taken a seat before he continued. "Kai, I know you. I know you would have offered very good and very cogent arguments for why I shouldn't resign. I would have listened to them all and weighed them and your final comment would have carried the most weight. You would have said to me, 'Victor, whatever you decide, I'll support you.' "

Kai frowned, then reached up into the branches of the low-hanging tree above him and plucked a pink cherry blossom. "How are you so sure I wouldn't have dissuaded you?"

"What could you have said, Kai? If I tried to remain as the head of the SLDF, Sun-Tzu would just have fired me. The Commander-in-Chief of the SLDF serves at the sufferance of the First Lord. I would have been stripped of power, which would have thrilled Sun-Tzu no end, and Katherine right along with him. The SLDF's loyalties would have been divided and the movement to have me kick Katherine off New Avalon would have taken on a life of its own. Hell, there are already rumors of people pledging their fealty to Arthur if he decides to oppose her."

"But you, Victor, walking away?" Kai twirled the pink flower around in his fingers. "I don't get it."

"Didn't you walk away from the military, too, Kai?" Victor gave him a wry grin. "I seem to recall your being Solaris' Champion, don't I?"

Kai's expression soured further. "Deirdre said you'd point that out."

"Smart woman, your wife." Victor sighed and sat down next to Kai. "Look, my friend, I've been kicked out of my home, stripped of power, and you know what? I don't think I've ever felt better. The pressure on my shoulders is lifted. I can be here, with Omi, and I don't have billions of people thinking I'm going to be giving their world to Theodore as part of Omi's bride price."

He fingered the front of his denim overalls. "This gardening stuff, it's a bit more difficult than I ever thought it would be. My back and legs hurt worse than they ever did in a 'Mech, but it's different."

He stood and tugged Kai over to a brown patch of earth in the garden. "There, you see, down there, those little green things. Those are flowers. Nasturtiums, I think—my Japanese is getting pretty good, but some technical terms escape me still. But, see, I planted those flowers and they're coming up."

"That's good, Victor, but you're too talented at what you do to remain here as a gardener."

"You're missing my point, Kai." Victor looked up into Kai's gray eyes. "This is the first time I've done something truly productive. I mean, you have David and Melissa as your contributions to the progression of life in the universe. Omi and I, someday, maybe, we'll have kids, but right now I'm exploring this. I'm working with my hands, I'm doing all the things that all the people who used to look to me for leadership do. Until I got dirt under my fingernails I didn't realize how isolated I really was."

He dug into his pocket and pulled out a fistful of crumpled Combine yen notes. "Do you have any idea how long it's been since I've actually carried money around with me? Not since getting out of the Nagelring, I think. I didn't know the price of milk or a cabbage or meat or anything. The concerns of the people I ruled were as alien to me as my ways were to them."

"But, Victor, you had other concerns, very strong concerns that you had to deal with." Kai rested his hands on Victor's shoulders. "Yes, you can lower yourself to the point where worrying about the price of milk or rice or cabbage is your main concern, but very few people can elevate themselves to the point where they can deal with the fate of nations. That's what you've been trained for.

"Make no mistake about it, Victor, I think you'll make a damned fine gardener, if you want to. With your drive I have no doubt you'll be turning out the Inner Sphere's finest roses and orchids or whatever you want to grow. There will be no stopping you. In fact, the only person who can stop you is you."

"I know." Victor looked down at the ground. "Minoru said some curious stuff to me on my first night here. He talked about my being a weapon and that, right now, I've been slipped into a scabbard. I guess, Kai, I just need time in the scabbard."

Kai's hands fell away from the Prince's shoulders. "I can understand it, Victor. I just don't know that now is the time for it."

"I know." Victor's breath hissed between his teeth. "If I were still in charge of the Federated Commonwealth, Sun-Tzu wouldn't be occupying the Compact. Data we get here is sketchy, but I guess things are heating up."

Kai nodded. "They are."

"You going down there to fight?"

"Not determined yet." Kai folded his arms across his chest. "I hope something is resolved before Tharkad. When I got back to Imperial City I had my invitation to the second Whitting Conference. Deirdre, David, and Melissa also had invites."

"A week ago they came for Theodore, his wife, Tomoe, Omi, and Hohiro. Yvonne and Tancred have also been invited."

"Nothing for you?"

"You've got to be kidding." Victor smiled. "Minoru and I will be 'batching it' while you're all gone."

"That sounds like fun."

"You don't know Minoru." Victor shook his head. "Actually I thought I'd head down to Komadorishima during the time of the conference. If I didn't, I'd be a junkie for any news coming out, and I know Katherine is going to have it all prepackaged. I'd just puke."

Kai got a mischievous grin on his face. "While Katherine is away from New Avalon, you ought to get Phelan and his Wolves to help you take it back."

"Now, there's a thought." The Prince shrugged. "Unfortunately Katherine invited Phelan, his sister, and their father to the conference. I thought Morgan was going to actually have to marry Candace before that happened, but I guess Katherine is adhering to the old dictum: keep your friends close and your enemies closer."

"Then she's making a mistake letting you be so far away."

"Could be, my friend, could be." Victor offered Kai his hand again. "Please give my best to everyone you see there who would care and, if you're not straight off to St. Ives after that, let me know how things went."

"I'll be your eyes and ears, Victor."

"Thanks, my friend." He walked Kai back into the palace. "Oh, yes, be sure to thank Sun-Tzu for his note."

"What?"

"Yeah, you haven't seen it. I had it framed." Victor led Kai down a small corridor to a where a framed message hung on the wall. "ComStar says he'll be sending me something more official, on Star League stationery and all, but this will do until the real thing arrives."

Kai peered closely at the document. "It is with great reluctance, Victor Davion, that I, Sun-Tzu Liao, First Lord of the Star League and Chancellor of the Capellan Confederation, do accept your resignation from the Star League Defense Force. In recognition of your service, I present you this hearty commendation for all you have done." Jaw open, he turned and looked at Victor. "That's it? That's all you get for kicking the Clans' collective butt?"

"It reads best in English. The German is pretty sad."

Kai peered closely at the Chinese translation. "You don't read Chinese, do you?"

"Nope."

"Just as well. You wouldn't like it."

"What a surprise." Victor sighed. "See why gardening looks like a nice alternative?"

"Yeah, I guess I do." Kai straightened up. "Well, I can promise you one thing that will come out of the Whitting Conference, and it's that the Lords will vote you a real commendation. This is a disgrace and I won't stand for it."

"Careful, Kai. You don't want to get involved in politics."

"No, I just want the others to think they don't want me involved. There's a difference."

"Politically noted."

"I learned well from you, Victor." Kai gave him a big smile. "And if it turns out I need some gardening done on St. Ives . . . ?"

"I don't know if I'm ever going to want to get back in the

traces, Kai. We'll have to see." Victor slapped him on the back. "No promises, my friend, but if I do come, I'll bring an OmniMech and we'll clear some serious acreage."

27

Kai Allard-Liao gave his wife a grateful smile as she surreptitiously smoothed the lapel on his jacket in the middle of the packed ballroom. "Thanks. Just one more thing to get used to."

Deirdre Lear returned his smile. "Actually, I like you better in a business suit like this, instead of a uniform. It's more subtle, more like you."

"I hope you're right." He frowned slightly. "You're not having problems with my doing this, are you? Since I've known you I've wanted nothing but to avoid politics, and here I am slipping into this stuff. To make matters worse, I'm a babe in the woods compared to the wolves lurking here."

Deirdre's blue eyes sparkled. "Kai, there are two things that are constants about you. The first is that you always do the utmost you can to help others. I've seen it firsthand and even though this tendency makes you do things you don't want to do, you go forward with your actions. You'd rather be miserable than to have someone else be miserable, and such a quality in a leader is a very good thing."

"But, Deirdre, you make it sound as if . . ."

She pressed a finger to his lips. "I'm not finished, my dear. The second thing about you is that you always excel at what you do. Prince Davion may learn very well and quickly, but you intuit a lot, and your learning abilities are not shabby at all. Your enemies won't know what hit them."

Kai rubbed a hand over his forehead. "But there's so much change now, so many things going on. Victor is out of power, Sun-Tzu has occupied the St. Ives Compact, and we have open warfare there." He sighed. "I've even heard a rumor the Precentor Martial might resign."

"But change is not all bad, Kai, and change means there are openings for you to move forward and establish yourself." Deirdre stroked his arm with a hand. "I want what you want, my love; and I know you want what is best for your people and friends. You'll find a way to get it. You'll grow into the role of a statesman."

"I will do my best to make you proud."

"You always do." Deirdre gave him a wink, then broadened her smile as a tall, black-haired man in gray Wolf Clan leathers approached them. "Khan Kell, it is an honor."

Phelan Kell smiled openly. "All mine, Dr. Lear. Kai, glad to see you back from Strana Mechty. From what I hear, you put Vlad down hard."

Kai, aware of his wife's discomfort, nodded. "He was an able foe. I could have the holocam footage of the battle sent to you."

"Already have it, from Vlad's point of view." Phelan's green eyes twinkled. "He has his agents, I have mine. You piloted a *Stormcrow* and beat him. That is no mean feat."

"Alas, we did not defeat the Wolves, but achieved a draw."

Phelan's leathers groaned as he shrugged his shoulders. "I could not prevent Katherine from taking Victor's realm, so neither of us were able to do for him what he asked us to do. My failure is the greater, of course."

Kai arched an eyebrow. "But what could you have done? If you had taken all your troops and conquered New Avalon, you would have put all of the Federated Commonwealth behind Katherine. There are enough people in the Inner Sphere who think your defection from the Wolves is a sham that you would have initiated a new war by your action."

Pain flashed through Phelan's eyes, and a weariness entered his voice. "You are right, of course, which is exactly what I have told myself every day since Katherine displaced Yvonne. In fact, I need to apologize to Yvonne for failing her. Have you seen her?"

Kai shook his head.

"I understand she's here," offered Deirdre. "I've not seen her either, but I believe Katherine ensconced her in the old château that Victor used as a getaway three years ago. I'm certain that has elevated her mood. When I last saw her on Luthien she was sliding into a severe depression."

"Not a good thing." Phelan's eyes focused distantly, then he narrowed his eyes. "Katherine has a lot to answer for. Part of me was hoping Victor would come back and roll over her, but I guess not."

Kai nodded slowly. "I last spoke in person with him in April. I think, at that time, he was just tired of war. I can't blame him. I even envy him a bit."

Phelan winced. "But become a gardener? Fighting aphids? I don't know. I thought Victor was made of sterner stuff."

"I think you will find, Khan Kell, that Victor still is made of sterner stuff." Omi Kurita touched the Wolf lightly on the shoulder and slipped into the circle between him and Deirdre. "Forgive my interruption, but I bear you all greetings from

248 Michael A. Stackpole

Victor. He wished very much to be remembered to you and said he wished he could be here."

"Thank you, Lady Omi." Kai bowed his head to her. "You will, of course, convey our best wishes to him. In fact, if you are returning immediately to Luthien, I have some things I would like to send to Victor."

"It would be my pleasure to carry them for you."

Phelan glanced down at Omi. "You said Victor still had his spine, but he is abandoning his people."

"No, Khan Kell, I said Victor was yet made of sterner stuff. Right now he has shifted his focus. He approaches gardening—and all of life—with the same intensity and passion he had for warfare. He is quite the same person you remember, but now he is embracing life, very much in a way he has never done before."

Kai nodded. "That's just about what he told me as well. Phelan, you never were isolated from real people—while your grandfather ruled Arc-Royal, you grew up with the Kell Hounds. Your career wasn't one of privilege and, as I recall, you did your best to reject all trappings of privilege that being Victor's cousin could have afforded you. And then, when you were taken by the Clans, you were a bondsman who worked his way up to becoming a Khan. You earned the respect you are given. Victor, born to privilege, never had a chance to face the challenges you did. He never had a normal life."

"This is one hell of a time to be looking for a normal life." Phelan shook his head. "No disrespect intended, but I expected better of Victor. I know this is a tough time for him, but he should be here."

"Should he, Khan Kell?" Deirdre's blue eyes became slits. "He has no standing here. For him to come and be turned away would be a tremendous loss of prestige. And you are missing the whole question of whether or not he feels he has any right to tear his realm apart with a civil war."

"Good points, Doctor, but I've been hearing that a civil war is brewing anyway." Phelan folded his arms across his chest.

"Arthur is fomenting trouble in the Draconis March, and various worlds that have rejected Katherine's power grab are facing serious shortages of imported items. Katherine doesn't seem interested in using troops to maintain order, but she will cause food shortages and disrupt economies to bring rebel planets to heel."

Omi reached out and rested a hand on Phelan's arm. "I would very much appreciate your giving me information about these worlds, so that I may communicate it to Victor."

Phelan's eyes narrowed. "So, you are not comfortable with Victor as gardener, either."

"I did not say that, Khan Kell." Omi's voice shrank to a whisper. "In my culture a warrior is lauded for being practiced in many different arts. Gardening, poetry, painting, all of these are acceptable."

Phelan rolled his eyes. "I remember reading some of Victor's poetry. If he's as much a gardener as he was a poet, I hope you have someone cleaning up after him."

Omi smiled for a moment. "*Hai*, Khan Kell, the gardens do not suffer. Victor, however, is withdrawing. As I left with my father to come here, Victor traveled to Komadorishima. Going there is to retreat from the world and from this age."

"It *is* very peaceful. Deirdre and I very much enjoyed our time there."

"Yes, but one goes there to contemplate the future, or to bask in the peace, not to hide from the world." Omi looked up and Kai felt the electricity in her blue-eyed gaze. "The lion in Victor slumbers, but it is important that someone awaken it."

The circle widened yet again as the Precentor Martial joined them. "You will find, Lady Omi, that the lion sleeps, but sleeps lightly. At your suggestion I visited Victor at Komadorishima after you departed. Though he claims no interest in what is happening here, he questioned me most keenly and has asked for reports afterward."

Kai raised a hand to shoulder height. "He asked me for the same sort of reports in April."

"Your concern over Victor is understandable, Lady Omi." Focht smiled very indulgently. "It is true, he is tired of fighting, but, more important, his responsibilities to the Star League and the Federated Commonwealth were ended at the same time. In essence, he lost momentum in his life and, for the first time, he has had a chance to rest. I find it difficult to begrudge him that rest."

Phelan smiled carefully. "The way you say that, it sounds as if you would like a rest as well."

Focht threw his head back in a throaty laugh. "Ah, rumors of my supposed resignation have already begun to circulate. I think you will find the Precentor Martial has lots of work yet to do, especially now that Victor has retired from public life."

The Wolf Khan frowned. "I never thought you had a taste for politics, especially in the Federated Suns half of the Federated Commonwealth."

Focht adjusted his eyepatch. "ComStar still maintains considerable assets in every nation of the Inner Sphere, save the League. Moreover, because we facilitate communications, we learn of many difficulties and would not be human if we did not suffer with the people of various worlds. Clearly, as was done over thirty years ago, a communications interdiction can be used to encourage compliance with humanitarian efforts on behalf of citizens. In the event of such an interdiction, the protection of ComStar's relay stations will be vital. We are not looking at conquest, but maintaining a defensive posture. Outside of that, we still have the question of what the Wolves will do when the truce expires. The Precentor Martial has plenty to keep him busy."

Kai smiled. "In fact, now that we only have six Lords in the Star League Council, you may be called upon to break ties, which is yet another duty for you."

"I think I would prefer combat."

"It is combat, Precentor Martial, just with more subtle weapons." Kai laughed. "I'd much prefer waging it from a 'Mech cockpit than a suit, though."

"Indeed." Focht bowed his head. "If you will excuse me, I see one of my aides looking for me."

Kai glanced off along the Precentor Martial's line of sight and saw a robed and hooded ComStar acolyte. *Red means Precentor, I think.* He shrugged. *I guess those sorts of details are the things I need to concentrate on now.*

As he turned back he saw Focht had departed, but a pretty young woman with long brown hair and brown eyes had joined them. She hugged Omi, then smiled at the rest of them. "I hope I'm not interrupting anything." She looked down sadly. "Duke Allard-Liao, I want to convey to you my deep regret at the state of affairs in St. Ives. I very much tried to convince Sun-Tzu that what he was doing was disruptive and foolish, but he did not listen to me. I know that probably sounds false coming from me, but . . ."

The pain in her voice sounded genuine to him, so Kai gave her a quick smile. "Isis, I thank you for using your influence over my cousin, and I regret as deeply as you that he did not heed your advice."

Isis Marik nodded, her lips pressed together in a solid line. "Thank you. I, ah, well, thanks."

Deirdre reached out and took one of the younger woman's hands into her own. "What is it, dear?"

Isis brushed a single tear away. "I'm sorry, I, ah, I just, ah, get a bit confused. Sun-Tzu has been distant, and growing more so. And my father's got a new son, a *legitimate* child, so my value in the universe is shrinking."

Kai struggled to conceal his surprise at seeing Isis in such a state. He didn't know her well, but she'd always seemed cool and collected.

Omi laid a hand on Isis' shoulder. "You have never struck me as one to see your own value as that placed on you by others. You were strong enough to endure at Hustaing. You have strength and worth even if your role as a political bargaining chip is over."

"But, Omi, I have not been prepared for a role as you have."

Phelan gave her a smile. "But you're smart enough to find yourself one."

Deirdre rolled her eyes. "I think, Phelan, you're missing her point. The role you wanted, Isis, was at Sun-Tzu's right hand. You still love him, don't you?"

Isis nodded mutely.

Phelan started to say something, but Kai reached out and poked him in the shoulder. "Don't. We're way out of our depth here, I think."

Deirdre looked at Kai and shot him a sharp glance. "That's right. You boys should go mingle or something—just try not to start any wars."

Phelan arched an eyebrow. "Now, where is the fun in that?"

Kai pulled Phelan away as the trio of women retreated toward one of the Grand Ballroom's corners. "Let them deal with Isis. I feel for her because I know my cousin can be very nasty and likely will discard her now that Thomas has someone who will no doubt take her place in the succession. Sun-Tzu can do better—at least he will think so."

"Better?" Phelan blinked. "Katherine?"

"I could wish. They would deserve each other." Kai smiled as he decided *that* marriage would be measured not in anniversaries but nanoseconds. "No, I was thinking the Periphery or, perhaps, Yvonne."

"Yvonne?" Phelan frowned. "I would think Sun-Tzu would be smarter than to again allow himself to have a realm dangled before him the way Thomas has been doing. Now, one of the Periphery states, that might work. Expand his realm bloodlessly, threaten either the FedCom or the League in doing so. Since things are not going well in St. Ives, he might need to do that."

"Well, whatever he's going to be doing, at least it won't be as the First Lord of the Star League." Kai shook his head. "It will be another fifteen years before he can drop into that post."

"I wonder how many of the people here will still be alive in fifteen years?" The Wolf's question came solemnly. "Kai, are you going to go fight in St. Ives?"

"I don't know yet. I'm going to do whatever is required to keep my homeland free. Right now my mother thinks my best use is here, so I'm here."

"Being here would be Victor's best use, too." Phelan sighed. "Then again, if Sun-Tzu takes St. Ives and Katherine decides to destroy the Arc-Royal Defense Cordon, maybe we'll just have to go to Luthien and help Victor in his war on aphids."

"I hope, my friend," Kai said, resting a hand on Phelan's shoulder, "it never comes to that."

28

**Royal Court, The Triad
Tharkad City, Tharkad
District of Donegal, Federated Commonwealth
3 November 3061**

Kai sighed. *Perhaps fighting aphids would be an improvement on this.* Sun-Tzu, as the First Lord of the Star League, presided over the meeting of the Lords and dictated the details of the various ceremonies surrounding the meeting. For this, the first session of the Council meeting, he had insisted upon full recognition for all the delegates and their aides, which produced hours of tedious introductions.

The council chamber had been set up much as Kai remembered it from three years earlier. The Grand Ballroom that housed the welcoming reception had been again transformed into a meeting hall. The long staircase down which each delegate entered was behind the speaker's podium. To the right of it sat a table for the Capellan Confederation, and to the right of that table was the one designated for the Draconis Combine. Next came the Free Worlds League and directly opposite the podium sat the table for the Federated Commonwealth. The St. Ives table diagonally opposed the Capellan Confederation table, placing it immediately to Katherine's right, then the Free Rasalhague Republic, and finally ComStar to the left of the podium.

At the first meeting ComStar and Rasalhague shared a table, but now Rasalhague has the one that would have been reserved for Victor's Federated Commonwealth. Kai glanced to his left at Katherine sitting at her table, her expression serene, but her eyes so very cold. Yvonne sat behind her and looked to be a million light years away. Kai wished Deirdre was there with him because she would be able to tell if Katherine had Yvonne doped up and presented as a show piece.

Because the St. Ives Compact was seen as one of the lesser nations of the Inner Sphere, Kai, his mother, Morgan Kell, and Phelan had been announced first and had to endure the parade of other delegates trickling into the room. Morgan Kell had been granted admission as an aide to Candace Liao, likewise Phelan. The Arc-Royal Defense Cordon might as well have been a realm unto itself. But Katherine had chosen to ignore the fact that Morgan wanted nothing to do with her. She still claimed it as part of her nation. If Morgan declared his full independence, Katherine would fight to pull him back into the fold, weakening the Lyran half of the Federated Commonwealth and allowing the Jade Falcons to sweep into the military vacuum left behind.

After them came the Free Rasalhague Republic, then ComStar and the Combine. The Free Worlds League came next, followed by Katherine—though here, in her realm, she was announced as Katrina. Kali Liao, the auburn-haired leader of a Thugee death cult, led the Capellan Confederation delegation down to the floor, then everyone waited for Sun-Tzu to appear.

Preceding him were members of the Black Watch Regiment, the First Lord's new personal bodyguard. They took up positions on the stairs as a ripple of barely concealed shock ran through the room. *So that's where they are. We should have known, considering who and what they are, that regardless of who holds the office of First Lord, they would be by his side.*

Next Sun-Tzu arrived. He was resplendent in a golden Han jacket worked with black tigers on the breasts and sleeves. The cloth of gold all but glowed, and the expression on Katherine's face showed she thought the display was so ostentatious as to be absurd, but Kai realized what was truly going on. *Gold was a color forbidden to all but the Emperor in Old China. The people of the Capellan Confederation will see him here, leading his peers, as imperial as ever. This show is for their benefit, not ours.*

Kai smiled, pleased that his jacket, likewise reminiscent of ancient Asian styling, had been cut from red cloth, but was embroidered with golden dragons. In China, the emperors had been seen as being dragons. The jacket, which his mother had supplied him, suggested subtly to Sun-Tzu that Kai was willing to oppose him as heir to the Liao throne. While that was the last thing Kai ever wanted, he knew it was a fear Sun-Tzu had long harbored, and doing anything that could unsettle him would be useful in the Compact's cause.

The Black Watch sergeant at arms announced Sun-Tzu in a loud and clear voice. "Lord and Ladies, I present to you His Excellency, the Duke of Castrovia, the Grand Duke of Sian, Chancellor of the Capellan Confederation, the First Lord of the Star League and Conqueror of the Clans, Sun-Tzu Liao."

Conqueror of the Clans? Kai exchanged glances across the way with Hohiro and shivered. *Yes, he was First Lord when the Clans were defeated, but he did nothing to help the cause.* He felt anger building in him as that phrase kept ringing in his ears. Normally he would have shunted his anger away, but he held on to it, letting it pool inside him.

Sun-Tzu slowly descended the steps, looking stately and calm, as if he were above any of the mundane political concerns of the assembly. His jet-black hair had been slicked back and golden lights flashed across it with each step. His jade eyes remained focused on a point well beyond Katherine. Finally he reached the floor, the heels of his boots clicking loudly on the parquet, then he mounted the steps to the podium dais and leaned forward on the podium as if he bore burdens that would have crushed a lesser man.

"We welcome you all to this tri-annual meeting of the Council of Lords—this second Whitting Conference. We thank Archon First Princess Katrina Steiner for her graciousness in hosting us yet again. Her willingness to organize these meetings speaks of her vast concern for the future of the Inner Sphere. Her contributions to the stability and safety of us all cannot be underestimated or ignored."

That remark can be taken two ways. Kai looked toward Katherine and saw her cheeks reddening. *And she took it the second way. Is Sun-Tzu warning us that her rapacious appetite for power could consume us?*

The First Lord continued. "There are many issues for us to discuss, but first we would report to you on the state of the Inner Sphere, if you would indulge us in this matter. As you are all aware, our agents were successful in defeating the Clans on Huntress and Strana Mechty. We would single out no person or nation's representatives for special praise because this was truly a united effort that has brought us freedom from oppression. This victory is a victory for all of us. While we were victorious during our holding the office of First Lord, this truly is a victory for all of you. Without your efforts, our victory would never have happened."

Kai's right hand tightened down into a fist. *The way he keeps hitting the words victory and victorious, he mocks Victor completely and totally.*

"Beyond that, we have accomplished much in our reign. We have suppressed banditry and promoted commerce. We have overseen the return of our warriors and their integration of our society. We have begun an exchange of diplomats who will allow us to broaden our contacts with the Clans and facilitate their integration into our society. These gains, meager though they may seem, are our legacy. We wish our successor as much good fortune as possible.

"I hereby call this session of the Council to order."

As Sun-Tzu looked out over the room, Kai slowly uncoiled himself from his seat. "I would be recognized, First Lord."

"Grand Duchess Liao, please instruct your aide that you are the Compact's chosen delegate."

Kai's mother, Candace, stood at his side. "Enough of your games, Sun-Tzu. You know who my son is, and you know he has a right to speak here. Just because you would not want your sister speaking for your nation is no reason you should assume I do not trust my son."

Sun-Tzu kept his face impassive despite the acid tones in Candace's words. "Very well, Grand Duchess, I shall allow him to speak, this time. Kai Allard-Liao, the floor is yours."

Kai swallowed hard and slowly let his anger drip into his words. "My Lords and Ladies, I stand before you as one of the warriors who left the Inner Sphere to represent the Star League. I was there and fought to defeat the Clans. I was but one of many who did your bidding, and I was glad to do it. I thought, as did those who fought by my side, that we were battling to preserve the Inner Sphere we knew and loved."

Kai lifted his chin, kept his voice strong and didn't let his nervousness make him speak too quickly. "There were changes in my absence, and I am certain those changes will be cause for further discussion here. The change I find most disturbing, however, is the complete absence of courtesy exhibited by the First Lord of the Inner Sphere."

Sun-Tzu snorted dismissively. "What are you talking about?"

Kai looked around the room, making eye contact with all the other leaders of the Inner Sphere. "What I am talking about, Sun-Tzu, is the disgraceful message you sent to Prince Victor Steiner-Davion. Having returned from defeating the

Clans at the head of an army that would do *anything* for him, he chose to resign his position instead of use it as a rallying point that would allow him to retake his realm and even to unseat you from the position you now hold. He accomplished what no other man could have by destroying the Clans, and then refrained from visiting war upon the Inner Sphere, and you send him a hastily worded message of thanks?"

"There was no haste used in composing that message."

"And there was no thought put into it either. How did it go? 'In recognition of your service, I present you this hearty commendation for all you have done.' "

The First Lord nodded once. "That sounds appropriate for the English translation. The original Chinese was more ceremonial."

Kai laughed at him. "You'll forgive me, Sun-Tzu, but I read the original Chinese. *That* version carried nuances that English won't allow, and that was even more insulting than the English. For this reason I move, here and now, that the First Lord of the Star League be required to record and communicate to Prince Victor Steiner-Davion a message of gratitude that is not insulting."

"It will take time to compose such a message." Sun-Tzu waved his hand dismissively. "We have more pressing business."

Theodore Kurita stood. "Do we, First Lord? I feel the petty nature of the message sent to Prince Victor was unworthy of him and the office of First Lord. I should like to see a new message sent to him, and made available to all the troops who accompanied him, so that they know the Star League valued their service. I do not think this is a matter that can be so casually overlooked. I will second the Compact motion."

Kai nodded at Theodore. "And, First Lord, I have taken the liberty of drafting the message for you to read. If you will allow me: 'I, Sun-Tzu Liao, First Lord of the Star League, speaking for all the Lords and Ladies of the Star League, do hereby commend you, Prince Victor Ian Steiner-Davion, for the leadership and courage you displayed in leading our forces to Strana Mechty to end the Clan threat to the Inner Sphere. All of us are aware of the great personal sacrifices that have resulted from your effort, and salute your selflessness in pursuing the task to which we set you. Without what you have accomplished, the Star League would have no future. To you go the utmost thanks of the people of the Inner Sphere and fond wishes for the same long life and happiness you have helped grant all of us.'"

The souring expression on Sun-Tzu's face told Kai he'd successfully pushed the wording to such an extreme that Sun-Tzu would choke on every other syllable. *Good, he deserves punishment for doing what he has done. I know this won't salve Victor's wounds, but it will teach Sun-Tzu he can't be so cavalier when his enemies still have friends.*

Sun-Tzu scowled. "You cannot be serious. We would never read such a sickly sweet message."

Katherine shot to her feet. "You *will* read it, if that is the message we decide you will read. Precentor Martial, would ComStar be willing to communicate this message to my brother immediately?"

Focht nodded. "Such an important message we would get to Luthien inside a day. It would be our pleasure to do so."

Katherine looked over at Kai. "If my colleague from the St. Ives Compact would be so kind as to amend his motion to include the text he has just read us, I would call for a vote."

"So amended."

"And seconded." Katherine smiled. "Is there any need for discussion?"

Prince Haakon Magnusson Rasalhague stood. "I would only suggest that passing this motion with any dissent would reflect most poorly on us all. I would ask that we accept it by acclamation."

Sun-Tzu's nostril's flared as his eyes rolled heavenward. "Seeing no opposition, the motion is passed."

Theodore smiled. "I would then move for adjournment so

the First Lord can record this message. I feel there should be no chance of delay."

Magnusson seconded the motion and it passed.

Kai sat back down as everyone else got up and started to head out of the hall. His mother swiveled in her chair and smiled at him. "Your first political battle, Kai, but you did well."

He turned to his right and looked at her. "But this was an easy one, mother. The other battles coming up will be tougher."

"You're learning to walk, later you can run."

"But run fast enough to save the Compact?"

Candace shrugged wearily. "You'll have to, won't you?"

Katrina suppressed a smile as Sun-Tzu stormed into her office. His gold jacket seemed too bright in the winter-white room, but it was nothing compared to the fury radiating off him. *He was expecting to be exalted and triumphant and instead his cousin stung him.* "To what do I owe this visit, Sun-Tzu?"

The First Lord raised his left hand, his index finger poised to point at her, but refrained from stabbing it in her direction. He quelled the trembling in his hand, then spitted her with a hellish glare. "You, I thought, were my *ally*. You wanted something from me, but you participated in my humiliation. The wording of that message will crystallize my blood, it's so sweet, and it's going to a brother you revile. How could you?"

"As I recall, Sun-Tzu, I sent you a message saying I thought it would be a wonderful tradition for the sitting First Lord to nominate his replacement. The response I got from you was tardy and non-committal." She picked up a platinum paper knife and tapped it against her desk's blotter. "I refrained from committing my troops and my assets in the St. Ives conflict, and I restrained George Hasek from sending his own troops or hiring mercenaries to intervene. I have not yet agreed with my military advisors to post the returning AFFC forces to the Capellan March or use them to occupy worlds you covet in the Chaos March. I have been good to you, and what do I get but insults in your opening remarks."

Sun-Tzu's face remained expressionless. "Insults? I praised you."

"Ha! You mocked me with your comments about stability and safety."

The First Lord stood there for a moment, his eyes glancing up and away. "Ah, I see how that could have been taken. I beg your pardon, Archon, but English is not my first tongue."

"Damn you, Sun-Tzu, but I will not accept that." Katrina leveled the paper knife at him. "Mock me again, think me stupid enough to believe you didn't know what you were doing, and I will bury your realm. I think you should remember that I managed to take the Federated Commonwealth from my brother and you can't even wrest the St. Ives Compact from your aunt. I can guarantee that will *never* happen."

"But you are willing to stay away if I nominate you as First Lord, my successor?" Sun-Tzu tapped a finger against his chin. "Thomas would back you, and perhaps Magnusson— one for peace and one for the promise of help to build his economy and fortify his realm. Theodore will oppose you, as will Candace. You need my vote to win."

"No, Sun-Tzu, you need to vote for me to win your little war." Katrina's eyes hardened. "If I don't have you with me, then I have to give Candace something, and I promise you won't like the deal I work with her at all. Vote for me, and St. Ives is an internal Capellan matter as far as I am concerned. Vote against me, insult me again, and you'll find I can be very passionate and dedicated to the rights of a subject people. I *am* my father's daughter and I could easily see completing his dream of conquering your realm."

Katrina smiled sweetly. "Your choice, Sun-Tzu. Make it quickly."

The Capellan bowed graciously to her. "I have every hope

that your tenure as First Lord will be as rewarding for you as mine has been for me."

"Oh, I am certain it shall be." Katrina laughed lightly. "Most rewarding indeed."

29

As he looked at her sitting there in the big leather chair at the consul's desk, it occurred to Kai for the first time that his mother was getting old. Her gray eyes still burned with the same fire, and her long black hair had not a strand of gray in it, but her shoulders had softened and her physical motions had slowed a bit. After seventy-three years and multiple injuries sustained in 'Mech combat, dealing with cancer and surviving an assassination attempt, some deterioration was to be expected, but she'd come through all those things very well.

The subjugation of her nation is grinding her down. Kai forced a smile onto his face and looked from her to her brother, Tormano. Eight years her junior, Tormano seemed older because of the white stealing through his hair. He'd also thickened appreciably, without being fat, and his various travails had tracked wrinkles across his brow, out from his eyes, and around the corners of his mouth. *His subjugation by Katherine has ground him down, too.*

Kai leaned forward, resting his elbows on his knees. "I thought we had a major concession out of Sun-Tzu yesterday. He says he's withdrawn all the SLDF forces he'd placed in the Compact."

Candace nodded. "Yes, he's replaced them with his own troops, so he'll be shedding his own people's blood. Unfortunately, they'll be spilling our people's blood."

Tormano sat back in his chair. "At least we had the Combine and the Republic backing your motion, Candace."

"True, this does set up an interesting scenario for today's vote on the new First Lord. Your mistress will no doubt be advanced and supported by Sun-Tzu."

"She will." Kai frowned. "Katherine spoke for your motion, and seemed to anger Sun-Tzu by it."

Tormano smiled weakly. "Of course she did, getting Sun-Tzu to withdraw was the carrot she held out to me and your mother for the Compact's support for her candidacy. The fact that Sun-Tzu anticipated her and pulled the troops means she no longer has anything to offer us, save military support."

Candace pressed her hands together, fingertip to fingertip. "She won't do that, of course, because she has set herself up to be a paragon of peace. So far her nations have only gone to war against the Clans. She has already offered me asylum within the Federated Commonwealth, but I'd sooner flee and exile myself to Arc-Royal. Since she cannot offer us anything substantial, she will promise Sun-Tzu to not interfere with his little war. You heard the language yesterday: that this was just an internal political matter of the Capellan Confederation."

Kai opened his hands. "Well, I can't let Sun-Tzu take the Compact. The moment we leave here, I'll take the First St. Ives Lancers and we'll give Sun-Tzu more war than he can handle."

"You'll not be alone, nephew." Tormano sat up straight.

"Once this conference is concluded, I will resign my position with Katrina and begin to actively direct the Free Capella Movement. I will bring my son in with me—it is time he has a direction in his life. We have assets that will make Sun-Tzu's life uncomfortable. More important, I know secrets that give me leverage with Katrina. She may not actively support us, but she will be turning a blind eye to any support we get from parts of her realm. Within the Capellan March there are a large number of expatriates who will give money and volunteer service to help us."

Candace sat there, stock still for a moment, her eyes closed. "For the better part of three years I feared for your safety so far from home, Kai, and now you come back safe only to move into danger again. And you, brother, I had long been afraid your association with this Steiner witch would end badly for you. And now this war may end badly for all of us. We *could* capitulate, save ourselves and our people the agony of this war."

"Leave them subject to Sun-Tzu's whims and Kali's madness?" Tormano solemnly shook his head. "You and I, Candace, escaped the madness of our father's realm, and what Romano did to it when she took over. Our freedom had a price, and now the bill is due. It's time for us to pay."

Candace smiled, displaying her teeth in the predatory grin Kai had seen often before. "My thoughts exactly, Tormano. It's a butcher's bill, and will be rendered in blood, but we have the coin to pay. Now we'll just have to see how much cost Sun-Tzu finds prohibitive."

Royal Court, The Triad
Tharkad City, Tharkad

Katrina sat on the couch in her office, opposite Thomas Marik. On the table in front of her had been laid out a silver coffee service and two china cups. The cups themselves were Steiner blue with the old armored fist crest on them. "These were my grandmother's favorites. You take your coffee with sugar, yes?"

Thomas nodded, the heavily scarred tissue on the right side of his face twisting unnaturally. Katrina did her best to look away from it—it repulsed her, but fascinated her at the same time. *To bear such hideous scars, to look each morning in a mirror and see your mortality etched into your flesh. I could never stand it.*

She put a single sugar lump into his cup, then poured thick black coffee over it. She offered it to him with a spoon and he stirred once. Her own coffee she prepared with cream and two lumps of sugar—doing as much as she could to make it taste like anything but coffee. She normally abhorred the beverage, but she had been told Thomas enjoyed it, so she indulged him.

Sitting back on the couch, she crossed her legs. "I don't wish to be abrupt, but our afternoon session begins in a couple of hours and we will be dealing with the election of the new First Lord of the Star League."

Thomas gave her a half smile. "You wish to know if the new First Lord will be you or me, then?"

"Most perceptive of you."

"Let me see if my other perceptions impress you." Thomas sipped his coffee, then let the cup and saucer rest on his left knee. "You wish to be First Lord for two precise reasons: neither your father nor your brother attained that goal in life."

Katrina allowed herself a little laugh. "The failures of the past are of no consequence to me. I have everything of my brother's that I could want. My desire to be First Lord comes from my intention to help the Inner Sphere through what should be an exciting and formative time. The peace with the Clans will initiate a prosperity of which we've not seen the like. Factories that have been turning out weapons will now produce consumer goods, and the Clans will have a voracious appetite for the same. The establishment of trade will benefit the Inner Sphere, and I mean to coordinate and develop that trade."

"I salute your vision." Thomas studied her thoughtfully for a moment. "Can you deliver the votes you'll need? Sun-Tzu's pulling SLDF troops from the Compact means you can't leverage their withdrawal for Candace's vote."

"I know, but no matter. Sun-Tzu is mine, and yesterday I had a long talk with Prince Magnusson. His paltry realm is in need of a lot of support, and I allowed as how the Federated Commonwealth would be happy to attend to his realm's needs in return for his support."

"That gives you the swing vote, provided you land me." Thomas nodded. "What will you give me for my support?"

Katrina smiled and nodded her head. "Directly asked, very good. What I shall do for you is keep Sun-Tzu distracted."

"Brightly colored objects could do that."

"His sister, perhaps, but not Sun-Tzu. The Compact war will divert his ambitions, and I can keep that war going for years."

"I will take that and one other thing."

"And that would be?"

Thomas set the cup down on the table then, tugging at his trouser leg, crossed his right leg over the left and sat back. "This commerce will benefit the Lyran half of your empire the most. I want favored-nation status, lowered tariffs, preferential shipping rates, and everything necessary to give me an equal shot at trading with the Clans. I have no doubt we will end up second to your efforts, but I will not be third or fourth. Is this acceptable?"

"Most." Katrina reached out with her cup and clicked it against his. "I believe, Thomas Marik, we have a deal."

Royal Court, The Triad
Tharkad City, Tharkad

Kai smiled slowly as the ComStar technicians set up the holoprojector unit off in the corner behind the Capellan Confederation's table, to the right of the podium. Sun-Tzu, standing at the podium and trying to take care of a number of minor procedural matters, kept glancing over at the workers. His annoyance came less, Kai expected, because of the red-robed and hooded acolytes working there than because of the message that would be displayed when they were finished.

One of the anonymous techs came over and whispered in the Precentor Martial's ear. Focht stood and nodded toward Sun-Tzu. "If the First Lord would permit?"

Sun-Tzu let the hint of a gracious smile flash across his face. "Please, Precentor Martial, let us not delay since we have important work to perform this afternoon."

"Your indulgence is appreciated." Focht clasped his hands at the small of his back and looked around the circle of delegations. "Two days ago you voted for the First Lord to record and transmit to Luthien a message of thanks and commendation to Prince Victor Davion. The message reached him at Komadorishima and he recorded the following reply, which he wished to have broadcast to all of you."

Focht nodded at the tech standing by the projector, and he hit a button to start the message. A white wall of static burned in the air for a moment, then color flooded it and resolved itself into an image of Victor standing in the foyer of Komadorishima's palace. Though the projector displayed Victor in life size, he still seemed very small to Kai. *An illusion caused by the distance.*

Victor's costume didn't help at all. He wore no shirt, and his overalls had only one suspender hitched to the front. The chest flap had flopped down, giving everyone a good look at the sword scar under his right nipple. The overalls were crusted at the knees with dirt, and the gardener's gloves he slowly pulled off were likewise soiled. A ragged cloth had been tied around his brow, and dirt smudged his nose and left cheek.

Victor smiled slightly. "I have received your message and I am deeply touched by it. It was the greatest of honors to lead brave men and women against the most serious threat the Inner Sphere has known since, perhaps, Stefan Amaris. It was their effort, their sacrifices, that won the day. I was merely fortunate that they allowed me to lead them."

The holocamera zoomed in on Victor's face. "I would return to you the hopes of a long life and happiness that you sent to me. There are aspects of my new life that I enjoy very much, and Tharkad seems a distant dream-world now. The trust you showed in me in sending me after the Clans, I return to you. I trust you to guide the Star League into a future that will be good for all of us."

The camera zoomed back out. "So, again, thank you very much. I hope similar messages of commendation will be sent to my troops so they, too, can know how much their efforts mean to the Star League and future. If you ever believe I can be of further service, you will know where to find me."

Reams of ComStar message routing data scrolled up over the image as it faded to black, then the acolyte punched another button and killed the picture.

Sun-Tzu, who had not even glanced at the message during its playing, smiled weakly. "Well, that was certainly worth the interruption of our schedule. If it is the will of this body, I shall record and have sent to the units involved in the invasion a supplementary message of congratulations and send it out with Victor's commendation and his reply to it."

Haakon Magnusson leaned heavily forward on his table. "Perhaps, First Lord, that is a job for your successor. We would not want it to seem that such a message was the last act of an outgoing First Lord. It might sully it a bit."

"I bow to your whim, Magnusson." Sun-Tzu straightened up to his full height. "It would seem, then, that it is time to open nominations for the office of First Lord. I should like to begin what I hope will be a tradition in the Star League, of the outgoing First Lord nominating his successor. Toward this end, I would put forward the name of a woman who has been vitally supportive of the Star League from the outset. She brought us here three years ago for the first Whitting Conference, and she has hosted us again this time. Her wisdom cannot be denied, nor can her compassion for her people. She has heard the cries of many and done everything in her power to offer them comfort. As First Lord of the Star League I am certain she will continue in this manner, bringing home to the peoples of our nations the reality of the Star League and its multitude of benefits to us all.

"I nominate Katrina Steiner of the Federated Commonwealth."

Katrina stood slowly, wearing a look of surprise on her face. "First Lord, you honor me. I would be glad to serve as your successor. If I am fortunate to be half as successful as you are, I will accomplish great things in our name."

Sun-Tzu smiled. "Is there a second?"

Thomas Marik raised a hand. "It is my honor to second the nomination."

"Very well." The First Lord leaned heavily on the podium. "The Star League constitution calls for us to vote on this candidate, and she must win by a simple majority. If there is a tie, ComStar will cast the deciding vote. If she fails to be elected, we will entertain subsequent nominations. I will now poll the delegations."

Sun-Tzu started at his right, with his sister voting in favor of Katrina. Theodore voted against, then Thomas for. Katrina voted for herself, and Candace voted against her. All attention then swung to Haakon Magnusson of the Free Rasalhague Republic.

Prince Magnusson glanced at Katherine, then shook his head. "The Free Rasalhague Republic votes no."

Kai caught a flicker of fury in Katrina's cold blue eyes, then she slowly lowered herself into her chair. *She must have thought she had Magnusson all wrapped up. He's made an enemy, which means Theodore must have made some sort of deal with him.*

Sun-Tzu looked over at the Precentor Martial. "We are at an impasse. Yours is the deciding vote to cast."

Focht stood slowly and very straight. His white robe could not hide the military bearing of his frame, nor his age. "This is perhaps the most important vote that will ever be cast in the history of the Star League. It will determine our future and set in motion many things. I am eighty-seven years old and the chances that I will live to see the fruits of this vote ripen are slender. It is for this reason that I choose to resign my position as the Precentor Martial of ComStar, and, instead, have my successor cast my vote."

What? Kai's jaw shot open. He looked over at Hohiro and saw that he and everyone else in the Combine delegation were equally surprised by Focht's announcement. Katrina's brow furrowed, and Thomas Marik covered his mouth with a hand. Haakon Magnusson seemed openly amused, and Kali Liao's glare seemed sufficient to cause the Precentor Martial to combust.

Sun-Tzu retained his composure. "Your announcement was not unexpected, Precentor Martial. Your choice of a melodramatic moment to make it was. Is your successor here?"

"Indeed, First Lord." Focht nodded at the hooded acolyte over by the holoprojector. "I give to you ComStar's new Precentor Martial."

When he lowered the hood, the new Precentor Martial wore a broad smile. "In this matter," said Victor Davion, "ComStar chooses to vote against Katherine."

30

Royal Palace, The Triad
Tharkad City, Tharkad
District of Donegal, Federated Commonwealth
5 November 3061

As the Council of Lords session broke up, Victor came around the ComStar desk and strode across the opening to the Combine delegation. He extended his hand to Theodore. "Congratulations on being elected First Lord of the Star League."

Theodore smiled. "And thank you for so quickly accepting leadership of the Star League Defense Force."

"I was honored by the appointment." Victor reached out his right hand and stroked Omi's arm. "I apologize to all of you for deceiving you."

Kai came over and shook Victor's hand. "I'm glad to see you here, Victor, but how did you get here? Even a command circuit couldn't have gotten you here from Luthien in response to our message."

"You're right. I actually got here before any of you." He

winced and felt his stomach tighten. "When the Precentor Martial came to me at Komadorishima I was already beginning to be uneasy about my retreat from life. Part of the reason I went there was to get as far away from the trappings of my old life as I could, so I wouldn't be homesick for it. When the Precentor Martial showed up, we had some long talks. Hohiro, you and Kai and I had all wondered about him and whether or not he was grooming one of us as his replacement. We were thinking about it in terms of becoming the point man to deal with the Clans. We were right, he was, but he was looking beyond that."

Victor felt Focht's hands land on his shoulders. "I was looking for someone to further the spirit of the new ComStar. When we secularized the organization, we came as close as possible to being akin to the old SLDF. We were a force that could be used to intervene in nasty situations—peacekeepers perhaps, but warriors needed to fight when a threat like the Clans arose. With the reformation of the Star League and the recreation of the SLDF, we had parallel organization. I wanted someone with the judgment and skill needed to lead a neutral force and use it to maintain the stability of the Inner Sphere. Any of you three would have been suitable candidates, but only Victor here was free of responsibility."

Hohiro smiled. "And he was the best choice."

"Thanks, Hohiro." Victor covered a light cough with his fist. "The Precentor Martial outlined for me his plans for the future and I accepted his offer to replace him. Kai, because you said you'd see to it that a new letter of commendation would be sent to me, we recorded the beginning and end of that message at Komadorishima. The middle, which referred to the text, I recorded in the ComStar compound yesterday. It was all spliced together and played today."

Omi looked at him. "And the message I sent to you?"

"Rerouted by ComStar to find me. ComStar also kept me up to speed on breaking events, so I could offer timely comments on things back on Luthien that you might expect me to now about." The new Precentor Martial looked down for a second. "I didn't want to fool any of you, but I needed to fool my sister."

"You didn't fool me, Victor." Katherine's whiplash voice brought him around and out from Focht's shadow. His sister, clad in white, stood there, her face crimson with fury. "I know your game, and I won't let you win. What is mine is *mine,* and you shall never have it."

Victor's eyes narrowed. "I'm going to say this *once,* Katherine. Believe it, act upon it. Ignore it at your peril. I am now the Precentor Martial of ComStar. My mission in life is to see to it that the Star League flourishes and does the most it can for all humanity. As long as you do nothing to interfere with my mission, you and I have no quarrel. If you choose, however, to make your problems *my* problems, you will not like my solutions to them. Am I making myself clear?"

"Crystal, Victor." Katherine's nostrils flared. "You have a week to leave my Tharkad, and a month to depart my realm. Don't come back without an invitation." With a flash of golden hair, she spun on her heel and walked off.

Victor turned back to his friends. "I think, someday, she'll come to a bad end."

"Better sooner than later." Phelan Kell and his father expanded the circle of people in the middle of the ballroom. "I look forward to dancing on her grave."

Victor sighed. "There are a few more immediate problems to deal with, however." He turned to Kai. "As SLDF Commander I can't commit troops in defense of St. Ives unless the Council votes for it. I can, however, send units there for exercises, and they would have the right of self defense. Perhaps you can tell me what spots would be good to train at."

Kai smiled. "You'll have the information you want before you leave Tharkad."

"Good. Morgan, does the Arc-Royal Defense Cordon need any bolstering?"

The elder Kell, his thick beard almost entirely white, shook his head. "Not at the moment, but I would be pleased to exchange liaison officers so we can come up with suitable procedures to coordinate activities in the future. We need to prepare for your sister's wrath, not provoke it at this point."

"True." Victor nodded thoughtfully, then smiled. "Thus ends the era of the Clans. Let us hope the future of the Star League will be bright indeed."

Bremmerton, Upano
Arc-Royal Defense Cordon

Francesca Jenkins paused inside the smoky pub's doorway, letting her eyes adjust to the dim light. The Archon's Mistress, as the pub was called, flickered with candles in red globes on each table, providing navigational beacons that allowed her to thread her way through the crowded common room. She forced herself to look around no more than she assumed her contact would expect. She had hoped to spot Curaitis somewhere in the room, but given the poor light and his ability to blend in almost anywhere when he put his mind to it, she couldn't find him.

Her target, on the other hand, might as well have been outlined in neon. The man was obese, and not just in the sense that his belly slopped over his belt. He'd managed to wedge himself sideways into a booth, and the fat on his flank rolled onto the table top as if the table were sawing deep into his chest. The man wore a flowing shirt that might once have been white, but rainbow splotches of color decorated it everywhere. The sleeves had been rolled up to mid-forearm, displaying thick-fingered hands that looked tiny because the rest of him was so large.

He hoisted a mug of beer and drank deeply, then licked his blubbery lips clean, save for a droplet that coursed down through his unshaven stubble to sink into a crevasse marking the first of his many chins. He set the mug down and spotted her, then tried to straighten up while pawing thin strands of blond hair over his shiny pate.

Francesca paused at the table's edge. "You're the artist known as Valerius?"

The man bobbed his head and waved her to the bench across from him. "I am. Your message said you were interested in some of my work?"

"Indeed, I am." Francesca brushed the bench clean of crumbs and slid in across from him. "I recall seeing some of your work on New Exford, about a year ago."

"Yes, I had pieces in a show there." The man shrugged as if that were no great feat. "New Exford bored me, though. I chose to come here, to Upano. Much more inspirational, this world."

She looked around and nodded carefully. "I can see that. You're doing lots of work here, then? Inundated with commissions."

"Oh, of course. Bremmerton may not look it, but there is a high demand for art."

"I understand that, Valerius." Francesca put an edge into her voice. "I've seen much of your work on the streets. You can hardly tell the hovercars were in an accident, you match paint so well."

The man's piggish eyes widened. "You insult me, madame. I don't have to listen to this."

Francesca pressed a heel to the top of one of his feet, pinning it in place. "You're going nowhere, Valerius, and it is time to get things straight between us. First, I know you're Valerie Symons and I know you left New Exford because Reginald Starling wanted to prosecute you for having forged a couple of his paintings. He would have, too, except he found it terribly amusing that you had been able to deceive the buyers. Your forgeries of his work were the best he'd seen and could easily pass for genuine."

Symons winced, then frowned. "Am I supposed to take that as a compliment?"

"Could be, or a preface."

"How about both?"

"Even better." Francesca gave him a smile. "I have an offer to make you. I'm going to offer you five thousand kroner for each Starling you produce in a new series. The series will consist of studies of the Archon Princess Katrina, but appropriate to a series titled 'Bloody Princess.' You will complete a dozen paintings along the lines I will dictate to you."

Symons shook his head. "Starling is dead, you know. No one will believe he did these paintings."

"Oh, but they shall, Val." Francesca smiled. *Actually only one person needs to believe, and that's the Archon herself.* "I knew Reg Starling and can forge documents in his handwriting that will pass inspection. Moreover, I also know the agent for his estate and I can guarantee he will authenticate the work."

Symon's brown eyes narrowed. "You'll sell the works for a lot of money. I want a royalty."

Francesca shook her head. "Royalties for art? We're not playing games here, Symons. Do the job you're asked to do and you will be amply rewarded. If you won't do it, I'll just find someone else who will, and you'll just have to live with knowing you passed up a chance to make money and fool the Inner Sphere's greatest art experts."

"Fool the art experts, eh?"

"Yes, the same ones who've claimed your work is pedestrian and derivative."

"Oh, yes, them." Symons thought for a moment, then tossed off the last of his beer, splashing little tendrils of it back over the tops of his rounded cheeks. "Okay, I'm in. Money up front."

"Five now, four on delivery of each of the first five pictures."

"Done." Symons began the laborious process of sliding himself out of the booth. "You got a studio, or do I need to find one?"

"Twenty-seven-forty East Greystone Avenue, second floor." Francesca suppressed a smile when Symons winced. "Be there tomorrow morning at ten. Everything you'll need will be there, including your money. We want your best work."

"You'll get it."

"Good. You're going to be fooling people in very high places."

"Don't worry." Symons patted himself on the chest. "When they see these, they'll be thinking Reg Starling is alive and well."

"That's exactly what we want, Mr. Symons." Francesca smiled broadly. "Exactly what we want."

Royal Court, The Triad
Tharkad City, Tharkad
15 December 3061

The man calling himself Harrison Harding nodded his thanks to the Archon Princess as he settled into the chair opposite the white leather couch in her office. On the table between them lay a coffee service and two cups. She reached out to pour, but he held a hand over the mouth of his cup. "No, thank you."

"Don't trust me, Mr. Harding?"

The man smiled. "I prefer to avoid caffeine and I know that you hate coffee, so I'd not have you feel obliged to join me."

Katrina sat back on the couch and drew her legs up beside her. "Not many know that about me. You discovered this how?"

"Research."

"For a job?"

"Personal interest. Had you been the object of an assignment, we'd not be having this conversation." He reached out and snagged a little biscuit from the small plate on the silver platter. "Almond."

Katrina smiled. "To cover the scent of cyanide."

"Quaint idea." He bit a piece off the biscuit, chewed and swallowed. "Good, but not poisoned."

"Are you certain?"

"Quite. If you wanted me dead you wouldn't have invited me here, and you'd not do the job yourself with sweets. First, you couldn't be certain that I'd succumb without a struggle. It wouldn't take much for me to shatter a saucer and slit your throat with a fragment of your grandmother's china."

Katrina's hand rose to cover her throat. "And the other reason you would cite?"

He smiled. "You'd put me on trial for your mother's murder and have me confess that your brother hired me."

Katrina nodded. "Very good. You impress me as much as your work. Ryan Steiner was yours, and your escape was brilliant. And then killing a whole government on Zurich, that was inspired."

"You are too kind."

"Hardly." Her blue eyes narrowed. "You've been idle since then."

"You may believe that if you wish, it matters not to me. Suffice it to say the money paid to me for your mother's death was enough to allow me to occupy my time in any way I wished." He nibbled more of the biscuit. "I chose to answer your summons because I found our previous work together very rewarding and quite the challenge. No one remembers Ryan's death, or the fall of the government on Zurich, but your mother's death, that they will never forget."

Katrina nodded slowly. "This one they won't forget either. I'm sure you've heard of my brother's new position. He chose to join ComStar specifically to humiliate me and deny me my rightful place as the First Lord of the Star League. Then he made me a laughingstock here on Tharkad and throughout the Inner Sphere last month. No one does that to me—no one— and gets away with it. He will pay."

"Undoubtedly." The man brushed crumbs from his pant leg. "But will you?"

"Forty million kroner."

It took some effort to maintain his composure. That was the most he'd ever been paid and double what Melissa's death had gotten him. "Interesting offer, but times have changed. Sixty."

"Fifty-five and you stop bargaining now." Katrina snaked a manila envelope from beneath the silver service and extended it to him. "Do we have a deal?"

"The money is right, Archon." He opened the envelope, pulled out a static holograph, glanced at it and smiled. "And the job doable."

"Excellent." Katrina's voice became as cold as her eyes. "Victor will pay."

"Indeed he shall, Archon." The man slipped the holograph back into the envelope. "As per your wish, Omi Kurita will die."

About the Author

Michael A. Stackpole, who has written more than twenty novels and numerous short stories and articles, is one of Roc Books' bestselling authors. Among his BattleTech® books are the *Blood of Kerensky* trilogy and the *Warrior* trilogy, both of which have been republished by popular demand. Other Stackpole novels, *Natural Selection, Assumption of Risk, Bred for War, Malicious Intent,* and *Grave Covenant,* also set in the BattleTech® universe, continue his chronicles of the turmoil in the Inner Sphere.

Michael A. Stackpole is also the author of *Wolf and Raven,* a braided novel set in the Shadowrun® universe. His other books include *Dementia,* the third volume in Roc's mutant series, and *Once a Hero,* an epic fantasy. *The Bacta War,* the last of Stackpole's four Star Wars® X-wing® novels, was recently published.

In addition to writing, Stackpole is an innovative game designer. A number of his designs have won awards, and in 1994 he was inducted into the Academy of Gaming Arts and Design's Hall of Fame.

**Next in the
Twilight of the Clans series**

Falcon Rising

by Robert Thurston

Coming in March 1999 from ROC Books

Falcon Caverns
Ironhold
Kerensky Cluster, Clan Space
13 March 3060

It had not been too difficult to lure Leif into Falconfire Cavern. Diana had known he was tracking her with his own active probe, and she had used the map of the whole Falcon Caverns system—with which she had spent a couple of early morning hours—to lead him by the fish-nose of his *Black Lanner*. She apparently headed toward him, only to divert into what must have seemed to him an unexpected tunnel.

She felt she was controlling the situation. Unless, of course, it was part of Leif's strategy to be lured into this cavern of rising smoke and sudden flames, of oil leaking in waterfalls from the walls, and pools with names like Styx.

Before coming into Falconfire Cavern, she had taken her 'Mech perilously close to a tunnel where Leif's 'Mech was proceeding slowly down a long, fairly steep descent. For a moment, standing in the intersection of two tunnels, she had seen the lower half of the *Black Lanner* in the distance. She could have sent a PPC blast at the legs and there was a chance she might have actually hit one, might have started a disablement that would have been finally fatal to the 'Mech. But she could not do it. She could not take a potshot, even for the bloodname. With all the taint that had accrued around her father's bloodname contest and other phases of his military career, she could not be even slightly dishonorable.

Would he have taken that shot? Joanna would probably say that he would. I do not think so. Anyway, it does not matter. My decision, not his.

Now, in the massive Falconfire Cavern, she awaited him. Her own probe had lost his whereabouts, perhaps due to interference in the air from the unusual geological activity. But she had led him along the center tunnel, and she expected him to emerge there, so she was surprised when he raced out of a tunnel to her right, fire shooting from his right-arm PPC and his left-arm medium lasers. Although much of the assault was apparently designed to surprise and rattle her, only some of it worked. The *Nova* vibrated from several minor hits, and a piece of armor fell into the pool called Styx, sending up a large sizzling geyser of its oily liquid. On the wall behind her, several chunks of rock fell and bounced along the cavern floor, one rolling quietly into the Styx, whose waters, if they could be called that, were barely stirred by it.

Diana responded with some rock-shattering fire of her own, concentrating on her left-torso, medium-pulse laser as she set the *Nova* on a path toward the *Black Lanner*.

Samatha nudged Grelev and said, "Well, there is a few hundred years of history going into the pool."

"With all due respect, Khan Samantha, they were just rocks. Think of it this way: Someday they may excavate that pool, find the piece of armor that also went in, and try to figure out what it could possibly be or could indicate about the civilization that once lived here."

In spite of the flurry of activity between the combatants, Samantha glanced at Grelev with raised eyebrows. "Are you saying the Clans will vanish and become forgotten history?"

He shrugged. "Everything is transitory, *quiaff?*"

"I suggest you keep that particular idea to yourself. Some might see it as treasonous. The Clans are forever—remember that."

In the dark Ironhold City tavern, Peri found watching the contest difficult once the shooting started. She gasped at each hit against the torso of Diana's *Nova,* and silently approved each of her successes against the *Black Lanner.* At the same time, the various pains in her body seemed to intensify.

"Are you all right?" Nomad asked.

"Of course I am. Why do you ask?"

"You look sick."

She gasped again as a PPC blast from the *Black Lanner* narrowly missed the *Nova*'s head.

"Or you're acting like a mother."

Diana kept edging her 'Mech sideways, causing Leif to counter her movements with shifts of his own. Leif maneuvered his vehicle very well. And why not? He was a Jade Falcon warrior, just as she was, well trained and fierce. The only real difference between them was, after all, the matter of birth. *Freebirth,* the derogatory name for a genetic type and the foulest Clan curse. Somebody had once said that nations could rise or fall on the strength of a single word. Whatever that meant, Diana thought, the lines and borders created by the word *freebirth* were considerable.

Even though Falconfire Cavern was huge, when a pair of raging BattleMechs inhabited it, it somehow seemed smaller. Where Diana had foreseen laser fire and charge-particle beams streaking across large distances, the combat was conducted at much closer range.

Diana had to swerve the *Nova* torso violently to escape a

PPC blast coming right at it. Immediately after, the cockpit rocked from the force of the impact. *"Freebirth!"* she muttered, then laughed to herself at her own use of the foul word.

Another hit, and the cockpit seemed to reel in the other direction. For a moment she was dizzy, but she remained in control of the 'Mech. Knowing the way was clear behind her, she moved the 'Mech three steps backward, each step maneuvering a bit to the side in order to confuse Leif's aim.

Leif's voice came suddenly over her commline, loud and clear. "Retreating, Diana?"

"Regrouping, stravag."

The sound that came next was perilously close to a sigh. A pilot did not hear many sighs through a commline. "Stravag, huh?" Leif said. "Do we need to go through the insult rituals just because we are pitted against each other? We are friends, Diana."

His voice sounded so warm, so—well—friendly.

Now she seemed to hear Joanna's voice through the commline. *Stop with that, idiot! Do you not see what he is up to? It is the strategy he has employed ever since the two of you met. I would not be surprised to find out that he planned the meeting, that he saw the possibility you would be his opponent in the final bloodname match, that he came to you to disconcert you with friendship. It is not friendship. It is a ploy, a vile ploy.* The words were so convincingly Joanna's that for a moment Diana, still fighting her way out of dizziness, thought she was really hearing her.

No, damn, it is just your own voice telling you to shape up. It does not matter who is in the cockpit of that Black Lanner! *Whoever he is, he wants your behind on a platter. This is a bloodname we are fighting for. He may be sincere, he may be a liar, but he wants that bloodname just as much as I do. But there is a difference. I need it. I need it. I need it.*

She kept the phrase going as a mantra as she shook the dizziness out of her head and swung her 'Mech's torso around to go face-to-face with the *Black Lanner.*